ISBN: 979-8-99-12332-5-5

Ebook ISBN: 979-8-9912332-4-8

Book Formatting: Fariss Ryan

@FarissRyan

Cover Design & Illustration: Victoria Davies

vcbookcovers.com

CONTENTS

In The Beginning   9
PART I: A REASON   11
1. When Souls Unite   13
2. Always Covered   20
3. Separated   25
4. Silent Fears   31
5. What's Done in the Dark   35
6. Conquests and Goals   44
7. Score   49
8. Glass Slippers   56
9. Torn   68
10. A Meeting at the Crossroads   76
11. Catch a Fallen Star   83
12. Topsy-Turvy   90
13. Two Trains in the Night   99
PART II: A SEASON   109
14. Disjointed   110
15. Can't Have It All   116
16. Game Time   121
17. Playing with Fire   129
18. Connected to My Soul   135
19. Tailspin   145
20. Revival   153
21. Finish Strong   161
PART III: A LIFETIME   169
22. Anticipation   170
23. Goodbye, Hello   175
24. Reunited   184
25. Aftershock   192
26. The Mothers   209
27. Coming Clean   219
EPILOGUE: A LIFETIME OF FOREVERS   225

Acknowledgments 231
Reviews 233
About the Author 235

"Born not of the same flesh, but realized in the splendor that is Alpha.
We have come to be one.
And I call her sister."

- Source Unknown

IN THE BEGINNING

Justine Chandler's parents met in Washington, DC. It was an overcast day at the cusp of Spring. The first budding hints of cherry blossoms were soon to make their debut. They were both in their early twenties and given their shared political aspirations, the nation's capital had been an obvious hub for both John Chandler and Barbie Whittaker to migrate from their southern roots. John was working part-time at the Attorney General's office while building his own company; Barbie was a paralegal for a prominent lawyer within the city. John, always grandiose in his retellings of their first encounter, claimed the moment he laid eyes on Barbie, the monuments faded into the background and only she remained. John described Barbie as a tall, slender goddess with an impeccably-coiffed afro.

By Barbie's account, prior to the moment they met, she had stopped at a bench to remedy a run in her pantyhose with a dab of clear nail polish. She was so preoccupied, she didn't realize she was being watched. As she strolled along the path, glancing cautiously at her stockinged leg every few steps to ensure the mishap hadn't worsened, she collided—quite literally—with John Chandler. From that moment, their stories matched. They had fallen hard and fast for one another. Their brief courtship was a whirlwind romance that carried them through a blurry rainbow of May flowers, and a heady, sun-drenched summer spent swimming and making love on the Jersey Shore. They married in an intimate wedding just before the leaves could turn colors. A move to Philadelphia soon followed, and not long after, the arrival of their first child, Justine Elizabeth, rooted their growing love into something that, for a time, felt unshakable.

John had always intended to surpass the Joneses—he insisted that his family maintain a certain level of prominence within the community. After Justine's birth, John asked Barbie to leave corporate America, focusing instead on philanthropic endeavors and raising Justine. Initially, Barbie wouldn't even consider the idea. Leaving her well-established position at the law firm and giving up her dream of being a career woman was completely out of the question. Seeing his young wife's resistance, John pulled a wild card: he contacted Barbie's mother.

"How's my favorite son-in-law doing?" Mrs. Whittaker fondly chimed, answering the phone on the first ring. John seized the moment, divulging his gripes and master plan. Mrs. Whittaker agreed wholeheartedly to get Barbie on board. One stiff tongue lashing from her mother haunted Barbie decades later. Every time she considered following her heart and rocking the boat, her mother's words replayed in her mind: *a woman's place is in the home... what you won't do, another woman will... I know you don't want to grow old alone.* The last one really frightened Barbie. From that day forward, she had kept her word and stayed in "a woman's place," just as her mother had taught her.

Fulfilling John's dreams and abandoning her own meant maintaining a level of airs that afforded Justine a life of privilege she had never been without. For this, Barbie was grateful. At a young age, it never occurred to Justine that most of her peers came from less fortunate backgrounds. Far be it from her to even know what a "broken family" was.

Yet.

PART I: A REASON

❧   I   ❧

WHEN SOULS UNITE

Justine

If ever there was a date that Justine would not soon forget, it was September 3, 1986—her first day of fourth grade at Martin Luther King, Jr. Elementary School. To say that she was excited was an understatement. Justine sprang up, bright-eyed, to the sound of her Care Bear alarm clock. Quickly pulling her pink ruffled bedspread into place, she greeted each of her beloved stuffed friends with fondness as she laid them one by one against her pillows.

"Good morning, Mr. Skittles. Hi Daisy... Wakey wakey Fluffy." She enthusiastically doled out greetings until each toy was placed in its designated home on her plush down feather comforter. Justine turned toward her walk-in closet and began picking out clothes for her big day. Mindful to avoid wrinkles, she carefully placed her favorite green denim overall dress, pink long-sleeved shirt, white tights, and brand-new brown loafers on her vanity chair. She stood back to assess her selections: not a single stitch was out of place. Justine nodded her head in approval.

"Perfect!" Justine walked into the adjoining bathroom and began to brush her teeth—thirty seconds per quadrant just as her mother had taught her.

"Good morning kiddo!" Barbie chimed as she waltzed into the bathroom, her silk robe leaving a river of fabric flowing generously behind her. "You're up early. I was just coming to wake you."

"Hi Mommy! I was so excited I couldn't sleep a moment longer. I have the perfect outfit picked out," Justine gushed, exaggerating the "er" sound in *perfect*. Without taking a breath she continued, "Can you do my hair in ping tails?" Her eyes sparkled. She was determined to put her best foot forward, so everything needed to be just right for today.

"It's *PIG*tails," Barbie corrected good-naturedly while laughing, "And yes, I will."

"Humph, that's what I said," Justine grunted. She had no idea what was so funny, but she hated being wrong. Her mother knew what she meant.

Barbie sensed her daughter's frustration and quickly changed the subject. "What are you most looking forward to today, honey?" *Too easy*, Justine thought.

"Meeting my teacher, making new friends, art class... ummm... Oh! I know—playing hopscotch and double dutch at recess! I *love* hopscotch—I can get all the way up to seven on one foot! I'm still working on getting to ten, but like you always say—"

"Practice makes perfect," the pair said together.

They continued laughing as they exited the bathroom and made their way toward the aroma of pancakes, eggs, uncured bacon, fresh fruit, and hand-squeezed orange juice waiting for them in the kitchen.

Story

Beep, Beep, Beep, Beep, Beep! Story's alarm blared, startling her out of a dream. In it, Story had found her estranged family and learned that she came from royalty. She was just about to be crowned princess when she was jolted from her sleep. Story had barely finished her curtsy when the annoying shriek of her alarm forced her to wake up. Story put the pillow over her head and rolled over, swatting aimlessly in the direction of her alarm clock, hoping to make contact with the snooze button.

A few more minutes, she thought. She was tired, not just physically, but emotionally. It was yet another first day at a *new* school with a *new* teacher and *new* friends. Not only had Story and her mother, Denise, moved from state to state (Connecticut to New Jersey and now Pennsylvania), but from town to town within each state.

Story had already switched schools four times during her short academic career, and right now, five more minutes in her familiar bed seemed far more enticing than restarting the ritual song and dance of being "the new kid." It was always so sudden. One day, Denise told Story she was looking for a change; the next, she had found a new job. They had relocated from Trenton only three weeks prior. Story hated having to leave her friends and start over so often; even now, she missed Mrs. Ford from her previous school.

"Storyyy, get up! You're going to be late," her mom yelled from the kitchen.

Peeking out from her warm cocoon to ensure her mother wasn't within eyesight, Story rolled her eyes as hard as she could without getting them stuck, before nestling deeper into her twin bed covers.

Not even two minutes later, her mom yelled out again, "Storyyyyyy! I don't hear you stirring!" The emphasis added to the last syllable of her name let her know her mom wasn't playing any games this morning.

Rolling her eyes again, Story responded "Coming Mom!" *Good grief,* she thought,

It's my first day. Doesn't she want me to be well rested? Mom never seems to let up on me.

"I laid out your outfit. Get dressed and come get your breakfast."

As soon as she heard that, her eyes shot open. Her mother always insisted on picking out what Story called "foo-foo frilly outfits." Her style was far too spunky to ever be caught dead looking like a girly girl. Besides, she could dress herself; even her mother said she was "a big girl" now.

Ugh! One glance at the selected outfit made her stomach turn: a purple dress with pleats and knee socks?! She hated that dress and there was no way she'd be caught in knee socks! Now inspired, she jumped out of bed and went to her closet. Quickly tossing on a pair of acid wash denim jeans, a purple pony t-shirt and purple high-tops with white glitter laces, Story stood back to admire her handiwork in the mirror.

Mom won't notice, she thought as she rushed into the kitchen.

"Good morning, Mom." She kissed her mother on the cheek before plopping into a chair to eat her oatmeal. "Mom, can we listen to the radio while I eat?"

"Sure baby." Denise turned to the boombox on the counter, switched it on and turned the dial to their favorite R&B station, Power 99 FM. The two began swaying to the beat as one of their favorite songs blasted through the speakers.

Justine

Justine's first day was going as well as could be expected. Ms. Lowery seemed nice and smiled warmly as she entered the classroom, pointing her to her desk, which was close to Ms. Lowery's. Her desk mate, Gina Blackwell, had been in Mr. Gregorio's third grade class. Gina was friendly enough for the arrangement to be peaceable. Behind Justine sat Joshua Brownling, who she recognized from her third grade class with Mrs. Cloud.

Justine felt relieved to see a couple of familiar faces, but as Justine glanced toward the door, her eyes stopped on a short girl entering the class. She wore a purple shirt, cornrows and matching hair beads. There was something about this girl.

Wow, she's so cool, Justine thought. *I hope she sits next to me.*

Ms. Lowery greeted the girl with the same warm smile, and pointed to the open seat to the right of Justine.

Yes! she thought before facing forward. The school day had officially begun.

Story

It was essential that her hair bead match her outfit. And it was this very reason that Story missed the bus after losing track of time. Sure, she had to endure a long lecture on responsibility, but the switch was well worth it. As her mom continued her diatribe, she nodded and agreed at all the right moments, topping it all off with a kiss of sincere gratitude as they pulled up in front of MLK Jr. Elementary. Beneath her cool demeanor, her mind reeled anxiously about all the ways this day could go wrong.

What if she didn't make any new friends? What if she couldn't find her class? What if her teacher turned out to be a real-life witch; she had heard stories about that happening to other kids. But as she approached the front of the building, an older lady in a colorful cardigan soothed those fears with a welcoming smile.

"Hi, my name is Story Brooks. I'm in Ms. Lowery's fourth grade class," Story recited, just as she had practiced with her mother. The nice lady assigned a student helper wearing a reflector vest and instructed her to walk Story to her class. As Story entered the classroom, the teacher greeted her with a big grin before asking her name.

"My name is Story Brooks; are you Ms. Lowery?"

"Yes, I am. It looks like you've found me," she said with a soft chuckle.

"Oh, were you lost?" Story asked innocently, oblivious to the cleverness in her own question.

"Er... no," Ms. Lowery replied, taken aback for a beat. "Anyway, there's your seat over there. We were just about to say the Pledge of Allegiance."

Story found the seat indicated by Ms. Lowery and sat down. As she got comfortable, the girl next to her smiled.

"Hi, I'm Justine Elizabeth Chandler, what's your name?"

"I'm Story Johnniece Brooks. Nice to meet you."

"Story? Now *that's* a crazy name! How'd you get a name like that?"

She was so used to this question, the words rolled off her tongue seamlessly. "Before I was born, my mom dreamt of being a writer for big time movies in Hollywood. But then she got pregnant with me and her dream of going to California was put on hold. She said she knew she still had a story to tell, so she named me *Story*. That way, every time she calls my name, she remembers her dream. Mom says one day she still plans to make it to Hollywood, and she's going to take me with her."

"Oh," Justine paused, listening politely. "Do you want to be friends?"

"Sure!" Excitement and relief filled her tiny body. This move might turn out better than she expected after all.

❧

The day progressed and Story learned all of her classmates' names during a game they played. At recess, she played hopscotch with Justine and a few other girls. When it was Justine's turn, she ran and jumped with so much strength that while trying to reach the number eight on one foot, she lost her footing and tumbled, landing on her knees instead. Story and the girls rushed to help her up.

As they got her to her feet, laughter could be heard behind them. Joshua and his friend, Kenny, were standing a small distance away, laughing, pointing and slapping each other high-five. When Justine looked down, she saw that she had torn her white leggings on the knee and began to cry.

Feeling suddenly protective over her newfound friend, Story turned around and marched over to the boys. "What's so funny?" she demanded, fists on hips, ready to pummel both boys if necessary.

"Ahhh, hahaha. Tumbleweed over there couldn't even jump on one foot. I could do that with my eyes closed," Kenny said in a thick southern accent. She learned during the icebreaker that Kenny and his family were new to Philly too; they had moved from Georgia during the summer.

"I'd like to see *you* try and do it Dun-lap!"

"Huh? Who's Dunlap? My name is Kenny."

"Well I coulda swore it was Dun-lap 'cause yo stomach sho nuff dun-lapped over your belt!" Story mocked in an exaggerated southern accent.

"Oooh," Joshua howled, "she got you man!" Joshua continued to cackle as he folded over with laughter.

"That's not funny man!" the pudgy-faced boy grumbled as he sulked away from the cluster of children who had gathered in anticipation of a fight. With that, Story felt more accomplished than ever strolling back to her friends. She had let everyone know just who she was and what she was about. Justine beamed at her as she neared the group.

"Thanks for taking up for me," she said appreciatively. "You're my new best friend now, deal?"

"Deal!" The two girls spit into their palms then tightly clasped their hands together as they rushed off to play on the monkey bars.

✵ 2 ✵

ALWAYS COVERED

Justine

The sun beat down on the exposed scalp between Justine's freshly-beaded cornrows. It had taken weeks of pleading, but Barbie had finally caved and allowed Justine to join in on the trend. She shook her head in frustration. Even in her tank top and cotton shorts, she could feel a bead of sweat slowly trail its way down her back. It was like being in an oven, far too hot to be comfortable. *Thank God Mom agreed to let me go to the pool today*, she thought while wiping her glistening brow and waiting for Story to exit Mr. Nick's local corner store. Just thinking about the promise of a water ice and soft pretzel made enduring this heatwave worth it. When Story said she found quarters under her couch cushions, Justine couldn't stop grinning. Her mom had given her just enough for admission to the neighborhood pool; she'd never approve of, or pay for, their indulgence in such "junk."

Since meeting in Ms. Lowery's class nearly three years prior, Justine and Story had been practically inseparable. More often than not, when one was seen, the other wasn't far away. When one had something, the other knew she had it too. They were close as sisters and many people often assumed they were. It didn't help that they dressed alike, finished each other's sentences, and even had their own secret language. As an added bonus, they lived in the same apartment building—Story living in a third floor apartment with her mother and terrier mix, while Justine resided in the penthouse condo with her parents. The girls were so close that they were affectionately referred to by others as "the Prospect Girls"—a play on the name of their high-rise housing complex, Prospect Gardens.

When Story exited Mr. Nick's, Justine licked her lips, in anticipation. If her mother caught her consuming such sweet-and-salty goodness, she likely would've given her an hour-long lecture about watching what she ate—and made her write a book report listing ten reasons why too much junk food is bad for you. That was all the more reason Justine planned to eat her snack outside on the playground, far from her mother's watchful eye.

When Story was within arm's reach, the girls locked hands and sprinted toward Griffin Park. They rushed over to the seesaws, sat down, digging into their snacks.

"Thanks girl! Mmm, mmm, mmm, lemon water ice is my favorite!" Justine gushed. She had been very strategic in her selection. Not only did she love the zesty sweetness of lemon water ice, she was also well aware that the lemon flavoring wouldn't stain her tongue—making it undetectable to her eagle-eyed mother.

"You know I got you, girl."

"Istersay, istersay, hatstay ymay istersay!" they recited together. Laughing, they gave each other a high five. After finishing, the girls threw away their trash, grabbed their towels and walked into the community pool. It didn't take long to realize everyone in Philly must have had the same idea about going to the pool that day. It was packed! At least a hundred people were splashing around in the water, and another fifty or so sunbathed in pool chairs. The line for the snack bar wrapped around the side of the pool house. Their idea to purchase and eat their snacks before arrival was genius.

Almost simultaneously, the girls spotted an older couple vacating their pool chairs. They quickly walked over to claim the seats before running toward the shallow end of the pool.

Tweeeeet! The lifeguard blew his whistle. "No running!" he yelled before returning to his seat. The pair ducked their heads as they continued toward the water.

Without hesitation, Justine jumped in. *Splash!* She immediately felt relief.

Story, a bit more hesitant around water, dipped her big toe into the pool, then quickly pulled it back. "It's cold!" she shrieked.

"Not if you jump in quickly," Justine replied. "You'll get used to it faster that way." She dipped under the water and made quick work of swimming to where Story stood at the pool's edge. Propelling herself out of the water, she rushed over and grabbed her friend's hand.

"Alright, let's do this together." Story tightly gripped her hand. She nodded as they began to count.

"One, two, three..."

On three, the girls jumped into the pool, still holding hands. In no time, they were splashing around and squealing—all signs of fear melted into fun. They played Marco Polo, Red Light/Green Light, and counted who could hold their breath underwater the longest.

After exhausting themselves with pool games, Justine excitedly suggested they go to the deep end and began swimming toward the diving board with expert precision. As her arms sliced through the water, she suddenly felt that unspoken fear resurfacing again. Justine turned to face her friend who was still standing on the deeper side of the shallow end, looking apprehensively at the deep waters where Justine now bobbed effortlessly. The more she thought about it, the more she realized she had only ever seen Story float on her back, doggie paddle, and hold her breath underwater—never truly *swim*.

"My dad taught me to swim when I was about four. I used to love spending time with him in the pool every summer." Letting her eyes drift toward a streak of light dancing on the pool's bottom, Justine continued. "But ever since his speaking engagements have been picking up, he doesn't have as much time anymore."

She swam closer to her frightened friend, reaching out her hand. "But I promise you, girl, I would never let anything happen to you— I've got you covered, Istersay."

Story still looked scared, but Justine meant every word.

"Fine," she conceded, taking Justine's hand, yet again. "Let's do this."

Story

"Cannonball!"

The word cracked the air a split second before a wave of water—and panic—capsized Story. If she had it her way, they would've stayed in the shallow end, playing until their fingertips wrinkled and prickly goosebumps bloomed on their arms. But Justine had gone ahead, and wherever Justine was, Story wanted to be. She had doggie-paddled, using all her strength and courage, splashing awkwardly toward the diving boards. By the time they reached nine feet, she was struggling to stay afloat, fighting to catch her breath while paddling in place. Her chest was tight, breath thin and quick.

She had no time to react as a gangly boy leapt off the diving board, hurled over her frame and clipped the back of her head with his heel just before crashing into the water. Stunned and disoriented, Story began flailing. Her arms and legs flopped erratically as she gulped down mouthfuls of pool water with every scream.

"Help!" she managed to belt out just before her head fully submerged beneath the water. She could hear the lifeguard's whistle, less piercing with the pressure of water building in her ears. It felt as though there was a magnet on the pool's floor, pulling her down rather than buoying her up. It was then she felt a forceful tug on her arm. Within seconds, she was above the surface, floating on her back, gagging and gasping from panic.

"Girl, stop swinging your arms or you're gonna pull us both under!"

An immediate calm came over her. It was Justine. She allowed her body to completely relax and before she knew it, they were at the pool's edge. The whistle-happy lifeguard met the girls and pulled Story out of the water in one swoop. It all happened so fast, she barely had a moment to process. They were immediately taken to the pool house for further assessment and given the all clear; however, the lifeguard asked for Denise's number.

"We have to release you to an adult after an incident like this," he said, almost apologetically. "It's protocol." Grateful to have not drowned, Story recited the number from memory to the diligent lifeguard before turning to Justine and dissolving into tears.

"I've got you girl. You're going to be fine." Justine wrapped her arms around the best friend whose life she had just saved, hugging her tight with no plans of letting go.

⚜

Wrapped in her towel and shivering slightly, Story sat in a trance mentally replaying the day's events. When she saw her mother's car pulled into the parking lot, she rushed to greet her. As soon as she reached her mother's arms, she broke into tears again.

"Mom!"

"Oh baby!" Denise hugged her daughter tightly as she smothered her face with kisses. "Sorry, it took me so long. That was the longest twenty minute drive of my life. I was just wrapping up my work day when they called."

"Mommy, I was so scared!" Story confessed—still refusing to release the firm grip she had on her mother.

"I prayed the whole drive here that you would be safe. You're all I've got." She inhaled deeply before asking, "What happened?"

"We were playing in the deep end, and some stupid boy hit me on the head when he jumped into the pool. I freaked out and almost drowned, but Justine saved me," she paused to catch her breath. "The lifeguards said I'm fine to go, but they needed to release me to an adult."

"My goodness! You scared the daylights out of me." Unclenching her jaw, she turned her daughter around slowly, inspecting for residual damage. After finding her daughter's body intact, she reached for Story's hand. "Let's get out of here."

"Mom, can you take Justine home too?"

Story noticed it took a moment for her mother to respond. "Sure. It's not like we're not going to the same place."

❧ 3 ❧

SEPARATED

Story

Since the near-drowning incident a week earlier, Story's mother had been keeping a much closer eye on her. She undoubtedly loved her mom, but she hated the tight rein she was now under. She couldn't even step outside without getting the third degree: *Why do you want to play outside? Who are you going to play with? Where will you be playing?*

For the life of her, Story couldn't understand why her mother even asked all those questions, especially since she hadn't been allowed to go outside once—not even after every single question had been answered. Had she known that getting knocked on the head and nearly drowning would lead to all this hoopla, she would've skipped the pool entirely last week.

Still, one good thing had come out of it: her mom changed her work hours so she could be home more during the day. And as much as she disliked being watched like a hawk, she had to admit it was nice having her mom around more for outings, laughs and dinners at night.

Denise, a community resource case worker at the local shelter, was responsible for making sure the residents had what they needed to get back on their feet. In the short time they had lived in Philly, she had successfully rehoused well over 150 individuals and families. Story loved that her mom was able to help others, but before the schedule change, the house often felt lonely—just her and her dog, Super Mario.

This past week, though, had felt like old times. Denise and Story went sightseeing, shopping, out to dinner and even visited the Philadelphia Zoo. Story soaked up the extra attention like a sunflower in the midday sun. The only thing that could have made their newfound quality time better was if her dad were there to complete the picture. For as long as she could remember, Story had dreamt of meeting her father. More than anything, she wanted to have a "normal" family like so many of her classmates. Like Justine. But for reasons she couldn't understand, her mother never spoke of him—and seemed to shut down, even get upset, whenever Story brought him up.

After sitting on the living room floor playing jacks for over an hour, she stood and stretched. Her right leg had started to fall asleep, and her toes felt like they were being pricked by a hundred tiny needles. Wandering into the kitchen in search of a snack, she found nothing that struck her fancy. Sulking back into the living room, she froze and stared at her mother for what felt like an eternity. Denise didn't flinch —her eyes were glued to *All My Children*. Story let out a dramatic exhale loud enough to rattle the curtains. Still nothing.

She did it again.

This time, she flung her arms in the air with flair, hoping for at least a glance. Nothing. Then the slightest smirk crept across her mother's face. Her gaze never left the screen though. She seemed determined not to let her daughter's theatrics interrupt her need to know the truth behind Erica's latest ordeal.

When the commercials rolled, Denise turned. "What's got you blowing all that hot air? Done with your jacks?"

"Yeah, Mom, I'm done. And I'm b-o-r-e-d. Bored! Wanna play Go Fish?"

"Baby, I'm finishing this episode of *All My Children*. Erica just woke up after fainting. *Again*. Give me thirty minutes, then we can play a round or two before I start dinner. How does that sound?"

Story rolled her eyes. "Well, can I go outside then?"

"It looks cloudy out. Not today." Her mother hadn't even glanced at the floor-to-ceiling window behind her.

"Well... can I just go to my dad's house, then?" she blurted in a last-ditch effort to get some kind of reaction. She knew she was poking the bear, but the boredom was getting to her.

Denise's eyes snapped from the television to her daughter. "What are you talking about? What would make you even say something like that?" She shifted on the couch to face Story more directly. "You know it's just me and you, baby. Your daddy is... away."

"Away where? It's been a loooong trip. I've never even met him!" Story's voice cracked slightly toward the end. She knew she was pressing her luck, but her desperation was louder than her caution. "You're always busy. So why can't I go stay with my dad? Just for a weekend."

"That's not possible," her mother replied flatly, turning back to face the television.

"Why not?"

"BECAUSE I SAID SO!" Her voice boomed through the room. "Now go to your room."

Story's eyes burned with the threat of angry tears as she turned on her heels. "Come on, Super Mario," she muttered, calling for her dog as she stomped down the hallway. She slammed her door and threw herself face-first onto the bed, letting out a muffled scream into her pillow. Flipping onto her back, she stared up at the ceiling, blinking hard. Super Mario tilted his head at her from the doorway, then, seeing no real distress, gave a little snort. He spun in a circle, scratched at the carpet, and plopped down for a nap. Story knew it had been a bad idea to bring up her dad—but she couldn't help it. With so much free time and no one to talk to, her thoughts kept circling back to the same place: she was the only one of her friends who didn't have her dad. Some days, that emptiness felt too big to ignore. She would've given *anything* for just one weekend with him.

Ugh! Her life sucked! Story could care less if she looked like a dying crab as she kicked and clawed at the air. She allowed a single tear to fall from her left eye and trail its way down the side of her neck before angrily wiping it away.

Write it out.

Even now, she could hear her mother speaking in her ear as clearly as if she were standing right beside her. Journaling was a way that Denise had taught her daughter to calm her feelings when she felt weighed down by her emotions, by life, by anything. Having exhausted all other options, Story grabbed her diary. She had some things she needed to get off of her chest.

June 30, 1989

Dear Diary,

I'm so mad right now! It's summertime. Do you know what that means? I'm on summer break from school? Do you know what I should be doing? Playing! Lots and lots of playing! Oh, and going to get ice cream with friends. Having sleepovers. Going to Rally's Roller Rink with Justine. But nooo! I almost drowned one measly time and now Mom won't let me out of her sight! I'm going to lose my mind. My life is so boring! And to make matters worse, I just finished a book called "Separated" a few days ago. It's a book I got from the library. We are required to read 15 books this summer. I'm up to book #2, I've got a ways to go. But where was I... oh yeah, the book. It's about this girl who was adopted at birth. When she's 11, she starts asking her adoptive parents about her real parents. Although her adoptive parents were the only parents that she had ever known they agreed to help her find her biological parents. It was kind of weird though because her real mom didn't really want to be found. But she eventually came around and they found a way to make things work for everyone.

After reading the book, it got me thinking about my own dad. I wonder where he lives. I wonder why he doesn't come to see me. Does he have another family? Does he even care if I exist? I picture my dad being really tall. So tall, he'd have to duck to enter our front door. He's also got smooth skin like chocolate. We have the same eyes and the same smile. When he talks, his voice carries, and everyone listens. On weekends, he'd come to take me to the park. Sometimes, I'd spend the night at his house. And sometimes, he'd stay at our place.

Eventually he'd fall in love with mom again and they'd get married. I'd be the junior bridesmaid in their wedding. And we'd all live happily ever after. Only one problem... I don't even know his name. Well, I hear my mom calling me for dinner. I'd better go before she has to come and get me. That never goes well. I'll write again soon, ok.

Until next time,
Story

Justine

Even though they lived in the same building, it felt like Story lived miles away lately. Ms. Brooks refused to let her out to play, and Justine had only managed to call once since the pool incident since her mother didn't want her phone line being "tied up."

This summer was not going at all as she had planned or hoped. Her daydreams had been filled with long afternoons spent running the block with Story, but that was far from reality. She had done the math: eight days, thirteen hours, fifty-two minutes and counting since she had last seen her best friend. She sighed for the fifth time in as many minutes.

In their forced separation, Justine did her best to stay busy. She rearranged her Barbie display, alphabetized her board games, and read four of the fifteen required books for the summer. She had even given her favorite doll, Daisy, a fresh haircut—with bangs. But as an only child, there were only so many things she could do alone.

Her dad had just returned from a speaking engagement in New York, but had already gone off to play golf with his buddies. Her mom was buried in her study, knee-deep in the seating chart for her next charity event.

Padding down the hallway, her bare feet sinking into the plush carpet, she made her way to her mother's study.

"Hi, Mommy."

"Hi, dear. What are you up to?"

"Nothing. I'm bored. Story hasn't been able to come outside to play."

"Well, what about your other friends? Courtney, Monica, and

Jasmine all live within walking distance. Maybe they would like to play?"

Justine sighed, her shoulders slumping. "It's not the same without Story, Mommy. She's the best Double Dutch jumper in our neighborhood. And she always finds the best hiding spots when we play Hide-and-Seek."

"Why can't she go with you?"

Justine exhaled with a hint of frustration. "Remember? I told you about what happened at the pool."

"Oh yes! What a pity she didn't know how to swim well enough to save herself."

She ignored the air of judgment lacing her mother's comment and pressed on. "Anyway, her mom hasn't let her come outside since."

Barbie looked up from her chart, her face softening slightly as she considered her daughter's words. "That's unfortunate, dear. But I imagine her mother is still shaken. Give her some more time—she'll come around."

As if to signal the end of the conversation, Barbie returned her attention to the seating chart, pen scratching softly against the paper. Deflated, Justine turned and sulked back to her room, no closer to solving her boredom.

She opened her bedroom's double doors and made her way to her vanity. Reaching to the left, she flipped the switch on her sound system and slipped on her headset—secular music was strictly off-limits in the Chandler household.

"We come together, 'cause opp-o-sites attract..." Justine closed her eyes and hummed along with Paula. For now, the music would have to do.

❧ 4 ❧

SILENT FEARS

Story

At last—*freedom*!

After what felt like an eternity on lockdown, Story's mother finally relented. Freedom was here, but not without a few stipulations. No pool. No wandering farther than her mother could see from the living room window. Remain with Justine, or at least one other friend, always. And, most importantly, be home before the streetlights come on. Story would have promised her firstborn child, if that's what it took to get her life back. She was all nods and "yes, ma'ams," her grin so wide it made her cheeks ache. She didn't even bother to sit down. With sneakers half-tied, heart pounding, she snatched the phone and called Justine.

"Finally!" Justine shrieked, before hanging up with a clatter.

Story practically flew to the elevator, terrified her mother might change her mind. The second the elevator doors slid open, there she was: Justine, waiting like Nettie returning to see Celie in *The Color Purple.* This had been the longest stretch of time they had gone without seeing each other since meeting three years prior; the girls crashed into each other, laughing and squeezing tight, chattering on top of each other without a bit of concern about being heard. They were together; that was all that mattered. As soon as they reached ground level, the girls grabbed hands and bolted toward the front door.

"Hey, hey! Slow down, girls," Arney, the doorman, called after them, shaking his head with a smile. He had grown accustomed to "the Prospect Girls'" bursts of energy and chatter, but he took his job of enforcing lobby rules seriously.

"Ok, Mr. Arney," the girls said in unison, slowing to a brisk walk as they made their way to the exit. When they spilled out the lobby doors, they allowed themselves to be swallowed whole by joy.

Their first stop was Mr. Nick's corner store for a bag of penny candy. In celebration of Story's return to the outside world, Justine's mom had, surprisingly, handed her a crisp dollar bill for them to share. Inside the shop, the girls carefully selected their candies, giggling between choices. Behind the counter, Mr. Nick's daughter, Nicole, raised an eyebrow in their direction. She knew this kind of excitement only meant one thing — "the Prospect Girls" were back in action. With their bags full and their change counted, Story and Justine emerged from the store, candy in tow, arms stretched wide, faces turned skyward. It felt like re-entering society, the generous rays of sun amplified the elation filling their bodies from the inside out.

Without a second thought about staying within eyesight of their building, the girls skipped excitedly toward Griffin Park. Upon arrival, they hopped on their favorite seesaw and picked up as though no time had passed at all.

"So what'd I miss?" Story asked, slurring her words while chewing a mouthful of Now and Laters.

Justine shrugged. "I don't know. I only went outside once. It was boring without you," she paused to eat her treats. "Courtney and Monica started arguing after they lost a relay race against me and Jasmine. Then everyone got all snippy, so I ended up just going home. Last Thursday, Jasmine called me and told me that Courtney and Monica were still upset with one another. I haven't been back outside since. Too much drama."

Story rolled her eyes in understanding. "Well, I've played enough jacks to be a pro by now. I made it through two of my summer reads.

Me and mom went a few places, but I think she finally got tired of me asking her to play," she lifted her arms triumphantly. "So here I am!"

The two cheered theatrically, hyped up off of sugar and togetherness. But even in their shared high, Story knew there were things, *important things*, she left out—like the blow up she had with her mom about her dad and how lonely she felt at home sometimes. She knew Justine wouldn't understand. How could she? Her dad lived with her. What could she possibly know about the ache of a dad that was M.I.A.?

Justine

"Mom, I'm home! ...Mom?"

The house was unusually quiet. Justine padded from room to room, her voice bouncing off the high ceilings. It wasn't unusual for the house to feel big—only her parents and Magda, the housekeeper, lived there — but today, the spaciousness felt heavier than usual.

Still, something smelled delicious. The aroma of beef and fried onions wafted through the air, making Justine's mouth water. Someone was definitely home—and by the smell of it, someone was cooking up something special. She rounded the corner into the great room, and before she could plant her feet, she was lifted clean off the ground.

"Hey there, Little Lady!" her dad called out, spinning her in the air like old times.

"Daddy!" Justine squealed, laughing as she wiggled to get free. "I'm too big for all that now!" She tried to sound annoyed, but secretly, she loved the attention.

John Chandler set her down gently, grinning from ear to ear.

"Your mother and I thought it was time for a surprise," he said. "Family movie and game night!" John spread his arms and turned showcasing the scene. Justine blinked, taking it in. Both the sofa and loveseat had been repositioned against the walls. The floor was lined with an assortment of colorful pillows and a tower of board games sat stacked next to the entertainment system. Atop the glass coffee table, a greasy brown paper bag basketed three foil-wrapped cheesesteaks— the family's favorite guilty pleasure.

Her mother held up a VHS tape with a hopeful smile: *Problem Child*, fresh from Blockbuster. "Your dad picked the movie," Barbie offered, glancing at her husband with a look of pride mixed with something else Justine couldn't quite name. She knew her mother had missed her father as much as she had. Although his frequent travel and speaking engagements afforded them a privileged lifestyle, Justine—and her mother—would have traded some, if not all, of those fancy things for her father's presence.

This night was a welcome delight, but she could still tell her parents had been arguing. Her mother's eyes were tinged pink and slightly puffy underneath a careful layer of makeup. Even her smile felt forced beneath the excitement Justine knew she felt at the rare opportunity for them to have quality time as a complete family. Her dad was laying on the charm extra thick, the way he always did when he was trying to smooth something over. And cheesesteaks for dinner? That was a dead giveaway.

In the Chandler household, cheesesteaks were reserved for birthdays and special occasions. Or, as Justine had learned just three months prior, nights for when her parents wanted to apologize. That night when her father left with a door slam and not so much as a goodbye, a cheesesteak hoagie had magically appeared for dinner. Her mother must have felt terrible for the arguing because she ordered Justine all the extra fixings. And last month, it had been a chicken cheesesteak—the "healthier" version—right before her annual physical, when her mom needed her buttered-up enough to forget about vaccinations until it was too late. Justine absentmindedly rubbed her arm at the memory.

She didn't know why her parents had been fighting this time, but deep down she felt it had something to do with her. Still, ever the good daughter, she did her best to push her worries aside, painted on her brightest smile and flopped down on a pillow pile. Tonight, she'd join the family and enjoy the greasy takeout, fun, movies and games. Tonight, she'd go with the flow. Tonight, she'd pretend, along with her parents, that everything was alright.

❧ 5 ❧

WHAT'S DONE IN THE DARK

Justine

It was Spring Break of 1990, and the girls were holed up in their favorite spot: Justine's bedroom. Barbie had asked her daughter to fold her laundry an hour prior, but at the moment, that chore was the furthest thing from either of their minds. A rerun of *Full House* flickered across the television screen, captivating both girls. Justine knew they were tempting fate by watching the show before doing chores; both parents were home and the house rules were clear: "work before play." But missing an episode of their favorite show was not an option. Not if they could help it.

Justine could hardly believe they were nearly in high school. Academically, she was thriving and well on her way to being the eighth grade valedictorian. She and Story were still thick as thieves with her captaining the school's soccer team and Story leading the cheer squad. As far as Justine was concerned, the only way from here was up.

As she lay on her queen-sized bed, half-watching the episode while daydreaming about her future, a soft knock broke her reverie. In a flash, she powered down the TV, sat up and grabbed a t-shirt to fold.

"Come in," she called innocently. Story followed suit, grabbing a pair of Justine's jeans, both girls hoping they hadn't been busted. When Justine's dad walked in, they let out a shared sigh of relief.

"Hey, ladies. Want to go for a drive?" John said with his characteristic ease and charming smile. "I need to swing by the office for some paperwork, and then I thought maybe we could go for ice cream."

"Yes!" the girls said in unison, their delight erasing all thoughts of chores and *Full House*.

"Umm, Mr. Chandler? I need to call my mom and let her know where we are going." Justine's father's brow furrowed briefly before he resumed his usual easygoing smile.

"Of course, Story. The phone is in the hall." After a quick call and getting the green light, the girls eagerly scurried to the elevator, and made their way down to the building's garage.

Justine absolutely cherished outings with her father. He traveled so often for work that when he was home, she savored every moment they had together. Her dad would tell her stories about his travels, share his thoughts on world affairs and speak of his big dreams for the future. He'd even offer unsolicited advice on staying away from what he called "fast boys," always with a knowing smile. Family meant everything to Justine's parents, and because of that, it held a sacred place in her heart too. And while she loved her mom, she was her daddy's princess through and through. Their connection was deeper than words, unspoken yet undeniable. Justine had heard the story of her father's humble beginnings and his rise to success countless times, and every time, she found herself even more enamored with him.

She stared out of the lightly-tinted rear window as houses and high-rises whizzed by. Narrow streets soon made way to open highways as the sedan powered forward to the city's business district: Center City. Justine's chest swelled with pride as she reflected on her father's journey to becoming a renowned powerhouse.

"Daddy, tell us again how you founded Dream Makers." Justine smiled in anticipation of Story hearing her father's journey—no one told it better than he did! The way he told it always ignited a spirit of becoming a change-maker in Justine's young mind.

"Again?" John mused, secretly relishing the interest his princess took in his career. "Ok, one more time." The two girls leaned as far forward as their seatbelts would allow. "I was born and raised in a small town in Mississippi, during the time of Jim Crow. You little ladies know what that meant, right?"

The girls nodded emphatically, hoping he'd continue his story. To their delight, he did. "Then you know because of segregation, I was well-versed in shrinking myself to make white folks appear greater. In such a small town, I was taught to have small dreams. Everywhere I went, my elders and white folk kept telling me, *'Mind yo'self, boy,'* and *'You betta know yo place.'*"

"Why'd they tell you that?!" Story blurted, not meaning to speak her thoughts aloud. John smiled.

"Well, it was dangerous. White folks said they were better than us, and if we did anything to step outside the rules they had, we were called 'uppity," John paused, looking at the two pairs of eyes gleaming back at him in the rearview mirror. "Even asking a simple question like you just did, Story, led to folk warning you, *'Don't get too uppity now.'*" Justine heard the emotion in her father's voice and leaned closer for comfort. "Yeah, I heard that plenty as a child, but I always knew I was different—I knew deep down there was more to life than 'Yes ma'am' and 'No sir' and accepting the unfair treatment of my people. One day, Ralph Abernathy—" John stopped, interrupting himself again. "You little ladies know who that is, right?"

Justine caught Story's look of confusion and piped up proudly. "A well-known Black minister and civil rights activist. Right Daddy?"

"That's right, Princess! He came to preach at my hometown church and from that moment, I knew I had found my calling—I was determined to be a voice for my people. From then on, I was focused. Every decision I made was so I could be who I knew I was meant to be. By twenty-one, I moved from Mississippi to Richmond—"

"That's in Virginia," Story added proudly. Justine smiled, happy her friend was as excited as she was about her father's tale.

"You're absolutely right, Story," John grinned. "I moved there and began working for a well-known activist with the county, and that's where I really spread my wings, found my voice and became a force for change…"

"Daddy?"

"Yes, Princess?"

"You always say you 'found' your voice. What does that mean?"

John was so excited with the conversation and the girls' engagement, he almost missed his turn. "Great question! I started to encourage those around me and speak up about my ideas. I got involved in the right circles so I could make real progress. When you get with the right people, you grow and your voice matters. This is why I always tell you both to watch the company you keep. The people you surround yourself with can make or break you."

The girls nodded to show they understood. "Before I knew it, I had become the Senior Victim Advocate for the Attorney General's office in Washington, D.C. By my thirties, I was known as 'The Dream Maker.'"

"That's where the name of his company came from," Justine told Story proudly.

"That's right. Soon after that, I was the proud founder of Dream Makers Grow, Inc., an organization dedicated to social justice and equality. Since then, I've led the charge for equal rights, spoken before Congress advocating for legislation to bridge the wealth gap, and toured the country motivating others, just like you two, to find their voices and use them for good." John's pride in himself was only rivaled by that of the girls beaming at him. He must have noticed a pensive look on Story's face because he asked, "You two have any questions for me?" Justine shook her head, but noticed Story was still deep in thought.

"So you just left the people in your small town? Do you ever miss them?" The car was quiet. For a reason Justine couldn't understand, she felt uncomfortable. All the times she had heard her father's story, she had never thought about those he left behind. Her father fidgeted in a way she had never seen him do before; Justine was eager for him to answer.

"You know what, Story, that's a great question," John took a deep breath. "With success comes great reward, but even though I can afford almost anything my heart desires, I never forget my humble beginnings. I am incredibly grateful for everything I've accomplished and the long journey from those backroads of Mississippi to the heights of international recognition. Everything I do is for my people and my hometown. I dedicate my work to them every day; I never leave those I love behind."

Justine felt like crying for a reason she couldn't name. She glanced over at her best friend in the whole world, and wondered if she felt the same.

Story

There was nothing Story loved more than hanging out with Justine. She was the best friend she had ever had. As an added bonus, she had become a second daughter of sorts to John and Barbie Chandler—being regularly included in family activities, dinners, sleepovers and outings. She had even traveled with them to Ocean City. Her mother, surprisingly, had agreed to the trip, but upon Story's return, it was clear that Denise had been a nervous wreck in her absence. While she remained respectful of her mother, she couldn't really grasp why she was so overprotective. On second thought, maybe her mother's feelings were warranted given her prior reports about Mrs. Chandler's behavior towards her.

"I think she thinks Justine is too good to be friends with someone like me," she had said, after recounting Mrs. Chandler's icy disposition, barely uttering *hello* before retreating to her room or office for the duration of Story's visits to their home.

"Someone like you?" Denise's feathers were clearly ruffled. She tried to downplay the statement.

"You know what I mean mom..." she said, hoping her mother would let it drop. From the way Denise stared back at her, Story knew she'd have to say it. *"Someone from a single-parent home."* she had softly finished, scared to meet her mother's gaze. When she had, she saw her mother blinking back tears and nodding gently. Neither she nor her mother ever brought it back up. But over time, Mrs. Chandler seemed to warm up to having her around, and in Story's eyes, she couldn't have found a more upright family to be welcomed into.

She hadn't mentioned it to her mother, but John felt like the father Story had always dreamt of. She smiled to herself, remembering how

Mr. Chandler had mistakenly claimed her as his own the weekend before:

"*That's my girl!*" he had shouted, grinning as he raised his hand for a high-five after she beat the whole family at Uno. Again. Catching Mrs. Chandler's stare, he quickly corrected himself—"*Great job, Little Lady!*"—but the first words had already etched themselves into Story's heart, as if he had truly meant them. Every moment with Mr. Chandler filled a space in her she rarely acknowledged, a quiet vacancy no one else seemed to notice. Though she'd never dare say it aloud, being with him felt as natural and binding as blood. Today was no different—she was thrilled to join Mr. Chandler and Justine, and deeply honored to hear the story of his rise to glory.

When the girls reached Dream Makers Grow's headquarters, they quickly jumped out of the car and headed into the building. The girls were far from strangers there; whenever they made an appearance, the staff always gave them small tasks to complete like making copies, sealing envelopes and using the shredder. While they enjoyed being office assistants, what they enjoyed most was raiding Ms. Vanessa's candy bowl. What could be better than all-you-can-eat candy—for FREE? As they burst through the doors, they immediately caught the eye of Ms. Vanessa, Mr. Chandler's executive assistant.

"Hi, Ms. Vanessa!" Story exclaimed, rushing expectantly toward her desk.

"Hi, baby! How have you been?" Ms. Vanessa hugged her so tightly it took the wind out of her.

"I'm good. Do you have any work for us today?"

"Oh, you know there's always work to be done. I'll grab the mail for you to sort in just a moment." Turning to Justine, Ms. Vanessa's face lit up again. "Hey, babydoll! How are you?"

"I'm doing well, Ms. Vanessa," Justine said politely, returning the hug.

"And how are *you*, Mr. Chandler?" Vanessa winked at John as she reached out for a hug. When she embraced him, Story noticed how her hands moved along his back and her cheek rested against the lapel of his impeccably tailored suit jacket.

John offered a guarded smile, catching Story's eye before taking a step back. "I'm just fine, Vanessa," he said, clearing his throat. "Can I speak with you in my office for a moment?" Without waiting for her response, he began walking down the hall.

"Absolutely, Mr. Chandler," Vanessa cooed, flashing a smile at the girls as she sashayed her ample hips into the office. "Girls, the mail is on the bottom shelf in the copy room. Separate it based on the recipient," she called over her shoulder.

Story and Justine made quick work of sorting the mail. Once they had completed the task and placed it in the designated boxes, they each made their candy selections from Ms. Vanessa's bowl and settled in the breakroom, eagerly awaiting the two adults' reemergence. About thirty minutes later, Story glimpsed Ms. Vanessa stepping out of Mr. Chandler's office, pausing to tuck her blouse before walking back to the front. Mr. Chandler walked up behind her and swatted her gently on the buttocks. The two shared a quiet laugh. Story quickly averted her eyes—not wanting to believe what they had just seen. Unsure of how to react and embarrassed on Justine's behalf, she busied herself by untying and retying her shoelace.

Justine

Justine was certain there had to be some explanation for what she had just witnessed. There was no way her father had just swatted Ms. Vanessa on the butt! Maybe there was something on the back of her dress that he was trying to swat away. *That makes more sense*, she thought, clinging to the idea like a life jacket. She refused to believe that her father could ever do something so inappropriate. *Doesn't Dad love Mom?* she wondered before checking to see if Story had seen what happened. She couldn't bring herself to say anything and risk shattering what had been, until now, a perfect afternoon. Justine decided to act as though she hadn't seen a thing.

"Are you little ladies ready?" John asked.

"Yes, Daddy," Justine replied.

"Yes, Mr. Chandler."

"Great," he said, eyes sparkling. "We have a small change of plans:

Ms. Vanessa is going to join us for ice cream. Is that alright with you two?"

The look the girls exchanged spoke volumes, but neither was brave enough to voice her truth aloud. So they politely nodded their acquiescence and silently made their way to the car.

At the ice cream parlor, Justine and Story chose their favorite sundaes and found a cozy spot to enjoy them. After Ms. Vanessa and her father had their cones of soft serve, they made their way over to the table sitting a bit *too* close for Justine's comfort.

Aren't they just the giggly bunch? she stewed, annoyed and confused at how her father could invite Ms. Vanessa to hijack their special time together. Chatting with Story was the only thing keeping her annoyance from showing, as her father and Ms. Vanessa's shared laughter grew in volume.

She couldn't believe this was happening. Not again. Last year, her dad had taken her school shopping at the mall where they met some mystery woman in the food court. As Justine hopped excitedly from store to store, she caught a glimpse of the two holding hands. She never spoke about the incident to anyone—especially not her mother. She could only imagine what it would do to her to know her father was going around town with another woman on his arm. Now here she sat, yet again, witnessing her father with another woman, and this time in front of her best friend.

After dropping Ms. Vanessa off at the office, John, Justine and Story headed home. "Did you girls enjoy our outing?"

"Yes, Daddy," Justine mumbled.

"Yes, Mr. Chandler."

"Well, you're both rather quiet. Everything alright?" Before the girls even had a chance to respond, he continued, "Listen, no need to mention our outing to your mother. We wouldn't want to rub it in that she didn't get to come, would we?"

"No Daddy." Justine's eyes remained glued on the window. She was unable to meet Story's gaze, but sensed her friend's concern.

Justine didn't know what to call what she was feeling. Embarrassment? Confusion? And something else she couldn't name. She only knew she wanted the day to end. No matter how hard she tried, the worries kept circling: *Are my parents getting a divorce? Does Daddy not love Mommy anymore? Does he not love me?*

A burning pressure crept behind her eyes. She blinked hard, willing the tears away. *What does Story think about all this?* She didn't have to wonder for long.

Without a word, her friend reached out, their fingers meeting and interlacing in the tiny space between them. That one, small, steady touch said it all: *I'm here.* And in the weight of the moment, that was enough.

Justine exhaled slowly, allowing a single tear to fall.

In the driver's seat, her father kept his eyes on the road, whistling a happy tune, oblivious to the hurt his actions had left behind.

❦ 6 ❦

CONQUESTS AND GOALS

Story

So, this is high school, huh? School had been in session for almost two weeks now, and things were going smoothly. Story surveyed the narrow hallways of Mary McLeod Bethune High, happy the rumors were true. Boys were *everywhere*, and the options were endless. She was determined to find her man before the first semester ended. She had never backed down from a challenge, and this was going to be no exception.

Strutting through the halls, she knew she looked good in her denim skirt, oversized windbreaker jacket, slouchy socks and classic high-top sneakers. Her hair was freshly styled into chunky braids, swept up into a high ponytail that bounced with every step. She swayed her hips just a little extra as she scanned the halls on her way to first period. That's when her eyes caught Travis'. He was leaning against his locker, watching her every move. He even blew her a kiss as she passed, but Story just rolled her eyes and chuckled under her breath. She had every intention of taking her time and weighing her options because she was set on finding her forever man.

After her morning man-scouting mission, she refocused on her real priority: finding Justine. They only shared one class, but they had the same lunch period and always walked home together. Outside of school, they spent pretty much all their time together, a bond so close that their classmates were already referring to them as "the twins." It was common knowledge that they were a package deal.

"Aye Justine!" Story yelled, waving her arms to get her friend's attention from across the hall. "Hey girl, what's up?"

"Same old, same old. What's up with you?" Justine said, leaning in for a hug.

"Nothing much. You look cuuuuute," Story stepped back to admire her bestie as Justine did a graceful twirl. "That set is perfect on you! Oooh! And I love the shoes! I couldn't have paired it better myself."

"That's because you *did* pair it *yourself*!"

The duo burst into laughter at Story's feigning surprise at her own talent. "Thank you, girl. You wouldn't believe how many compliments I've gotten today."

Story had convinced Justine to buy the two-piece orange blazer and shorts set during their most recent mall trip. With Story's keen eye for fashion and Justine's willingness, it was like having her own personal mannequin.

"Girl, you know you're always welcome," Story replied sincerely. "Now, let's get to this boring class." Justine linked arms with her for support, while Story dragged her feet, rolling her eyes and popping her gum.

If it weren't for being with Justine, Algebra I would be, without a doubt, her least favorite class of the day.

Justine

High school was proving to be a success so far. Not only had Justine had managed to coordinate her schedule to near perfection, but thanks to her stellar academic performance throughout middle school, she had been accepted into Honors Math and English. Her schedule also included Spanish II, Computer Science and Orchestra as electives. After a successful audition, she had earned a coveted spot as first chair clarinet and had made the school's soccer team. As a freshman, she would have to start on junior varsity, but she already had her sights set on trying out for varsity at the end of the spring season.

Justine's circle of friends had grown, but she wouldn't exactly call herself "popular." If anything, people mostly knew her by default. Sticking close to Story had brought a lot of friendships her way, but Justine had never been the social butterfly Story was. She wasn't shy, just... different. Her energy went into college prep more than parties or hangouts. Her parents expected a lot, and she understood high school for what it was: a stepping stone, not a destination. If she wanted to be a lawyer someday, she didn't have much room for playing around.

Story

By lunch, Story had made her pick: Rakim Arthur was going to be her man.

He didn't know it yet, but her sights were set. *He is sooo fine,* she thought, practically swooning. With his creamy brown skin, high-top fade and single gold earring, he checked every box in the looks department. But more importantly, he was one of Bethune's star wide receivers. To top it off, he was an upperclassman, which was a major score for a freshman.

After asking around, Story learned a little more about her dream guy. Not only was he fine, but he also had a reputation as a dope boy, known for supplying classmates with nickel bags of Mary Jane—or something a little harder—for the right price. But even that didn't faze Story. In fact, she liked the added edge his side hustle brought. It only made him more intriguing.

Confident in her ability to catch his eye, Story felt like the stars were finally aligning. She and Rakim shared the same gym class, and thanks to her gift of gab, she had already made small talk with him during warm-ups on the track field. She was certain it wouldn't be long before she worked her magic and sealed the deal. In fact, she was already planning to brainstorm with Justine after school.

. . .

Justine

By the end of the day, exhaustion had settled in her bones. She had started the day with her usual gusto, clinging to her family's mantra: *work before play*. But deep down, Justine was still a teenager. Part of her ached to experience the kind of love and carefree moments her friends seemed to have. As she watched them, she couldn't help but feel a quiet longing. They moved through their days so effortlessly, laughing, kissing, and daring to be free.

All day, she observed clusters of friends: some wandering the halls, caught up in gossip; others sharing heated kisses with their latest crush before rushing off to class; and still others standing in the hallway, hands in their pockets, scanning for the next fleeting connection.

How do they balance it all—fun, love and priorities? Curiosity tugged at the edges of her heart. She made a mental note to figure it out... and maybe, just maybe, let herself open to the possibility of love too— when the time was right.

For now, she had a mountain of homework waiting for her. Between the tests, reports, and reading assignments, almost every class had something looming on the horizon. But secretly, Justine thrived on the pressure, the busywork, the sense of moving toward a future goal. She actually looked forward to getting home and diving in.

She also had a second mission in mind: convincing her mother to go out for dinner that evening. With her father away at a conference in Atlanta, Justine thought it was the perfect opportunity. A new Italian restaurant, Salvatore's, had just opened a few blocks from their high-rise, and she had been itching to try it. With a little finessing, she was confident she could sway her mother. After all, if there was one thing consistent about Barbie Chandler, it was that she loved being on the forefront of whatever was trending.

She was walking toward her locker, mentally mapping out her evening, when Story rushed up, grabbed both her hands and practically pulled her out of her head.

"Girl, I think I'm in love!" Story squealed, jumping up and down. "Come on, let's go. We need to work on a plan for me to get my man!"

And just like that, Justine knew her night wasn't going to go as planned. Shaking off the flicker of disappointment, she put on her most supportive smile. She prided herself on being a good friend, and a little change of plans wasn't the end of the world. That could be sorted out later. Right now, her best friend needed her. And that always came first.

🙟 7 🙝

SCORE

Story

By February 1991, Story and Rakim were practically high school royalty. It hadn't taken long for her to win him over, even with half the girls at Bethune throwing themselves at him. Constantly. Story felt special: Rakim had looked past all of them and seen her—really *seen* her. She wasn't just pretty or popular. She was magnetic—a diamond in the rough, but still shining all the same.

They had been "official" since December, and with each passing day, Story fell harder. She felt certain that what they had together would stand the test of time. Sure, their love story was cliché on the surface—a tale of a star football player falling for a bright, spirited cheerleader. But to Story, it was much more: Rakim was her soulmate. On more than one occasion he had reassured her, "I only have eyes for you, boo," and Story, hungry for his devotion, believed him. She would've gone to the moon and back for Rakim. So one evening, under the cool hum of stadium lights and the crisp bite of winter, she agreed to venture into uncharted territory.

"Let's take things to the next level," Rakim proffered, eyes glinting with what Story perceived to be devotion.

"Ok," she replied breathlessly, too blinded by emotion to recall all the times she'd had to check Rakim about flirting with other girls.

It finally happened on a Saturday while chilling inside Rakim's grandmother's basement. Story took shallow breaths through her mouth to avoid ingesting the pungent smell of mildew that saturated the basement's walls. The two pretended to watch the latest block-buster release while sitting hip to hip on the old plastic-covered couch. She squirmed uncomfortably as cracks in the heavy material imprinted markings on her thighs. *What is he waiting on?* she thought as the couple's charade continued and they pretended to be unbothered by what lay ahead.

Rakim's grandmother had left for a meeting at the Senior Citizens' Center, promising to be back at eight. When Rakim placed his hand on Story's thigh, she didn't move. She barely breathed. Instead, she pretended not to notice, even as her heart loudly thudded against her rib cage. Rakim advanced, hungrily kissing and sucking her neck. Story pretended not to notice this either, but her body told a different story. With each moment, heat rose and bubbled over with anticipation. Part of her swelled with excitement, desire and disbelief that she was actu-ally about to take it "all the way"; another part of her curled up protec-tively, unsure about the repercussions of this decision.

Rakim tickled the lobe of her ear with his tongue as he leaned in to whisper, "You ready for all of this, baby?"

A chill shimmied down her spine as she noticed the rapid rise and fall of his chest as he spoke. Fear wouldn't allow her to meet his gaze. *All of what?* she thought in a small panic, while offering a feeble, "Yeah" instead.

She vividly recalled some of her friends' horror stories about their first times—tales of pain, disappointment and regret. But the manda-tory sex-ed classes and extensive talks with Justine weren't any comfort now either. Being inexperienced and newly in love, she had not taken the time to discern the real from the exaggerated; all she knew is that she was here now and a choice needed to be made. With every tongue swirl and kiss trailing down the trunk of her body, it became harder to think clearly. Caught between her body, heart and mind, Story didn't know which to follow—and there was no time to call Justine for a pep talk.

Left to her own devices, Story followed her body—she mirrored Rakim's movements, learning by feel. He kissed her neck, she kissed his. He rubbed her nipples, she traced slow, uncertain circles around the fuzzy tufts of hair on his chest. When Rakim's hand slipped under her skirt, she nearly bolted. Her body burned with a sensation that teetered on overwhelming. And dangerous. But before she could reconsider what she was doing—or not doing—Rakim's expert fingertips had found her panties. A few inches lower, he parted her lips and began to stroke, featherlight.

"Mmmm," Story groaned, her panic giving way to the pleasurable sensation.

"You like that, huh?" Rakim expertly increased his rhythm.

It felt... incredible. Sensually inebriated and disoriented, Story pressed into his fingers, feeling she was going to burst. Then, just as quickly as it all began, Rakim stood and began tugging his shirt over his head. As he fumbled hastily with the waistband of his jeans, he glanced over, voice low and rough:

"Do you have protection?"

"Huh? Umm... no," Story replied confused. "I thought you did." In all the movies she had watched, providing protection was always the guy's responsibility. A sound of frustration escaped Rakim's darkened lips as he put his head in his hands while Story kept her eyes downcast, feeling personally responsible and embarrassed for messing up "the mood" by being ill-prepared. As her disappointment morphed into shame, she wondered why they couldn't continue with their usual caressing sessions. Just then, Rakim spoke assuredly, making a decision for the both of them.

"It's ok," he said huskily. "I'll just use the tip."

"Ok," Story consented, not considering—or knowing—the significance or mechanics of just using "the tip." Struggling to regain her cool and keep the air of confidence she usually possessed, she began to peel off her blouse, followed by her skirt, while gazing brazenly into Rakim's eyes, the way she had seen them do in movies. As she did, the fear began to fade; if he still wanted her, she was ready. Story loved the feeling of being... desired. She craved it.

"You are so... doggone... beautiful," Rakim mused, allowing his roughneck persona to give way to mesmerization. He stood in the middle of the basement, naked and unashamed, his member at full attention as his eyes gulped down her raw beauty.

Story's heart melted feeling his eyes soften and seeing his body harden; she knew he was the one for her. Feeding on his unsheathed admiration, she whispered, "Thanks," while blushing and lying back on the couch.

Before she could take another breath, Rakim was on top of her.

Things escalated quickly: arms, legs and lips intertwined and reconfigured punctuated by gasps of air. The couch's sticky plastic cover did nothing to slow the lovers' passion. Rakim grunted and gyrated as he poked, preparing to enter her. Suddenly with one huge thrust, Story felt her insides nearly split in two.

She gasped, arching her back instinctively from the searing pain.

Her mind went blank. Sound ceased. For a moment, she thought she might even vomit.

"Sorry," Rakim grunted, "it slipped. You aight?"

She wasn't sure. Between the enormity of the sensation and the tidal wave of emotions threatening to break free, all she could utter was a shaky, "Yeah." Barely breathing, she made the quick decision to "woman up" and welcome his fullness.

Hearing no objection, Rakim began slowly rocking in and out of Story's body. As he did, the initial pain subsided, as Story attempted to catch and match his tempo. Sounds of pleasure escaped her lips. His thrusts sped up. Story gripped the back of the couch, ripping the plastic in a new place on the cushion. She was bracing herself for—what turned out to be—Rakim exploding inside her, too far gone to consider the ramifications of their actions. Five minutes after their escapade began, they both lay breathless and spent.

"You were amazing," he confessed before reassuming his usual arrogance. "I bet you liked that didn't you?"

"I was?" Story blushed initially before meeting his pretense with one of her own.. "I mean ... yeah. That was dope."

She sat up with only one thing on her mind: *Wait until Justine hears about this.*

Justine

Something was off—Justine couldn't feel Story. It was as though their usual connection was somehow blocked. As she sat on the couch with her parents staring at the game show, she kept wondering about her friend. Speaking with Ms. Denise earlier that evening, she was informed that Story was at their homegirl, Nora's, house, but it wasn't like Story to keep things from her.

"I'm surprised you're not there yourself," Ms. Denise prodded gently with a hint of suspicion. "Story told me you'd be there—"

"Oh, yeah..." Justine scrambled. "I'm headed there now. My parents made me... um... clean my room before I left. I was just double checking if Story had left yet."

Her cover seemed to work, but knowing nothing about this supposed "gathering" at Nora's nor where Story *actually* was concerned her. More than likely, she had run off with Rakim since the two had been practically attached at the hip since they started dating. While she was happy for her girl, she also saw legitimate red flags. It wasn't just her jealousy speaking. Sure, she wanted a boyfriend of her own, but what she *really* wanted was her friend back—the one she could count on not to put her in a position to lie.

Story offered to hook her up with one of Rakim's friends, but Justine was more than capable of finding her own boyfriend, when *she* was ready. And whoever she chose would certainly have more standards for himself than some low-level drug dealer: he *had* to be just right. She didn't dare confess this truth to Story—about the loneliness or difference in their standards. Instead, she let her studies take the place Story left empty. For now. She knew this affair with Rakim wouldn't last; until then, she'd just bide her time and continue listening to her best friend gush.

What could possibly be more fun than that, she thought facetiously, dreading the topic of what she anticipated would be her and Story's very next conversation. Just then, her father yelled out the winning answer to the show. His volume snatched Justine into the moment, where she feigned interest by cheering on his big win just as she'd do with Story later on.

⁙

"Girl, where have you been? I had to cover for you earlier with your mom." It was half past eight by the time Story finally called back.

"Oh my gosh! Did she call your house looking for me?" she whispered, panicked. "What did she say?"

"Don't worry about it," Justine tried to hide her disgust. "I covered for you, but where were you actually? Although—" she interrupted herself, "I'm pretty sure I can guess. The better question is: where were you *and* Rakim?"

"Girl," Story spoke conspiratorially. "We did it tonight at his grandmother's house and it was *amaaaazing*." Misreading the silence on the other end, she continued. "I love him soooooo much, Justine! After we finished, I started talking to him about when we get married and what our babies will look like—"

"Marriage? *Babies*?!" Justine almost choked. "You need to slow it down, girl! Let's rewind this. First off, I can't believe you had *sex*. Did you at least use protection?"

Silence.

"Story, *please* tell me you used a condom!" Again. Silence. "What if you catch an STD? What if you get pregnant?!"

"Girl, re-lax," She spoke a little too confidently for Justine's comfort. "That's not going to happen; Rakim would never cheat on me, one, and TWO, he said he pulled out."

It took all Justine's strength not to suck her teeth. She knew this was a special moment for her friend, but she wanted more for her, and wished she would choose more for herself. Relegated to rolling her eyes—since Story couldn't see through the phone—she simply replied, "For both of our sakes, I sure hope that you're right. Your mother would kill us both!"

"Why would she come after you?"

"Because I was your alibi, Einstein!" The love they shared broke through the wall of mounting emotions as they laughed together for the first time that night. "All jokes aside, you've got to be more careful, girl. We've got futures to think about. Please promise me you will do better!"

"Ok, ok," Story yawned, conceding. "I hear you *mom*. It won't happen again. Promise."

"Good," Justine yawned too. She still had more homework to finish. "Now that that's settled, I have to talk to you later girl. *Some* of us have work to do."

"Oh, I know." Pausing for dramatic effect, she added, "But I *did* my work for the night." Justine laughed along, but deep inside she cringed at the thought.

8

GLASS SLIPPERS

Justine

True to herself, Justine spent the rest of ninth grade fully committed to her studies. By the time sophomore year rolled around, she finally let herself loosen the reins just a bit—and began dating Daniel McClendon, a friend from Math Club. Daniel stood about 5'9" and weighed barely 145 pounds soaking wet. He was unassumingly handsome with smooth chocolate-brown skin, a neat low-top fade with a side part, square-framed glasses, and a chill, steady way about him that instantly reassured Justine.

Story, on the other hand, could never figure out what she saw in "Dorky Daniel," which is what she teasingly called him behind his back. But Justine was smitten. Even her parents—especially her dad—liked him, which was no small feat. He made her feel safe and valued, the way a good book wraps you up and carries you somewhere better. They could talk for hours about anything—math homework, civil rights issues, college dreams. Sometimes, they'd even imagined their futures together. Being with him felt as natural as breathing, as if he had been hand selected by God just for her.

Even now, as Justine pushed through endless racks of formal dresses at Vickie's Couture Boutique, searching for the one for the

Homecoming dance, she couldn't help but smile—thinking about something Daniel had said during their morning call.

"What are you over there looking all starry-eyed about?" Story teased.

Startled, Justine quickly looked away, trying to hide her smile. She wanted to keep this one thing to herself. "Nothing important."

Story had always been her ace, but Justine wasn't sure she'd understand this. "Did you find anything yet?" she asked, eager to change the subject.

"Nah, this store is lame. We can hit the mall after this, if you want," Story said, waving her hand dismissively. "But you're not getting off that easy. What's got you cheesing like that?"

Justine hesitated. "It's nothing. Really."

Story gave a mock pout. "Since when did we start keeping secrets from each other?"

Justine caved. "Fine," she said, still unsure. "This morning I was talking to Daniel on the phone and we were talking about astrology. He told me he had a dream that there was a constellation named Justine—"

A smirk teased Story's face, stopping her mid-sentence. "You know what? It's nothing—"

"Girl, go ahead! You already started, you may as well finish."

Justine exhaled.

"But when he woke up, he said he realized the constellation in his dream shined nowhere near as brightly as I do. He's just... so romantic."

She rushed the words out, only to have her brief moment of reverie shattered by Story's guffaws.

"I honestly had no idea how corny you two could get. This takes the cake! Or should I say *the stars*?!" Story's laughter gained momentum as she collapsed dramatically onto Justine's shoulder.

"You know what..." Justine began, agitation and hurt rising from some vaulted space within her. "This is why I didn't want to say anything."

Story sobered instantly. Justine wasn't just annoyed, she was genuinely hurt. "I'm... I'm really sorry, girl. I wasn't trying to hurt your feelings—"

"But you *did*, Story!" Justine surprised herself with the force behind her own words.

A pause fell between them—one of those rare moments where neither knew what to say or do. Story chewed her bottom lip, uncharacteristically pensive.

"You and Daniel seem to be... I don't know... *made* for each other," she said, eyes distant. Then more firmly, "It's no secret: me and you like different things in our men, but one thing's for sure, he's *definitely* for you... and I love that."

Justine smiled, softening a little. But deep down, she couldn't ignore another feeling: vexation. A small, yet threatening spark. Lately, all Story seemed to do was clown her relationship with Daniel—and even Daniel himself. After all the times she listened to her prattle on about that good-for-nothing Rakim?! And when Justine finally entrusted her with a sacred moment, *this* was the response she received? Something didn't feel quite the same between them anymore.

"Hey," Story gently interrupted, speaking softer than normal. "Are we good?" Seeing the concern in her friend's eye compelled her to shake it all off. At least for now. Besides, they were running out of time to find dresses for Homecoming—a once-in-a-lifetime moment and memory they would make together.

"Yeah, girl," Justine said, struggling to mean it. "We're good."

Story

Standing in front of her mirror admiring herself in a fitted red cocktail dress she'd fallen in love with, Story beamed. It was Homecoming night and her heart was doing flips. As she angled this way and that, she couldn't deny those 3-D rose florets flowering along the hemline. She slipped on her second gold hoop earring right when the doorbell rang.

Her new boyfriend, Jonathan Banks, had just arrived to pick her up. They met at Teen Night at the local skating rink. She remembered it clearly—the way he glided across the floor, smooth and flashing a smile that could melt steel. From the second their eyes met, she was hooked! Never one to sit back and wait, she skated onto the floor, grabbed his hand and introduced herself as they whirled together under the rink's strobe lights.

Jonathan attended a technical high school in North Philly, but that hadn't stopped them from seeing each other whenever they could, spending hours whispering on the phone, and laughing late into the night. Tonight's dance would be their first formal date and Story intended for it to be one to remember. She'd already given him strict instructions—red tie and a red carnations corsage to complement her dress. Jonathan had chuckled good-naturedly as he reassured her, "I got you."

Still barefoot, one heel dangling from her fingers, Story bolted from her room and toward the front door. She was too late. Denise was already welcoming Jonathan with a warm smile.

"How's it going, Jonathan?" her mother said brightly, leaning casually against the doorframe.

"It's going aight, Mrs. Brooks," he said shyly, shifting foot to foot.

"It's just *Ms.* Brooks," Story interjected, glancing at her mother for confirmation.

Denise rolled her eyes. "Yup. Juuust *Ms.* Brooks," she said dryly, before sauntering back toward her bedroom.

Story grabbed Jonathan's hand, flashing him an eager smile. "Ok, Mom, we're headed out!" she yelled over her shoulder. "Come on, before she makes us sit down for a bunch of questions," she commanded him in a hushed whisper, bumping him with her hip out of the door.

"Have fun Sweetie, don't stay out too late," Denise hollered back.

"Ok, Mom. Later!" Story tossed just as the door closed. Tonight was going to be one for the books—Story could feel it.

Justine

This night felt... *significant* for some reason. Justine did one final spin for her mother while gazing into the full-length mirror and smoothing her butter-cream yellow, A-line cocktail dress with her hands.

"Aw, baby!" Barbie exclaimed, clasping her hands together. "You look so beautiful!"

"You sure do, Little Lady," John bellowed over Barbie's shoulder. "Now let's get you off to this dance."

As she entered the living room with her parents in tow, Daniel quickly rose to his feet. When he saw Justine, his mouth parted. "You look amazing!"

Reaching out to Justine, he met John's broad chest instead. "Thanks son, but keep your hands to yourself, you hear?" Justine could see the tension in her father's jaw and feel the strain in his voice. "This is *my* baby girl I'm entrusting you with. You treat her with respect at all times and we won't have a problem. Protect her like the princess she is," her father continued, his chest puffed like the proud papa bear he was. "If you hurt her, you're hurting me. You hurt me... and I'll find you. That's a promise."

"Daddyyy... " Justine half-groaned, half-begged. This was getting embarrassing.

"Yes, sir, Mr. Chandler, you have my word," Daniel stood at attention. "Would it be alright if I gave her the corsage now, Sir?" He sheepishly held out the container for Justine to put it on herself.

Just then, the doorbell rang, breaking the awkward silence. Barbie hurried to answer it almost apologetically, warmly greeting Story and Jonathan.

"Hi you two," Barbie greeted.

Peeking his head around the corner, John bellowed, "You look pretty, Miss Story." He bent to give Story a warm embrace.

"Pictures," Barbie said suddenly, seeming moved by the scene. "We need pictures." As she rushed off to grab her disposable camera, Justine thought she detected a crack in her mother's voice, but shrugged it off assuming it was some mixture of her "little girl growing up" and "the change" her mother was always whispering about on the phone.

The two couples took pictures until their cheeks began to hurt. When Barbie insisted, "Just a few more," John placed his hand tenderly on her shoulder.

"I think they best be hurrying along, Barb. My driver is waiting for them downstairs." There was a moment of softness, when everything felt oddly... *complete*. "Be home by midnight. And have fun, but not too much," John directed, giving both young men a pointed stare. Justine and Story shared a knowing glance, happy to have each other for support.

"Yes Sir," Daniel and Jonathan said in unison as all four scurried to make their exit.

Story

The night was going amazingly well. Story and Jonathan were dancing up a storm, and she'd already introduced him to all her friends. Even better, he seemed to be getting along rather well with Daniel. Story could already see double dates in their future. *Who would've known?* As the night wound down, Principal Cloake took the stage to announce the Homecoming Court. Beside him stood Mrs. Baude—the Homecoming Chair, school guidance counselor, varsity cheer coach and Story's unofficial mentor. She caught Story's eye from the stage and gave her a quick wink. The simple gesture steadied her jitters, a little.

Story was up for Sophomore Class Queen. And she wanted it— badly. But she also knew competition was tough. Her cheermate Kendra Johnson could easily cause a split vote, they would likely have the support of the same jocks and squad mates. Then there was

Stephanie Satori. She had been handing out laminated *'vote for me'* flyers all week.

"Ladies and gentlemen, your sophomore class queen is..." Mr. Cloake paused dramatically, awaiting everyone's full attention, St–"

Just as her mind began drifting to worst-case scenarios, she heard her name called.

She had won!

Grinning, Story floated onto the stage. On the floor, Justine was screaming like a lunatic. Her heart swelled seeing—and hearing—her usually-composed bestie go all out to celebrate her tonight.

"That's my queen!" Jonathan proudly yelled as he pumped his fist in the air. He gave her an affectionate wink and dramatic bow when they made eye contact.

After each queen was crowned, Mr. Cloake moved on to the kings. As fate would have it, Rakim was pronounced Junior Class King. Story almost gagged.

Rakim.

The boy who shattered her heart just a few short months ago by tossing her aside with some tired excuse about her being "too clingy," was now in closer proximity than he had been in weeks.

His loss, Story beamed, grateful she was now with Jonathan—and finally realized Rakim wasn't the end-all be-all. She looked at him again. Jonathan emitted a proud, raucous cheer while holding her gaze, eliciting laughter from the crowd. Glancing back toward Rakim, Story felt herself slipping.

He does look too good in that suit tonight though.

She snapped out of it just in time for Mr. Cloake to announce the Court's first dance. One by one, the kings and queens paired off. Just as Story was making her way toward the sophomore king, the junior queen swooped in possessively. Story had almost forgotten that they were going steady. That left her only one option: Rakim.

Begrudgingly she grabbed his hand, avoiding eye contact with him, Jonathan and Justine.

"Let's get this over with," she muttered, leading him to the floor. On the way, she conveniently made a sharp turn by the table, causing Rakim's leg to clip the end of it. He released an expletive after stubbing his toe while Story scoffed, feeling the slightest sense of vindication.

"Dang, why you gotta be like that?" Rakim tossed, barely catching himself before he face planted. "You know you wanna dance with me. How could you resist all this?" Regaining his balance, he licked his lips and stroked the struggling peach fuzz on his chin.

Story rolled her eyes so hard it could be considered a workout. But as they both stood in the center of the dance floor, enfolded in each other's arms, chest-to-chest, the old familiarity hit like a punch to the gut. Something was happening.

He pressed his tall frame against Story's body, allowing his lips to brush her ear. "Congratulations on your win. You look really good tonight."

"Thanks," she offered coolly, trying her best to withstand the electricity between them.

Rakim pulled back just enough to meet her eyes. "Don't be mad, baby. I miss you." He almost seemed sincere. "I messed up." He looked around.

"Seeing you with that dweeb tonight... made me realize that you're meant for me. I can't just stand back and watch some other dude put his hands all over my lady." He slid his hands lower, settling at the small of Story's back. Her breath caught.

"*Your* lady?" she echoed, her resolve crumbling. She could see Jonathan out of her peripheral vision, and even if she couldn't see him, she could *feel* him. He was staring intently. Jaw tight. Unblinking. Fists clenched.

Justine stood next to him, as though in solidarity. Her gaze volleyed nervously, pleading with Story, between Jonathan and her best friend. As Story continued the obligatory ritual, or so she told herself, she felt her best friend's eyes flare with a fierce admonishment.

When Story finally met her gaze, she heard Justine loud and clear: *WHAT ARE YOU DOING?!* Story ignored the question, her face hot with overwhelming sensations. She was trapped between what *was* right and what *felt* right. It was too much for one moment considering how good those hands felt sliding lower down her body. She chose to refocus on Rakim.

"Look at him over there mad as hell," he continued.

Before she could catch herself, a giggle escaped. "Cut it out, Rakim. You're the one who broke up with me, remember? Don't be mad because I've moved on," she blushed. "What do you want from me anyway?"

"I want you back," he said simply. "Besides, he doesn't know how to handle a woman like you."

Her knees went jelly. "And what am I supposed to tell... him?" Story asked, relinquishing the little that was left of her better judgment.

"He'll catch the hint," Rakim said before leaning down to kiss her. Sloppy. Ravenous. Familiar.

Story didn't hesitate. She fell right back into that familiar dance, matching his passion like no time had passed. When she finally pulled away and looked around, Jonathan—and Justine—were nowhere to be found.

Justine

Story was tripping! Justine couldn't fathom any reason Story would jeopardize her relationship with Jonathan for the likes of Rakim, and all the drama that came with him. All the nights she listened to Story mourn the loss of their "storybook" romance were now going to waste; she was about to repeat the pattern all over again.

"*I just don't get it,*" Story had cried on Justine's shoulder. "*Can you believe he called me clingy? Like I was sweating him or something.*" As the sadness rose to the surface, she'd wrestle with denial, "*We were supposed to be forever.*"

"*Maybe it's for the best, you did say—*"

"*What?!*" Story had screeched, raw from the pain of a first time heartbreak. "*No way! Rakim is my soulmate.*"

At that, Justine decided to let time take its course, and to be a listening ear and loving presence instead. She spent weeks nursing her weepy friend back to sound mind. And when Story met Jonathan, things seemed to have gotten better all around—Justine and Story spent more time together, Story was more focused with her studies and Jonathan was a way better catch overall. He had a good head on his shoulders and legitimate plans to make his dreams a reality.

Now Justine watched helplessly as Story fell back into Rakim's snare. She couldn't understand why he had such a hold on her, but she wished he didn't. She wished she could break her best friend out of whatever spell he had her under, but she was powerless to change the course of events. Story would have to learn this lesson the hard way.

"You wrong," she mouthed to Story before her friend's face was swallowed by that obnoxious, and disrespectful kiss. At that, she had enough. She stalked out of the gymnasium with Daniel and Jonathan in tow. Even with the music, the crowd, and Rakim staking claim to her like a fresh pair of Timbs, she knew her friend had heard her.

Story

In the school's darkened auditorium, Story used muscle memory to find empty seats in the far corner. The guttural moans and smell of sweat in close proximity let her know they weren't alone. An hour later, they exited the auditorium feeling accomplished in what they'd set out to do—get *reacquainted.*

Since Rakim had driven to the dance in his used Hyundai Sonata, he offered to drive Story home. The car was baby blue with tan doors and cracked leather seats. You could hear the engine blocks before seeing the vehicle, and although it coughed black smoke while idling, Story couldn't be prouder of riding shotgun in his most prized possession. On the way home, Story reflected on the fact that she'd won *her* man back. *Who could have imagined the night would end like this?* she mused.

On cloud nine, she barely made it out of Rakim's car. Following another round of "reacquainting," she glided into her apartment building, and exited the elevator at her floor. But just as she stepped off, she caught a glimpse of her mother kissing a tall man with his back to Story. Upon hearing the *ding* of the elevator car, he quickly jumped on the other elevator.

"Hey... Mom," Story began hesitantly, "Who was that?"

Denise was unusually flustered, blinking rapidly, chest rising and falling as she swallowed hard. "Hey baby..." she stalled, "Uh, you're back early. How was the dance?"

Story ignored her mother's deflection.

"It was fine. Who was that?" Story had never seen her mother so much as give a man a double take, let alone kiss one.

"Who was *who?*"

"Ok," Story relented, too sex-weary to play Inspector Gadget. "Whatever."

As they both entered their home, she decided to let her mom keep her secret. After all, she certainly had no intention of divulging her new relationship status to her mother. Story retreated to her room, daydreaming about "her boo." All the while that tan trench coat, brown leather loafers and scent of vanilla sandalwood kept interrupting her memories. It all reminded her a lot of Mr. John. *But that's... impossi-*

ble. Still, she knew no one else who had a style quite like his. Without concrete proof, her suspicions were just that: suspicions. She took out her diary, determined to capture all the juicy details from her night with Rakim instead.

There were some things about this night she could not afford to forget.

$$\text{\textbf{9}}$$

TORN

Justine

After a lot of hard work—and even more convincing—Justine finally landed a summer internship at Dream Makers Grow. It was the summer before senior year, and so far, it was shaping up to be everything she'd hoped for. Having always looked up to her father, she knew from a young age she wanted to follow in his footsteps, especially when it came to advocacy work. Justine's dream was clear: she would become a civil rights lawyer.

Now, every morning felt like stepping into that dream. She and her father shared a pot of coffee, discussed the morning news and waved goodbye to her mother as they headed out for their day. It felt natural —like she was exactly where she was meant to be. And she loved everything about it: the business suits, the rhythm of the streets, the sense of purpose humming through her veins and, most importantly, working alongside her hero. She already knew most of her father's staff, and the ones she didn't yet know had quickly taken her under their wing. Working closely with her father's new executive assistant, Kimberly, Justine soaked it all in.

Kimberly was a well spoken twenty-two year old career woman. She possessed an undeniable zest for life and the drive to bring others into her experience. Unlike John's prior assistants, Kimberly was all business. She'd never given Justine any indication that she was there for anything but change for the people. Given their closeness in age, the two related well to one another. In time, they developed a friendship in addition to an exceptional professional relationship.

Kimberly showed Justine everything from how the team chose which injustices to rally behind to how speeches were written, edited and sharpened for maximum impact. She shook hands with politicians, pastors, community organizers—more connections than she could've ever imagined. Interning at Dream Makers Grow didn't just give her experience, it gave her a voice. Standing beside her father, fighting for justice, Justine felt powerful. She finally felt seen.

As her skills grew, so did her father's faith in her. Before long, he was inviting her to join him on the road. That weekend, they were flying to Los Angeles, where he'd speak at a major social justice roundup alongside some of the country's leading civil rights activists. She had spent the entire week bubbling with excitement, picturing the city lights, the energy and the history unfolding around her. By the time they finally touched down in L.A., standing beside her father felt like living the dream. She could see herself doing this work with him for as long as life allowed.

Justine couldn't wait to share every detail with her two favorite people: Daniel and Story.

Story

There were four things Story Johnniece Brooks didn't play about: Justine, fashion, her man and academics. Justine was her ride or die. There wasn't a single thing Story wouldn't do for her. After years of friendship that bordered on being family, they kept all—well, *almost* all —of each other's secrets and admitted their bond was destined to last a lifetime.

Even after the stunt she pulled at Homecoming their sophomore year, when Justine had been incredibly disappointed in her, they hashed and hugged it out after a few days. It took time, but Story could finally admit her wrongdoing. While she was elated to have her man back, she could have handled the whole situation better with Jonathan. He didn't deserve the way she went about things. Justine had been right about that. That hiccup was far from unusual. The girls fought like sisters, not always seeing eye to eye, but if there was one thing they could always depend on, it was making up.

Among her peers, Story had a reputation: she was *that* girl. The one who floated down Bethune's halls with a flawless yet fearless style. No one could match her attentiveness to detail or dared push the limits stylistically the way she did. She never shied away from bold colors that accentuated her complexion, mixing patterns and textures, high end with lower end brands.

As a trendsetter, she was the go-to girl for fashion advice—first for friends, then for anyone who had twenty bucks, materials and full trust in Story's creative vision. After styling her and Justine's Homecoming looks, her clientele skyrocketed. She had a knack for dressing people for their personalities so that *they* owned the look. From the first day of school to date night apparel—Story could whip up a fit so memorable, she stayed booked and busy. Being well-versed on how to flip a dollar didn't hurt either. While Denise and her daughter had never lived in excess, they had also never felt lack—for the most part. Story's grades remained steady. This was part of the agreement she made with her mother when Denise became concerned about Story spending so much time with clothing.

"I see you spending a lot of time with these clothes and things, but I need you to remember how this household works," her mother had said. "Education first, entertainment after. As long as your grades stay up, you are free to style to your heart's content."

"You've got yourself a deal, Mother Dear," Story had said, extending her right palm formally for Denise to accept. They shook on it, and from that moment on, Story's M.O. had been, *Work hard, play harder.* The A's and B's on her report card kept Denise happy, and Story free to play to her heart's content.

By the end of junior year, word of Story's talents—both with a sewing machine and a store rack—had traveled fast, earning her five personal stylist orders before summer even began. She was confident more would follow and looked forward to pocketing a pretty penny from her growing side hustle. It was a good thing she worked well under pressure and thrived on multitasking because Rakim demanded a fair share of her time also. Not that she minded. Since they had found their way back to each other more than a year ago, they had broken up—and made up—at least twice. Still, her love for his unapologetic ways and insatiable sexual appetite deepened. He was *it* for her—funny, manly, sexy, about his business and never shy about showing Story off to his friends.

Unfortunately, Story couldn't do the same. When she wasn't working, she was torn between spending time with Justine or Rakim—two people she loved deeply, but who couldn't seem to share the same space without tension. And lately, there was a new reason for the growing distance—one that Story couldn't bring herself to tell anyone.

Rakim had asked Story for a threesome. With Justine.

Not only did Story feel crushed that the man of her dreams would be fantasizing about her best friend, but she felt diminished and disrespected, as though she wasn't *enough*. This latest obsession of his had crossed the line. Sharing her best friend in such an intimate way was absolutely out of the question. And if Justine only knew, Story would never hear the end of it. It was Justine who constantly reminded her of her big dreams of being a fashion designer. And over the past year, Story spent a lot of time learning from Mr. Chandler, too, about the importance of watering dreams.

In fact, he was the inspiration behind her restructuring of her budding fashion business—*he* had given her the idea about being a personal stylist. She remembered his words clearly, "Manage the three C's: your craft, your clients and your cash the way *YOU* want to. Always remember that, Little Lady. Stay in control of *your* business."

There was another significant relationship that bloomed during Story's sophomore year—Mrs. Baude, the cheer coach. Between academics and sports, they spent a lot of time together, and the woman had become more than a mentor to her. When a city-sponsored summer program needed a counselor, Mrs. Baude handpicked Story. Given their close relationship, Story couldn't say no; if her coach saw something in her, she trusted that. Between her commissions, chilling with Justine, keeping Rakim "satisfied," and now cheer camp, Story's plate was full. She had everything mapped out and in its proper place when the thing she least expected happened.

Story fell in love. Again.

This time it was with her job. She wasn't just great at it; connecting with children came naturally. The more time she spent with the camp kids, the more she grew as a person. Story began thinking before she spoke, taking on more responsibility and reflecting more deeply on her actions. Those twenty-five pairs of eyes watching her each day pushed her to consider the kind of woman she wanted to become. She was becoming a mentor to those girls just as Mrs. Baude was for her. As her love for nurturing children strengthened, Story considered a new possibility. Maybe she'd like to become a teacher. Everyone she shared it with was supportive, especially Justine, Mrs. Baude and her mother.

Still, one part of her life remained messy and tangled—Rakim. And his fantasy.

With so much pressure from various aspects of her life, Story finally decided to ask her mentor for advice on her love life debacle. As the two wiped down mats and put back equipment one evening, Story tentatively broached her concerns.

"Mrs. Baude, can we have some girl talk?"

"Ohhh," Mrs. Baude teased. "This sounds serious. Do we need to go grab a couple of containers of ice cream and sit down?" Seeing the somber look on Story's face, she became serious. "Absolutely. What's on your mind, hun?"

Story looked around to ensure there weren't any little ears in sight. "It looks like everyone is gone for the evening. Can we go sit in your office?"

"Sure, let me just go lock up. I'll meet you there."

As Story contemplated the best way to share her dilemma, she shuffled to her mentor's office and took a seat. Head down and hands tucked beneath her knees, she felt like her heart would burst out of her chest. Instead, tears raced down her face as soon as Mrs. Baude entered the office.

"Oh no! What's wrong, honey?" Mrs. Baude gushed, stooping at Story's side and handing her a box of tissues.

She worked to compose herself and glanced up apprehensively.

"This is just so embarrassing," she sniffed. "I really need your advice, but please promise you won't judge me."

"Story," Mrs. Baude began, "I am your coach, and now your boss. But I hope you would know that the most important position that you hold in my life is my mentee. I take pride in our relationship. It's my personal mission to ensure you have all the tools you need in life to be the best version of yourself. There isn't anything you could tell me or ask me that would make me think any differently of you."

"Well, I'm sure it's stupid really," Story giggled nervously, "I'm having guy troubles."

"Haven't we all?" the willowy brunette scoffed, fluttering her eyes. "So let's hear it. What's on your heart?"

Relationship advice was something the middle-aged woman felt she could handle although she knew teens nowadays had much more on their plate than she did at their age. She had heard it all: *This girl looked at my man. I have a crush on such and such. Who should I take to prom?* She braced herself for more of the like.

"I've been dating Rakim off and on for a while now. And I thought things were going well, until he started suggesting we 'spice things up,'" Story paused, glancing to gauge her coach's reaction. The same caring expression rested on her unlined face. "He wants to have a threesome with my best friend, Justine. I don't get it. I know that I'm new to this sex thing, but I thought I was enough. Lord knows we get enough practice."

Mrs. Baude stifled a cough. She had no idea they would be traveling down this lane.

"Now this?" Story's eyes were pleading. "I love Rakim, but I love Justine too. And as much as Rakim means to me, I would never jeopardize my relationship with her like that. So what should I do?"

There was a moment of quiet filled only by the buzz of fluorescent lights. They seemed to join the two women—one young, one experienced—in contemplation. Deep in thought, Mrs. Baude paused to consider her response. And collect herself from the shock she was working hard to hide.

"Let me ask you this: what is your gut telling you?"

"There is no way I'd ever do such a thing. I can't even bring myself to tell Justine, but I also don't want to lose Rakim," Story wrung her hands. "I guess my gut tells me to figure out a way to make us all happy? But I don't know how to do that."

There was another pause.

"How do you think you would feel if you gave in to Rakim's request?" Mrs. Baude's tone was cautious.

"I can't imagine I'd feel very good about myself. My mom always tells me to never compromise my integrity for the sake of quick satisfaction. You've told me to never accept less than my worth. And I know that I'm deserving of respect and love without conditions," she paused, regaining her composition. "And I don't like sharing my dessert."

Mrs. Baude's smooth face suddenly came alive with unabashed laughter, lines appearing only when she smiled. *Beauty lines,* Story thought, joining her. She watched the woman take a swig from her water bottle and felt relieved they could share a laugh at a time like this.

"You are absolutely right in all that you've said, my dear. I can't say that I'm pleased to hear that you're having sex, but you are your own person. So, all I can do is encourage you to act responsibly. Are you using protection at least?"

"Yeah. When I told my mom, we had a long talk. She set up an appointment and I was prescribed the pill. She also gave me a pack of condoms and told me to let her know if I ran out." They laughed again at Denise's vigilance.

"It's clear your mother doesn't play when it comes to her baby," Mrs. Baude said finally. "I can't say I blame her."

"Yeah, I can pretty much talk to her about anything, but THIS... " Story added quickly. "She's not the biggest Rakim fan."

"Can't say I blame her there," was all Mrs. Baude could muster. "Look, you have too bright a future ahead of you to ever allow anyone to put you in a position you're not comfortable in."

"You sound like Justine now."

"*She* sounds like a friend worth keeping," her mentor gave her a knowing look. Story agreed. She knew she had to protect her friendship at all costs. "I know a star when I see one, and you're a bright girl with the world at your fingertips. Anyone who presses you to go against that isn't meant for you." There was a deep affection in her words.

"Sometimes we gotta learn to make peace with letting go of dead weight when someone's season has ended. Do you understand what I'm telling you?"

"I do."

"Trust me, I'm speaking from personal experience." Story wondered what experience had put so much certainty in the woman's tone, but she had her own life to live right now. After a few moments, she stretched, feeling lighter and more energized.

"Thanks for hearing me out, Mrs. Baude. I think I know what I need to do."

"I KNOW you know." They both smiled.

"Aaaaannnnd...is that offer for ice cream still good?"

"You read my mind, Miss Lady. I think we've earned it if I do say so myself."

❧ 10 ☙

A MEETING AT THE CROSSROADS

Justine

Day one of the conference in L.A. felt nothing short of magical. Justine watched in awe as her father took the stage at the opening luncheon, commanding the room with more than his words. His voice shifted effortlessly to emphasize key points. His eyes met those in the audience, drawing them in with unspoken dialogue and warm, improvisational banter. Justine absorbed every moment, watching as the room leaned in with her. Her father was captivating, and though she was his daughter, she was also his biggest fan.

Afterward, the networking was nonstop. It felt like they spent hours shaking hands, exchanging stories and weaving connections. Justine met the mayor of Los Angeles, a bishop from South Central, a host of activists and even a survivor of a racially-motivated attack. Each encounter left her more inspired—their paths were different, but their purpose was shared.

In the afternoon, the crowd split into smaller groups to collaborate on addressing the injustices facing their respective communities. Justine was electrified by the conversations. Though the youngest in her group, she felt anything but out of place. In fact, she was giddy—like she'd finally found where she belonged. That night, there was no doubt in her mind: this was her life path. Law wasn't just a goal anymore—it was her calling.

By the time Justine finally returned to her hotel room for the evening, she was on such a high, she couldn't sleep. She reached for a stack of postcards she had purchased from a local vendor at the conference. She pulled out one with a photograph of Santa Monica Beach at nightfall and wrote to Daniel. She told him how alive she felt, how deeply connected she was to the movement, how much she missed him—and promised to see him as soon as she returned to the East Coast. After lining her lips with her favorite fuchsia lipstick, she sealed the note with a kiss.

Next came a postcard of Rodeo Drive. She gushed to Story about the fashion, promising they would come back one day to shop to their hearts' content, spot celebrities and track down every local hotspot. She ended the note with their signature chant: *Istersay istersay, hatstay ymay istersay!*

The final postcard revealed a red-brick chapel with stained-glass windows, built in 1908 and tucked in the heart of L.A. Word was that Dr. King had spoken there just months before his assassination. Justine penned a short note to her mother, assuring her that Dad was taking good care of her, that she had met some wonderful people and that she couldn't wait to share everything when she returned home. They'd chat over a meal at Salvatore's, which had become her and Barbie's local favorite food spot. She gave the postcard a light spritz of her favorite perfume, a touch her mother had taught her, then added it to the pile.

Moments later, she was at the front desk, requesting the postcards be sent out with the morning mail. Hopefully, they would make it back to Philly before she did.

Feeling accomplished, Justine finally began winding down. Day two of the conference promised to be even bigger than the first, and she was determined to hit the ground running. After her shower and skin-care routine, she steamed her blush-pink two-piece suit, then laid out her comfortable—yet commanding—four-inch black pumps, a simple gold herringbone necklace and the earrings Story had sworn would complete the look. With her hair pinned in soft curls, Justine slipped under the covers, ready for a sweet slumber.

Her father had arranged for the entire Dream Makers Grow team to stay in an upscale hotel in the heart of Los Angeles—just a short walk from the conference center. For her mother's peace of mind and Justine's safety, he'd requested that her room be adjoined to Kimberly's, his sharp and ever-efficient executive assistant. When they checked in, Justine promised she'd bang on the wall at bedtime to say goodnight. It was partly a joke, but now, remembering her promise, she got up to do exactly that.

As she neared the adjoining door, she heard voices. Kimberly's unmistakably light and conversational timbre. And then—her father's. Followed by soft giggles.

Justine froze. Her heart ticked faster. Without knowing why, she darted to the other side of the room and jumped back into bed, staring at the ceiling as questions buzzed through her mind.

She turned onto her side, catching sight of the clock on the nightstand: 11:07 p.m.

What is he doing in Kimberly's room at this hour? Whatever it was, couldn't it wait until morning?

Her stomach twisted in guilt. For her mother's sake, Justine felt like she had to know. Quietly, she crept back toward the door, pressing her ear against it, hoping to catch another clue. But the room had gone silent. *Maybe it wasn't him,* she reasoned. For all she knew, Kimberly had just been watching TV. As a dry laugh escaped her lips, she stepped away from the door, calmer this time. As she climbed into bed for good she thought, *Look at you, playing detective in silk pajamas.* Justine knotted her head scarf at the nape of her neck before reclining onto the soft downy pillows. *I must be quite the sight right now.*

And while the thought evoked a shallow chuckle, it still took her a while to fall asleep.

Story

"Yoooo, that was bomb!" Rakim panted as he rolled to his side. "But you know what would make it better, right?"

Story's expression immediately shifted from satisfaction to huffed annoyance.

"What's that, Rakim?" she asked condescendingly. "And make sure you *think* before you speak. Because if you say what I think you're about to say, I swear I'm gonna flip out."

"Dang, boo, chill! I was just gonna remind you that your girl Justine is always welcome... if you know what I mean." He chuckled to himself, too proud of his one-sided joke.

Story's face was deadpan. Her glare made it clear she knew exactly what he meant, and she wasn't amused. Not even a little. Closing her eyes, she slowly counted to ten. Then she got up and began collecting her clothes from where they were tossed around the room.

"Where you goin', girl? I was just kidding," Rakim laughed nervously, trying to sound casual. "I ain't even peeped that young jawn like that, forreal forreal. You need to stop being so sensitive."

She couldn't believe it! He was talking like she had offended him. She fastened the last two buttons on her oversized cardigan before turning to face him—fury blazing in her eyes. Her voice smoked.

"Rakim, let me tell you something: you *ain't* all that! You're scum. The kind that sticks to the bottom of your shoe—no, worse. You're straight from the gutter. I don't know what I was thinking getting with you, let alone giving you a second, third, fourth and fifth chance."

"A second chance?" he scoffed. "Wait... I forgave *you*! You practically begged me to come back!"

"If that's what you took from everything I just said, you're more delusional than I thought. Let's get something straight—maybe I entertained your little pasty behind, but my girl Justine? She's never been your concern. Ever. I don't roll like that, and neither does she." Story's voice shook, not with fear, but fury.

"Forget 'sharing is caring.' Have you ever heard 'three's a crowd'? I would *never* disrespect myself—or my best friend—like that. Justine's like a sister to me. She's my ace. But you wouldn't understand that kind of loyalty. And for the record, she would *never* think to come for my man or rock the boat." She paused, her voice simmering. "Tuh. Rock the boat—you wouldn't know anything about that either. You and your little pee-wee can go find your next victim because I'm done. And when I walk out that door, do me a favor: lose my number, *scrub*."

"You'll be back!" Rakim called out trying to salvage the last bit of his dignity.

The door slammed behind her in response.

Story stormed out of his grandmother's basement, her head held high. She had never felt so furious—and never so free. Justine, Mrs. Baude and her mother were going to get a real kick when they heard this one.

For the first time, Story had truly stood up to Rakim. And it felt good.

Justine

Day two was finally here! Justine awoke the next morning feeling refreshed and ready for whatever the day had in store. She sprang out of bed and dove into her morning routine. One thousand sit-ups and five hundred jumping jacks later, she took a quick shower and slipped into her carefully planned outfit. Before leaving, she banged briskly on the adjoining door to alert Kimberly she was heading downstairs to join the rest of the team.

"Kim! I'm out!"

But as she stepped out of her suite and turned toward the elevators, she ran smack into her father—mid-stride, apparently attempting to make a quick exit from... was it *Kimberly's* room?

John froze, panic flashing across his face.

Justine's eyes darted from the suit jacket draped over his arm to his wrinkled shirt and slightly unkempt 'fro. Then to Kimberly's door. And back again.

Her stomach dropped. "No. No. No, no, no!" she shouted, fumbling with her room key, desperate to get as far away as possible.

John stepped forward, closing the space between them and wrapping her in a tight bear hug just as Kimberly peeked out from her suite. Upon seeing Justine, she gasped and quickly slammed the door.

"It's not what you think. I'm sorry, baby girl," John repeated, clinging to her. "It's not what you think."

"Let go of me!" Justine screamed, thrashing, trying to break free.

John wrested the key from her hand, unlocked her door and ushered her inside before the entire floor caught wind of the scene.

"How could you? What about Mom?" Justine cried, collapsing onto the bed.

"Baby girl, this is all a misunderstanding," John said, his tone shifting wildly between pleading and commanding. "I don't know what you think you saw, but I can explain. Calm down."

Justine struggled to steady her breath.

"She just needed help with some paperwork before today's session —" John insisted.

"Liar!" she snapped. "How would you feel if it were your mom getting screwed over? I know Grandma raised you better than this!" Her voice cracked under the weight of heartbreak.

"You've always told me to carry myself with integrity. With *standards*. To do the *right* thing even when it's hard. And this—" she gestured wildly toward the adjoining wall, "—is how you live that out?"

John inhaled sharply as if her words had knocked the breath from his lungs. Justine continued, angrily wiping free-flying spittle mixed with tears from her face. "Let me tell you, you're missing the mark by a long shot these days!"

"Hey! Watch yourself, young lady! I'm still your—" he began to bark, but caught himself. His voice softened, pathetically so. "I'm sorry. Kimberly tricked me. She called last night needing help, and I... I got caught up. But you don't need to worry. I already fired her. She's done. Gone. I'll give her a severance package, but she's not going to ruin this family more than she already has. I swear it."

"*Her* ruin the family?"

"You know what I mean... I should've seen through Kimberly, but I didn't. That's on me. But I swear to you, my eyes are open now."

He reached for Justine, but she recoiled. "Don't."

"Whatever you want, baby girl... whatever you want," he murmured desperately.

Justine stared at him, expression blank, her chest rising and falling with quiet intensity.

Her father dropped his head and rubbed the back of his neck, as if trying to press away the shame. "I messed up. I know I did. Damn it," he muttered, more to himself than to her. "But we can move past this. Your mother doesn't need to know."

"Of course. Just like the back-to-school shopping spree and the ice cream. Can't say I haven't heard that one before," she spat facetiously.

John didn't chide her this time. It was clear Justine had been paying attention all those times. It was evident that her grace had run its course.

"I'll fix it. I'm a man, and I made a mistake. But this doesn't define me. I've never done anything like this before. I love your mother. Please don't tell her. You want us to stay together, don't you?"

He paused, as though the silence would grant the absolution he sought. Justine said nothing. She could only stare.

This was her father—her motivator, her voice of reason, her hero. The one who had taught her how to dream big and stand tall. But now, all she saw was a man. *Just* a man. With every word he spoke, something inside her broke. And with each break, her heart hardened a little more. Tears rushed down her cheeks carrying traces of liner and mascara, dripping onto and darkening the fabric of her pink suit. She didn't speak. She didn't need to.

In that moment, Justine understood something no daughter ever wants to realize: even heroes fall. Even fathers lie. Even changemakers cheat.

There were no fairytales: only secrets.

Just then, she thought of her mother, and how she seemed to revere her father. This would break her. But *John*, as she now thought of him, had made his bed.

One day, he'd have to lie in it. And maybe even make it up.

If he could.

CATCH A FALLEN STAR

Story

After the initial adrenaline rush of checking Rakim, Story crashed —hard. She went home, crawled into bed and cried her way through the remainder of the weekend. Under normal circumstances, she would've leaned on Justine to help her navigate the heartbreak. But Justine was still in L.A., unreachable until her return.

When Story tearfully recounted everything that transpired with Rakim, Denise was furious that "that boy" had treated her daughter with such disrespect. Still, her mother also seemed proud. Story had stood up for herself: she had drawn a line, spoken her truth and walked away.

"I get it baby" Denise sat on the edge of Story's bed after watching helplessly for days as her only child fought to manage her emotions. "We've all been there and had our share of heartbreaks, missteps and lessons learned the hard way," she continued.

Story looked up at her mother and sniffled in response. She knew her mother was doing her best to console her, but she could also feel her mother's relief at knowing Rakim was finally out of her daughter's life—a feeling she couldn't yet access for herself. Her mother continued.

"It wasn't very long ago at all, I fell hard for someone that should have been off-limits. My parents would have killed me had they known." Denise inhaled shakily. "My family had their issues, but my parents did teach me right from wrong. I knew better... but the heart wants what the heart wants."

Story nodded, perking up at this rare moment of intimacy between her and her mother. "What did you do? How did you fix it?" Story greedily ingested these morsels of her mother's past love life.

"I eventually allowed myself space to mature and grow into someone I could be proud of. That's not to say I didn't stumble. I went back to that man plenty of times before finding my footing and standing strong in my decision to leave." She rested her hand on Story's thigh. "Of course... I always prayed your path would be easier than mine. You have the tools to weather any storm, Story." Denise looked directly into her daughter's eyes.

"Thanks Mommy," Story hugged her mother's neck.

"You're welcome."

As Denise stood to leave, she paused at the door. A current of love seemed to flood the room. Story felt it before her mother said a word: "And baby, no matter what, I'll always be here to guide you back to your center. Whatever it takes."

Story nodded gratefully, seeing her mother as a woman, perhaps for the first time ever.

Justine

For more than two hours, John had begged, pleaded, groveled—offering apology after apology, trying desperately to salvage his "Little Lady's" silence. He dangled promises like carrots: a brand-new car, a lavish vacation to anywhere she desired, stacks of hard cash. But when he stooped low enough to guilt her, saying that telling her mother would "break up the family,"Justine hit her breaking point. She was done—emotionally drained and physically incapable of putting on a united front with the man she now despised.

She had no idea what to do next. A part of her felt she had no choice but to tell her mother the truth: that her father had been unfaithful. Over the years, there had been moments—whispers, inconsistencies, things she chose to overlook. But this wasn't speculation anymore. This wasn't a misread moment or some optical illusion. John had been caught red-handed and had no choice but to confess. Now, the weight of that truth sat squarely on Justine's shoulders, threatening to crush her.

She knew the truth would shatter her mother. Barbie's whole identity was her family. To be the one who pulled that world apart? Justine couldn't bear it. It was at that moment she decided her mother didn't deserve this heartbreak—not now, not ever. So if Justine had to carry the weight of this secret to protect her, she would.

When her father finally left her hotel room, she lay in bed crying until she couldn't cry anymore. Puffy-eyed and emotionally spent, she longed to be back in Philly—with people who truly loved her, with clarity, with peace. After hours of misery, Justine finally drifted off. She never made it to another day of the five-day conference.

❦

On the final day, as the group checked out, Justine could hardly look at her father without tears threatening to spill. Kimberly was nowhere to be seen. Allegedly, she had been sent home early due to a "family emergency." The irony was almost comical.

When the plane touched down, she avoided John entirely and hitched a ride from her colleague, Gladis. As soon as she walked into the family's condo, she embraced her mother tightly. Barbie's radiant smile nearly broke her. Less than an hour later, she knew she couldn't stay in the same home as her mother without the events of her trip spilling over.

"Mom, I'm going to see Daniel for a bit."

"That's fine, dear," Barbie chimed easily, sensing her daughter needed space. She quietly welcomed the chance to spend some rare alone time with her husband.

As Justine walked through the summer heat to Daniel's house, her thoughts churned. She was resolved not to tell her mother, but didn't know how to face her father either. The moment Daniel opened the door, Justine's façade crumbled. Tears poured from her eyes like an overdue rain cloud finally fulfilling the forecast.

Daniel said nothing. He simply held her.

It took nearly twenty minutes to coax her inside, and another fifteen before her sobs slowed into words. She told him everything—every detail. Daniel listened without interruption, quietly absorbing the story that fractured his image of Mr. Chandler. The man who had always seemed unshakeable now appeared deeply flawed. *Treat her with respect at all times... Protect her like the princess that she is... If you hurt her, you're hurting me.* Mr. Chandler had said each of these statements to him on more than one occasion.

Well what happens when YOU hurt her? Daniel rebutted his own memory. *One thing's for certain, I will never break MY end of our bargain.* He held Justine a little closer.

"Wow," he said, carefully. "That's... a lot."

"I'm just so lost, Daniel. Not just hurt—*lost*. This affects everything. My mom, my job... my peace. My dad was reckless. This could ruin us all."

"What are you going to do?" he asked gently.

"I can't tell my mom—it would devastate her. I can't tell anyone at Dream Makers Grow either. It's his company. No one would believe me, or worse, they'd cover for him. I feel like I'm stuck... like I just have to carry this and pray I'm never in this situation again." She paused, then added, "This wasn't the first time I saw something like this. I just... always looked away. But this time, I couldn't. I just couldn't." The tears came again. Softer this time.

She laid her head in Daniel's lap, lost in thought.

Daniel stroked her hair. "You're not alone in this. We'll figure it out."

Justine looked up at him. She was aching for comfort, for love, for something she could trust. She reached up and kissed him.

What started soft quickly grew intense. Her hands roamed. Daniel's body responded. He matched Justine's efforts—kissing, caressing, sucking. Swept up in the moment, she began fumbling with his belt. He pulled back abruptly.

"What are you doing?" she asked. "Please don't stop."

"You're hurting right now," he said, cupping her face. "Are you sure this is what you want? I want our first time to be special."

"This *is* special," she whined. "I love you and you make me feel good. There's no one or nowhere else I'd rather be, and I need you. Right now. I need you to hold me. I need to be as close to you as I can. I need to feel connected to something... *someone*... real. I need to feel the realness of your love for me."

Daniel was still. Then he stood. "Give me fifteen minutes."

He darted from the room, leaving Justine confused but smiling. She could hear him scrambling through different rooms, gathering... something. Things clinked, rattled and even dropped a few times. Her upset began to dissipate with the sounds of his frantic scavenger hunt.

Exactly fifteen minutes later, Daniel returned with a silk scarf and handed it to her. "Put this over your eyes."

She laughed. "Why?"

"Trust me?"

"Always."

He guided her carefully downstairs to the family room. "Ok," he said. "Take it off."

Justine removed the blindfold and gasped.

He had laid out a makeshift picnic: a soft blanket, scattered rose petals, candlelight flickering in a heart-shaped pattern. Two wine glasses filled with apple juice. A bowl of strawberries. Her heart swelled.

Tears filled her eyes. Happy ones this time. "Daniel... this is beautiful."

He wiped her tears tenderly. They sat, sipped, fed each other strawberries and talked softly in the golden glow. Then Justine turned to him, her eyes heavy with longing. Their kiss reignited, deeper now. Clothes came off more slowly, thoughtfully. Daniel planted kisses wherever he saw skin as though simultaneously asking permission and giving thanks.

Justine's fingers grazed his manhood. And when Daniel hesitated again, Justine met his gaze and gave him a simple, steady "Yes."

Daniel lifted the hem of Justine's dress, pressing kisses to every inch of newly revealed skin. She grew greedy with anticipation, easing his shorts down until they pooled at his feet. She gasped—his manhood stood thick and fully engorged. Wrapping her fingers around his shaft, she began to stroke him, tentatively at first, then with growing confidence as his reaction affirmed her touch.

Daniel gently guided her back until she was reclined on the makeshift pallet, his body hovering just above hers. Their eyes remained locked, Daniel silently asking the question neither of them had to say aloud. Justine, dizzy with desire, nodded and shifted her hips to slide off her panties.

With a nudge of his knee, Daniel parted her legs, and she felt the firm press of him at her entrance. To her own surprise, her body welcomed him, already slick and swollen with yearning. Still, Daniel took his time, easing into her with care. He never took his eyes from hers. He remained watching, listening, feeling, making sure her *Yes* remained intact.

Justine answered him wordlessly, lifting her hips to meet him fully, drawing in the length of him with a soft gasp. Their bodies found rhythm instinctively, a gentle dance building toward a fevered crescendo. The pace quickened, their breaths shortened and Justine gripped Daniel as waves of pleasure surged through her.

Within minutes, he spilled into her with a guttural moan and she trembled beneath him, lost in the bliss of release.

They lay tangled together, bodies damp and hearts racing. Daniel grinned, breathless. "I never would've guessed it could feel that good."

Justine smiled lazily, a satisfied gleam in her eye. "I think I just took a trip to the North Star."

Silence stretched between them like a warm blanket. Then Justine turned to him, voice playful, "Wanna do that again?"

Daniel's grin was all the answer she needed.

Story

Story awakened from a restless sleep with a start.

She rolled over, rubbing the sleep from her eyes. *12:11 a.m.* Justine should have returned hours ago. *Where is she and why can't she sense that I need her?* The questions looped in her mind, but it was too late at night to call Justine's home phone. She would just have to wait until tomorrow to unload.

❧ 12 ❦

TOPSY-TURVY

Story

The rest of the summer passed quietly. Without Rakim, Story felt a bit distant from the social scene. Justine was wrapped up in her relationship with Daniel, and though she and Story remained close friends, Justine's priorities had clearly shifted. Most of Story's other friends were coupled up too, which made her feel like a third wheel more often than not.

Lately, her creative juices refused to flow, which put a huge damper on her styling business. With her lack of focus, she was weeks behind on getting clothing bundles out. Eventually, she decided to contact her remaining clientele, feigning an unexpected emergency. She refunded their initial deposits. It seemed that nearly everything that was important to her was falling apart.

Story tried journaling to release the internal pressure. She couldn't find the words. She poured herself into cheer camp. She confided in her mother and Mrs. Baude, though there wasn't much to report these days. Both women remained incredibly proud of her for standing her ground with Rakim—and for not going back. But it wasn't as easy as it sounded.

When Mrs. Baude noticed Story's increased withdrawal from the things she had once enjoyed, she encouraged her to start thinking about life after high school.

"What do you dream of for yourself, Story?" Mrs. Baude prodded. "Allow yourself to put *you* first in this moment. Where do you want to be in a year?"

Though she hadn't nailed down exactly what she wanted to do, Story was finally starting to take the question seriously.

"I mean... lately, I guess I've been considering a future in education—maybe even becoming a teacher like you." The impact Mrs. Baude had on her life was indescribable. Deep down, she believed she could be that kind of force for someone else one day. She *wanted* to.

"But my passion for fashion hasn't *completely* gone away," Story added, popping her collar in jest. "I could easily imagine myself designing clothes in New York City, strutting through Fashion Week in Paris, Milan or Tokyo, chasing the glitz and glamour of the fast-paced creative life."

Mrs. Baude nodded with a knowing smile. "Whether you choose the classroom or the catwalk, I just want you to always know you aren't alone; every cheerleader needs a squad of her own. You've got your mother. Me. And Justine."

"Thanks," Story smiled feebly, grateful for the kind words and reassurance. She was beginning to feel the possibilities come into view, but what she yearned for most was for her and Justine to be the way they used to be. Without that, nothing much seemed to matter.

Justine

By summer's end, life was quietly unraveling. Justine still wasn't speaking to her father and hadn't completely processed what had happened. The shame clung to her like smoke—thick and suffocating. Only Daniel knew the whole truth. She couldn't even bring herself to tell Story.

She had been avoiding her calls, keeping things short and surface level when Story did catch her. Justine was disappointed in her father, yes—but more than that, she couldn't bear seeing that same disappointment in Story's eyes. He had been as much of a father figure to her as he was a biological one to Justine. She didn't want to be the one to shatter that image, to hand over the heaviness she was already struggling to carry.

Work was a drag.

Since the conference, she and her father barely acknowledged each other unless they were under the watchful eye of Barbie. Yes, he had followed through on his empty promise and bought her a car after she got her license, but Justine saw it as a guilt gift. Still, she accepted, knowing it meant she wouldn't have to commute with him. At the office, she took direction from his new assistant, Bianca, and avoided him at all costs. John seemed relieved by the distance. And the times their eyes did meet, his were heavy with shame. Justine felt no sympathy. As far as she was concerned, he wasn't sorry for his actions—just that he had been caught.

Then came the fatigue. The nausea. Her appetite vanished. Even her favorite perfume turned her stomach. At first, she thought it was a stomach bug—until she realized her period was late.

Panic set in.

She called Daniel. They drove to the drugstore, then straight to his place. Five minutes after taking the test, she had her answer.

Pregnant.

Daniel purchased four more tests. All positive. They stood together in his tiny mint green powder room, not speaking, barely breathing. Then, as if all the vaults in her heart had finally been granted permission, Justine let out a shaky breath and collapsed into tears. Daniel caught her before she hit the floor.

Story

Story arrived to an empty house after the final day of cheer camp. Exhausted but buzzing with a forgotten excitement, she couldn't wait to tell her mother how the end-of-summer showcase had gone. Each counselor had choreographed a five-minute routine with their assigned group, and Story's had nailed theirs. She assisted in developing the concept, solved hiccups along the way, and even picked out their outfits. When a few girls clashed during rehearsals, Story stepped in before things got out of hand, reestablishing harmony among the team. This only affirmed her growing confidence in working with kids long-term.

Seeing as her mother wasn't home, Story dialed Justine to see if she wanted to hang. She was eager to share her day with someone. Plopping down on the couch with one leg folded under her, she reached for the house phone and dialed Justine's number. Three rings later, Mrs. Chandler answered.

"Hello?" she said, a hint of surprise in her voice.

"Hi, Mrs. Chandler! How are you?"

"I'm well, thank you," Barbie replied warmly. "Let me guess—you're calling for Justine?"

Story laughed. "You guessed right. Is she around? I promise I won't tie up the line."

"Actually, she went for ice cream with Daniel."

"Oh... ok. Will you let her know I called?"

"Of course. I'm expecting her back any minute, so I'll have her call you. I've got to run—bridge game."

"Yes ma'am. Thanks, Mrs. Chandler."

Story placed the phone back in its cradle, her smile fading. Lately, Justine always seemed to be busy. With a sigh, she headed to the kitchen to start dinner. The phone rang again.

"Hello?" she answered.

"Yes, we're trying to reach the next of kin for... Ms. Denise Brooks."

Story froze. "This is her daughter, Story Brooks."

"Miss Brooks, my name is Olive Rose. I'm a social worker at

Jackson Memorial Hospital. I'm calling because your mother's been in an accident."

"An accident?" Story's voice cracked as she shot back to the couch, the phone cord stretched to its limit. "Is she ok?"

"We really can't discuss details over the phone," Olive said gently. "But your mother is awake—that's about all I can share. She asked us to contact you. If you can come to the hospital, we'll explain everything there."

"Jackson Memorial, right? I'm on my way!" Story hung up before Olive could respond.

She didn't have a car—didn't even have a license—but none of that mattered. She needed to get to her mom. Panic swelled in her chest as she realized they had no family nearby, and the little extended family they did have never bothered to check in.

Trying not to spiral, Story ran through her mental contact list. Justine and Daniel had new licenses and cars—maybe they could help. She doubted they were actually out for ice cream, so she called Daniel's house directly.

"Hello?" Daniel sounded distracted.

"Daniel, it's Story. I need a huge favor," she said, urgency in her voice.

"Umm... now's not really a good time," he replied, clearly flustered.

Story heard muffled voices in the background. "Is that Justine? Can I talk to her?"

He sighed and handed over the phone. Justine sounded off—voice shaky, sniffling. "Hello?"

"Justine, are you ok? Look, I really need your help. My mom's been in an accident—I need a ride to Jackson Memorial."

Justine hesitated. "It's... not a good time, Story. We just got some news and—"

"You're *serious* right now?" Story snapped. "My mom's in the *ho-spit-al*, and you're telling me it's 'not a good time'? You know what? Don't even worry about it. I'll find someone who actually shows up when it matters." She hung up, seething.

She hated what she was about to do next, but she was out of options. She called Rakim.

"Yeah, who dis?" he answered.

Story rolled her eyes and took a breath. "It's me. Story."

He chuckled. "Ahh, I knew you'd be back. What's up? Miss ya boy?"

She cut him off. "Rakim, listen. I know things ended badly, and I'm not trying to rehash it. My mom's in the hospital and I need a ride to Jackson Memorial. Please."

"I mean, I could. But what's in it for me?"

Story clenched her jaw. After everything he had done, he still had the nerve—but she needed that ride. "If you get me there, I'll do whatever you want after I see my mom. Deal?"

"Word? I'll be there in ten minutes."

She was already waiting by the doors when Rakim pulled up in his beat-up Sonata. Story ran out, jumped in, and slammed the door behind her. They made small talk on the way, but her mind was somewhere else entirely.

As soon as they pulled up to the ER, she was out the door before the car stopped.

"So when can I see you again?" Rakim asked, grinning.

"Never," she said, slamming the door.

"I shoulda left you in the gutter where I found you, hoe!" he yelled as his smoke-belching jalopy coughed a plume of black soot before peeling away with less speed than the sound of the strained engine let on.

❧

When Story entered the Emergency Room and gave her name at the front desk, the receptionist immediately paged Denise's nurse to escort her. With no idea of what she'd find, Story counted her blessings that they were taking her to a room instead of the morgue. *That's a good sign,* she thought, trying to prepare herself.

Outside room 171, the nurse paused. "She's in pretty rough shape. Try not to get her too worked up—she's already been through a lot and needs rest."

"I'll do my best."

She knocked gently before stepping into the room. Nothing could have prepared Story for what she saw. Denise sat upright on the bed, eyes closed. Her left eye was swollen shut, her bottom lip split and badly swollen. Dark red bruises wrapped around her neck, and her right arm was in a cast.

Hearing the door, Denise struggled to open her better eye and offered a faint smile. "Hey baby, I'm glad they called you."

Tears were already rolling down Story's face. "Mom, what happened to you?" she asked, rushing to her side.

"Oh, I got in a fight with the ground—and the ground won," Denise said weakly, attempting a joke. But seeing Story's face, Denise sighed and turned serious.

"I stayed late at work finishing prep for a briefing. I was the last one out, locking up, when I felt someone behind me. I turned—and there he was. Wearing a ski mask. Whoever it was punched me hard. I hit the ground, and he was on me before I could get up. I tried to shield myself, but he kept yelling things like, 'I knew I'd catch you slipping! Now you're gonna pay, skank!' I screamed, I fought—but he was too strong. I think I passed out."

Story didn't interrupt. She had no words. It was hard to even breathe. A solitary tear squeezed from between Denise's swollen eye.

"At some point, I heard someone down the street yell, 'Hey man! What are you doing?' It must've scared him because he stopped. But before he ran, he said something I'll never forget, 'I know where you live. You tell anyone who I am, and I'll finish what I started.'"

Just then, Denise's monitors began spiking, sending off all kinds of beeps and chimes. Story looked from the monitors to her mother, mentally shushing the world and praying for everything to be alright. Instinctively, she began stroking her mother's hand and shaking her head as fresh hot tears made rivers on her face. A nurse rushed to the room, but paused when she saw mother and daughter cradled on the bed. She watched from the doorway, and seeing Denise's vitals settle, quietly withdrew.

"I think I blacked out again. Next thing I knew, I was here. Thankfully."

Story felt violated by the experience her mother had just recounted. She relived the terror of not only the actual incident, but the unspoken "what if's" as she and her mother cried silently together. Too shaken to move, she sat terrified at the thought of how close she was to losing the only person who had ever always been there.

Justine

A week after learning she was pregnant, Justine and Daniel still didn't know what to do. Justine wanted desperately to tell Story, but with Ms. Brooks just home from the hospital, it didn't feel right to burden her. She couldn't talk to her mother either—Barbie would probably disown her. That left one option: John. Her father owed her. And this was far too big for her and Daniel to handle alone.

She waited until her mother was off on a shopping trip with a friend, before finding her father nestled in his study after a work trip.

"Daddy, can I talk to you for a minute?" she asked, hesitantly stepping inside.

"Of course," John perked up, surprised that his daughter was speaking to him. "I've been meaning to tell you again how sorry I am about what happened. I appreciate you not saying anything to your mother and—"

"Daddy, that's not why I'm here." Her voice was hollow. "You and Mom will have to figure out your own stuff."

He nodded. "Ok... so what's on your mind, baby girl?"

"Don't call me that," she said, shaking her head. Her voice caught in her throat. "Daddy, I'm..." She paused, unsure she could say it out loud. Then, in one breath, "I'm pregnant."

John blinked, stunned. "Well... I certainly wasn't expecting that." He sat back, trying to absorb it. "How?"

Justine gave him a look, eyes glossy with fresh tears.

"I mean—not how, how. I mean... why? When? How far along?"

When she didn't answer, he threw up his hands. "Justine, honey, you're not ready to be a mother. What about all the dreams we had for you? How could you be so irresponsible?" He stood, agitated. "I need to take some time to think—can you imagine how this *looks*?"

Justine was stunned into silence as she watched her father—lost in his own spiral.

"No daughter of mine is going to be a teenage mom. We've worked too hard for your future to fall apart like this. Go to your room. I need some air."

"But—Daddy—"

"I said go to your room!" His voice thundered through the house.

Shocked, Justine stumbled to her room, eyes blurred with tears. She barely heard the front door slam as her father stormed out.

When he returned hours later, Justine was asleep on her bed, curled in a fetal position, clutching her childhood doll, Daisy.

"Little Lady," John said gently, shaking her awake.

Her eyes fluttered open, unsure what to expect.

"You've gotten yourself into a real mess. And believe me, I could kill Daniel." He sighed, rubbing his temples. "But this? This can't happen."

He crossed the room, placed a thick wad of cash on her desk, then turned toward the door. Without looking back, he said, "You're a smart girl. You know what to do. And your mother can never know. Do you understand?"

Justine stared at the money, heart sinking. Was he really asking her to get rid of her baby?

Too stunned to argue, she whispered, "Ok.

❧ 13 ❧

TWO TRAINS IN THE NIGHT

Justine

Less than a week had passed before Justine and Daniel found themselves in his car, headed down the interstate toward a family planning clinic in South Philadelphia—one Daniel had found in the Yellow Pages.

"Are you sure about this, Justine?" Daniel asked.

"Yeah. We've been over this. Neither of us can afford to support a baby. My dad made it clear my parents won't help, and your parents would kill you, too. What other choice do we have?" she snapped. But as they neared the clinic, her own doubts began creeping in.

They didn't speak another word until they arrived. At the front desk, Justine was asked to complete a health questionnaire and take a seat in the waiting area. The couple chose two corner chairs closest to the door. Justine discretely glanced in the direction of a young girl who couldn't have been more than a few years older than her. The girl sat quietly trying to suppress her sobs. As though she could feel Justine watching her silent progression of tears, their eyes met. And they both screamed the same thing: _I'd rather be anywhere but here._

Sitting cross-legged next to the girl was an older woman, presumably her mother. The tension between the two was palpable as the woman vigorously swung her crossed leg, lips pressed in a tight line. Feeling exposed, Justine looked at the paperwork in her own lap as Daniel leaned in.

"Justine, I still don't know how I feel about this," Daniel began. Justine shot him a look. "But I love you, and I'm here to support you no matter what."

She paused, her pen hovering over a blank line. "Thanks," she said quietly, shifting her gaze as she filled in the necessary health information.

Within minutes, a staff member called them to a back room. As they stood, they locked hands instinctively—two teenagers, overwhelmed and underprepared, trying their best to appear united.

"Ms. Randolph," the staff member said, glancing at Justine's paperwork. "My name is Joelle. I'll be performing your ultrasound before we begin the procedure."

She could feel Daniel's confusion. Keeping her eyes fixed straight ahead, she did everything to avoid his gaze. She had lied about her name because she needed to be certain this couldn't be traced back to her or her family. Once they left the clinic, she planned to forget it ever happened.

"That's fine," she said to Joelle.

"Please undress from the waist down and cover yourself with this drape. I'll be back in a moment." Joelle left the room.

Justine did as instructed, folding her clothes into a pristine pile before lying on the table.

She stared determinedly at the ceiling. Her mind was set on not allowing Daniel's stance to sway her decision once Joelle returned. As the ultrasound began, Justine refused to look at the monitor. Daniel held her hand steadily, watching her face closely for signs of distress. Once Joelle captured the necessary images, she quietly told them she would need to return with the doctor to review everything.

Less than five minutes later, there was a soft knock.

"Come in," Justine said.

"Hi, Jennifer, I'm Dr. Wilcheck." A bubbly older man with a balding hairline and rosy cheeks entered the room. His voice had a rehearsed kindness to it, the kind people used when they were practiced at delivering bad news. "I'd like to repeat your ultrasound to be absolutely sure of what we're seeing."

"Is something wrong?" Daniel asked, speaking up as Justine sat upright on the table.

"The ultrasound helps us determine how far along you are and the placement of the pregnancy," Dr. Wilcheck explained. "In Ms. Randolph's case, the images Joelle took left me with some questions. I'd just like to confirm a few things before we proceed. This will only take a moment." He patted Justine's knee haphazardly.

"Oh," was all Justine could say as she glanced nervously at Daniel and reclined again. They locked eyes for a moment. He kissed her hand.

Dr. Wilcheck moved the probe side to side, capturing more images. "Just as I suspected. Jennifer, it appears you have what's called a blighted ovum—or, medically speaking, an anembryonic pregnancy."

"What's that?" Justine clutched the drape to her chest, her eyes welled with tears at the thought of things possibly getting any worse. She didn't think she could handle any more unexpected news. *God help me.*

"A blighted ovum happens when a fertilized egg implants in the uterus but doesn't develop into an embryo. So technically, a pregnancy began, but it never progressed far enough to be viable. If you look here," he gestured to the monitor, "this dark circle is the gestational sac—but as you can see, it's empty. A pregnancy like this will inevitably end in miscarriage."

He continued routinely, not giving either parent a chance to digest what this all meant. Especially for their situation.

"You're still early in your first trimester, based on your last period. I'd recommend either allowing the miscarriage to happen naturally or using medication. I don't believe surgery is necessary at this point. We'll also monitor your hormone levels with bloodwork to ensure they return to normal."

Justine looked to Daniel for clarity.

Daniel struggled to meet Justine's gaze. He feared her scrutiny the moment she realized he didn't have the answers either. He didn't know if they should cheer, cry or both.

A spacious feeling bloomed in her chest, as though the news had pulled something out of her she didn't know was there.

"So what you're saying is, she's pregnant—but not really?" Daniel spoke up. He shifted uncomfortably in the clinic's hard folding chair to gain a firmer grip of Justine's increasingly sweaty hand.

"That's one way to put it," Dr. Wilcheck replied. "There's no embryo, so the pregnancy can't continue. The next step is making sure all products of conception are safely expelled."

"Oh my goodness," Justine finally said. "Thank you, Doctor. Daniel, let's go."

Story

Denise continued to recover at home after her release from the hospital. Thankfully, Story's summer job had ended, allowing her to stay home and care for her mother. Just days after Denise had settled in, she received a call from the detective assigned to her case: the assailant had been captured and confessed to everything.

It turned out he was a former client of Denise's at the resource center—a man named Kevin Halter. Denise had been forced to terminate the agency's contract with Kevin after discovering a parole violation.

She had no idea what happened to him after he lost housing and was made to serve the remainder of his original sentence, but according to the detective, Kevin had developed a personal vendetta against anyone he believed had wronged him. They found a list in his wallet, naming various staff members and an ex-girlfriend he had planned to target.

Denise's name was number six of fifteen.

On the outside, her mother tried her best to appear unbothered, but Story knew the truth. She noticed her mother was constantly on edge, startling even at the sound of Super Mario padding into her room. She hadn't slept a full night since the attack. Story knew because neither had she. Every creak and sigh woke her with a start.

"Mom, you're safe now." She was trying to convince her mother and herself.

"Who's to say he won't follow through on his vow to finish what he started?" Denise half-asked, half-wondered aloud.

"We can't think like that."

She lay with her mother until she heard the soft rumble of her mother's snores. Rolling away from her mother's line of vision, Story nibbled the inner corner of her lip. She wasn't sure she believed her own reassurances. All of those *what if's* had yet to leave her mind.

⚜

Needing a break from her new role as full-time caregiver, Story called Justine and asked to meet for a walk; she could use some fresh air. To her surprise, Justine eagerly agreed. The two had missed each other and were overdue for a proper catch-up.

When the elevator doors opened on Story's floor, she rushed in and wrapped Justine in a warm embrace. Not ready to let go, she relished in how a simple hug from her best friend could bring such tranquility.

"Look, I know it's been a long summer for both of us," Story cleared her throat in an attempt to ward off the emotions threatening to crack her composure. "But I hate being mad at you. Let's catch up. I've missed you, bestie."

"Ditto," Justine acknowledged, grabbing Story's hand.

As they walked toward Griffin Park, Story thanked Justine for the flower arrangement her parents had sent her mother after the accident, then told her everything—including Rakim's "raunchy request."

"Can you believe he was trying to double dip?"

"Ugh," Justine spat in disgust. "Nothing against you, but that's not my vibe *at all*. He's proving to be an even bigger loser than I thought."

Story let out a gut-busting laugh. "Dang! Tell me how you really feel girl..." Proudly lifting her chin, she continued, "...Well, we don't have to worry about him anymore: I told that busta to kick rocks!"

Justine squealed in delight as Story chronicled their breakup and how she had tricked him into giving her a ride to the hospital. She also shared how well her summer job had gone, her new education aspirations and the latest developments in her mother's assault case.

By the time she finished, Story felt free as a bird. Spreading her arms wide, she took off—completing a victory lap around the playground.

"Dang! You had as much going on as me," Justine paused, uncertain of how much she should share.

No more secrets, she lectured herself. She launched into a recap of her own summer—her job, catching her father having an affair, and, with a proud grin, revealing that she and Daniel were no longer virgins. After enduring Story's congratulatory theatrics, Justine turned to face her.

"Listen, for this next part, we need to sit down."

Story audibly sighed and followed Justine's lead to the bench. She should have guessed that there was more. She remembered the uneasy feeling that persisted for days whenever she thought of Justine, and braced herself for whatever her friend had to say next.

For a moment, they sat in silence, letting the breeze wash over them.

"It's weird because for days now, my brain has felt crowded every time you come to mind." Story was the first to break the silence.

Justine hung her head.

"What is it, Justine? You're starting to worry me. Whatever it is can't be *that* bad."

Justine unpacked the rest—the pregnancy, the miscarriage and even how her father had quietly given her the money to terminate.

Story was speechless as the two sat in silence for an uncomfortable amount of time. Seven Septa metro buses passed before she was able to steady her mental dialogue. She felt Justine glance at her a few times, but still said nothing out loud. Unsure how to proceed, Justine quietly waited for her friend's reaction—mindlessly toeing a pebble between her two soiled sneakers.

Finally, Story nodded her head, in what Justine interpreted as acceptance.

Story could see Justine's shoulders drop. More relaxed. Less guarded. They both stared into the distance as two little girls—no older than four—squealed with laughter, chasing each other around the swing set.

Story watched Justine as her eyes followed the jubilant duo, her mouth curled into a strained smile. She knew in that moment they shared the same thought: if things had gone differently, that could've been *her* child playing with a friend. The idea stirred a strange blend of relief and sadness deep in Story's chest.

"Why didn't you tell me?"

"Well, every time I thought I could, I just... chickened out," Justine admitted. "I didn't want you to think less of me, or of Daniel—or my dad. It's all heavy stuff, ya know?"

"But I'm your *best* friend. We talk about everything..." Story stumbled over her words, "Or at least, we used to." With a sharp intake of breath, her voice became more pointed. "I bet *Daniel* knew everything." Justine didn't take the bait. "And after all the times you lectured me about using protection with Rakim—how could you be so stupid and slip up with Daniel?"

"Come on, Story, that's a little harsh, don't you think?" Justine looked taken aback.

"No. It's real, is what it is! You better thank God you weren't able to keep that pregnancy, girl. You almost completely ruined your life—"

"But I didn't," Justine's shoulders were tense again.

"But you *could* have!" Story huffed, propelled by something old and bitter. "And we both know your dad can be a twatwaffle. He's been recklessly slapping bellies with more women than just the one you caught him with. I just wish I could have been there for you."

Justine turned to face Story. "And what would you have done that Daniel didn't do, huh? Why are you buggin' like this? I *finally* open up to you, and *this* is what I get?" Her voice cracked. Story could see the hurt in her friend's eyes.

She softened. "I'm just saying, these days you seem to care more about Daniel than anyone or anything else. You've gotten reckless, Justine—*you*, of all people! And as for your dad—I've seen him out around town with women who definitely weren't your mom. Shoot, he even tried to hit on my mom once!"

"What the heck are you talking about?" Justine's voice rose. "Say what you want about me—I really don't care—but don't start making stuff up about my family!"

"I've got no reason to lie, Justine. Your dad gets around. And not just on business trips," Story added with a shrug.

"Whoa. You're going way too far, Story. You need to take that back."

"Sorry, girl. I wish I could..." she paused for a moment. "I can't believe I used to wish he was my dad too. Talk about a change of heart."

Despite her bluntness, Story did feel sorry for Justine. She loved her and would never wish her harm—but part of her was still stung that Justine had kept so much from her. Maybe, just for a second, she wanted to bruise Justine's ego and knock her down a peg. She needed Justine that summer, but instead of being there, she had been off getting herself knocked up by Daniel.

Like father, like daughter, she thought bitterly.

Justine shook her head in disbelief. "I don't know where all this is coming from, but it feels like you're intentionally trying to hurt me. And that's not fair—"

"But it's true, right?" Story quipped, head whipping with fresh attitude.

"You know what else is true," Justine piped back. "He's *not* your father. So just... stop drawlin'!" The jab hung in the air between them: the two now even in dishing insults.

"Look, I get it—I could've been more available to you this summer," Justine began, trying to find a path to peace. "But you heard what I've been dealing with."

"And you heard what I've been going through too!"

"Everything can't always be all about you, Story. For once, can you support me like I've always done for you? Fine—maybe I made some bad decisions, but all I can do is deal with the hand I've been dealt."

Story sucked her teeth before muttering, "Looks like it took more than Daddy's wad of cash to win that hand if you ask me."

Justine flinched.

Story knew she had crossed the line, but before she could say anything, her friend was on her feet, huge tears plopping from her lashes to the ground. "For as long as we've been friends, I've bent over backwards to be there for you. I've shared what I had—including my father, as flawed as he is—with you. I never asked you for anything in return. Your friendship was enough. But I take just a couple of weeks of me choosing me—and *this* is where it gets us?"

Story was shattered. She'd gotten caught up in winning the argument and overlooked the repercussions of her words. Still, she didn't know where to go from here.

Justine continued, "I can't deal with this right now. I'll catch you later."

And with that, she walked away.

Story sat frozen, regretting the words she'd said and how she'd said them.

Justine was right: she didn't deserve the way Story had just unloaded on her. Not now, not ever. She knew she let her frustrations get the best of her, and it stung to see the damage done. Still, pride wouldn't let her call out after Justine.

I'll call her in a few days and apologize, she told herself.

But that day never came.

Three days later, Story's mother woke her at the crack of dawn.

"Pack up," she said softly. "We've got to go."

Kevin Halter had been released on bond, and Denise had no intention of waiting around to see if he planned to act on his threats.

It was time for the Brooks to move on. Again.

PART II: A SEASON

❧ 14 ☙

DISJOINTED

Story

August 5, 1996

Dear Diary,

No one ever told me that with growth, life held so many changes, losses, and hurdles. I've always been an easygoing and optimistic person—so hopeful for the future and all life has to offer. Today was no different. My mom and I just finished successfully moving me into my freshman dorm room at Virginia State University in Petersburg, Virginia. I'm actually writing this while she's off filling her gas tank before hitting the road home. And while I'm ecstatic about the opportunities ahead, I can't help but find it bittersweet that, in just a few hours, I'll be setting out on this new life adventure alone.

Going off to college was something Justine and I always dreamt of doing together. I planned to major in Early Education or Fashion Design, and Justine in Sociology with a minor in Humanitarian Studies. But our dream never came to fruition after me and my mom abruptly moved to Raleigh, North Carolina. That was right before my senior year of high school. Ultimately, I chose to

attend college closer to her, and VSU is just a 2.5-hour bus ride from Raleigh—
close enough to make getting home easy when, or if, I need to. I've also narrowed
down my major to Elementary Education.

Though things didn't go quite as planned, I think I'm ready for college. It is a
means to an end, but I can't shake the nerves that come along with this next step.
I still wonder about Justine: where she is… if she's been accepted into New York
University as we planned… if Daniel is still chasing after her like a lost puppy. I
even think about her parents from time to time. During my last talk with her,
the night everything fell apart, I learned of Mr. Chandler's latest rendezvous
with someone who wasn't Mrs. Chandler. And while I couldn't say I was
surprised, I didn't want to see the Chandlers break up. They were the closest
thing to a normal family I've ever had. I wonder if Justine ever told her mom
what Mr. Chandler was up to?

Even with all of the hiccups, at least Mr. and Mrs. Chandler had each other.
And Justine had her dad. I can't recall a time when I've ever had a complete
family. Don't get me wrong, I'm beyond appreciative of my mother, but having
my father in my corner always felt like it would have settled things somehow…

Just as Story turned the page to continue writing, a faint knock came at her door.

"Come in," she said, quickly closing her diary and slipping it under her pillow. Denise walked in and sat on the edge of Story's bed. Together they surveyed her newly-unpacked and organized room. Her face laced with uncertainty, she mustered all the zeal she could and said, "I think that's everything."

Denise scanned the room from left to right, taking it in. "Seems to be," she replied sadly, half to Story, half to herself.

They had fully stocked Story's room with all the dormitory essentials: wall art, bedding, mini fridge, shower caddy, toiletries, bath towels, cleaning supplies, boxes of snacks and even a hidden hot pot. Denise could stall no longer. She sat with a gut-wrenching sadness over her inevitable departure.

Something about this moment reminded Story of her final days in Philly. After saying some terrible things in the heat of the moment, she lived with regret. There wasn't a day that went by when she didn't wish she could take it all back—*had* taken those words back the moment she spoke them. They left Philly in such a rush, she hadn't had the chance to call Justine and apologize, and when Story did call the Chandler home, once she and her mother got settled in North Carolina, Mrs. Chandler had made it quite clear her calls were far from welcome. She could never forget the coldness with which Justine's mother had spoken to her:

"Hi Mrs. Chandler," Story began politely. "How are you?"

"Who is this?" Barbie snapped.

"It's Story," she replied with an awkward laugh.

"Oh. YOU. Hello there." Barbie's voice was cool. "Listen Justine isn't here… she told me you two had a falling out. I'm surprised we haven't heard from you sooner, but it's for the best. Justine came home VERY upset after your little alter- cation. She wouldn't tell me exactly what you did, but I know you hurt my baby very deeply. And that's enough for me.

Barbie continued, her voice clipped, *"She's finally starting to act like her old self again, and with college applications, school and work, she doesn't need distractions or drama. Maybe it's time for a clean break."* She paused briefly before ending the call with, *"It was brought to my attention that you and your mother have moved. I wish you well in your future endeavors, but I would appreciate you giving Justine the space she needs to focus on the things that are really important. She will call you if or when she's ready. Otherwise, please don't call here again."*

Story had been so taken aback, she had said nothing. She simply stood there blinking in silence trying her best to process the words Mrs. Chandler had spoken.

"Are you there?" Barbie probed. *"Well, that was easier than I thought,"* she said to herself before hanging up, having assumed that Story had long since hung up the telephone.

Story never had the chance to share her forwarding address or phone number. She held the phone long after the call ended, unsure of how she'd ever reconnect with Justine.

A deep breath brought her back from her memory. Mrs. Chandler's words stung. Badly. But she owned her part in creating the divide that now existed. In spite of it all, Story passed her entire senior year hopeful that Justine would one day call her and make things right again. When that day never arrived, she slowly began to put the pieces of her life, and heart, back together again. Moving south was the perfect opportunity for Story to reinvent herself. She made a personal commitment to be a better version of herself; namely, she promised to never take another friend for granted.

She had been through a lot in her eighteen years of life, and she was unwilling to let a childhood mistake keep her down. With time, Story finally learned to forgive herself. If it were meant to be, she felt confident that one day she'd have the opportunity to reconnect with Justine. Their bond had been entirely too deep for this to be the end.

Based on her mother's refusal to make eye contact with her, Story could tell Denise was deep in her own thoughts, and likely on the verge of tears. *Your baby girl is officially ready to face life on her own, Mommy,* Story mused, knowing her mother was excited for her even as she wrestled with completely releasing the reins.

"How about we grab lunch before I hit the road?"

"Ok, but we'll have to make it quick, Mom. They're doing a freshman welcome at the Student Union in about an hour."

"Wow, how quickly you've pushed aside your little *old* mother," Denise joked.

"It's not like that, Mom. I just don't want to miss a minute of my college experience," she reassured Denise, looping their arms. "Plus, I hear the Greeks are going to be there later. *All* the fine boys are in fraternities, and everybody knows joining a sorority is like a rite of passage in college. So, I need to make my presence known."

Denise gave her a look that said, *Alright now.*

"I know I know: education first, entertainment after. I got this, Ma." Story winked as her mother shook her head laughing. She still missed Justine, but Story was happy to be feeling a bit like her old self.

Justine

At LaGuardia airport's baggage claim, Justine walked stoically toward the man holding a whiteboard with her family's name on it. Her parents trailed silently behind her. The flight had been uneventful, but tension simmered between them. Justine had no interest in their drama—not today. She had enough on her mind.

She couldn't help but feel energized at the thought of starting her freshman year of college in the Big Apple. But something was missing: Story. Today was supposed to be their day. At fourteen, both girls made a pact to attend NYU together. Sadly, a lot had changed over the past year, and now Justine found herself beginning this new chapter without one of her closest confidants. Granted, Daniel would be joining her as planned, but it wasn't the same.

It had been over a year since their falling out, and while much had happened in that time, nothing felt complete since their argument. Justine never had the chance to tell Story that the day after their big argument, she officially started to miscarry. She spent a little over a week discretely managing her pain and bleeding, doing her best to keep her mother from suspecting anything was amiss. She and Daniel also returned—secretly—to the clinic in South Philly, as instructed, to confirm everything had passed. The entire ordeal couldn't have come at a worse time. And without her best friend to support her through it, the remainder of Justine's summer became a nightmare.

Before she even had time to fully process what happened—with her bestie, the miscarriage, everything—Story and her mother had moved. Justine wasn't sure when or why, and with no forwarding number or address, she had no way of finding out.

For the past year, Justine had replayed the events of their altercation in her mind. In time, she reconciled some of the hurtful things Story had said; as blunt as she had been, time helped her realize that much of it was actually true.

Justine had spent a good part of her senior year reflecting on how easy it could be to get caught up in a momentary high—a dangerously enlightening ride, even if a little fun. Doing the unexpected was undoubtedly a thrill, but in the end, it wasn't her speed. As much as she hated to admit it, her fall hadn't been any more graceful than her father's. Without Story to help her fully process the experience, Justine sank her teeth into books that motivated her from the local library. She had become enamored with the life and works of Maya Angelou.

As the town car navigated the packed streets of New York City, she recited lines from one of her favorite poems, "Still I Rise":

Out of the huts of history's shame
I rise
Up from a past that's rooted in pain
I rise
I'm a black ocean, leaping and wide,
Welling and swelling I bear in the tide.

Justine knew things could have turned out very differently if she hadn't miscarried. She had long since forgiven Story, and only one hope remained: that they might reconnect in college. Justine felt certain that if Story had stuck to their plan, like she did, their paths would cross. Hopefully sooner rather than later.

15

CAN'T HAVE IT ALL

Justine

After three months at university, Justine hadn't run into Story. She had even gone as far as to go to the registrar's office and inquire about her attendance at the school.

"Due to the school's privacy policies, I am unable to confirm or deny if anyone by that name is registered as a student," a short lady with a Jheri curl and glasses the size of saucers said. Her voice was impatient.

Undeterred, Justine politely thanked her and left the office. She made it a habit to pass by the education and liberal studies buildings whenever she could, hoping to spot Story among the crowd. But so far, their paths hadn't crossed. Justine had even asked her small group of acquaintances at the university; not one had heard of Story.

Time passed and she gradually relinquished all hope of seeing Story at NYU. As disappointing as it was, Justine felt in her soul that they would be reunited. She couldn't figure out why fate pushed them apart, but she trusted that one day it would all make sense. She even found herself still humming their secret chant from time to time. *Istersay istersay, hatstay ymay istersay!* She believed maybe, just maybe, Story would receive the message telepathically, and hoped with all her might that her dearest friend hadn't given up on her.

On a positive note, Justine and Daniel were sticking to their plan: she worked toward her Sociology degree with plans to attend law school afterwards, while Daniel pursued his Biology Pre-Med major. The two often joked that once they completed their respective schooling, they would be just like the Huxtables. There was no more idyllic version of "the American Dream" for them.

Their coursework was intense, but even as first-year students, they made every effort to connect whenever possible, whether between classes or after school. Most of their outings were study sessions at the school's library or grabbing pizza with a side of study cards at their favorite pizzeria.

Since the loss of their baby, the two had grown even closer—but they were connected by more than just trauma. Daniel was her person. He still gave her butterflies, still made her laugh until she cried and still wooed her with love letters and flowers. After three years together, he now felt even more familiar and safe.

There was only one problem: Gregory.

Gregory was a classmate who recently caught Justine's interest. He was different. With the build of a football player, the grace of a ballet dancer, the confidence of Don Juan and the insight of a man far beyond his years, he was a unicorn. Gregory was from Brooklyn—"born and raised," as he often proudly reminded her. He, too, aspired to become a lawyer, which made him all the more tempting.

From the moment he shared his "why" during their first-day class introductions, Justine was smitten.

"My older brother, Adam, is my 'why.'" He shared with the collective. The sound of Gregory's voice alone has been enough to capture her attention. His deep baritone stirred something within her.

"When my bruh was nineteen, he was unlawfully stopped on his way to work. To this day he doesn't remember a thing about how he ended up in the hospital with two broken ribs, brain bleeding and permanent loss of function in his right arm."

Justine could feel the experience through Gregory's words as though she were standing beside him in the hospital room.

"We still haven't recovered. The entire community felt every blow. I was only fourteen when the case made national news, but from that point, I committed myself academically." Gregory paused to ensure he had the attention of his peers. He reminded her of her father in that way. "I'm here so my brother's story doesn't have to happen to anyone else."

During their shared freshman-level public speaking class, he went on to share that he eventually wanted to open his own practice—one that catered specifically to the underprivileged. Justine was captivated, especially given her own drive toward advocacy.

Gregory knew Justine had a boyfriend, but he seemed set on winning her over. As time progressed, the small kind gestures from Gregory ballooned into more significant advances. Before she knew it, she had caught feelings and didn't know how to navigate them. Like a slow steady leak that weakens a foundation, he wore away her defenses. Gregory was like a shiny new toy, while Daniel was the constant. She appreciated them both, craved them both. Without trying, she soon found herself torn between the two.

Story

In Virginia, Story was juggling school and her own man troubles. Academically, she was excelling—as she always had. She loved her course load for the semester and had begun working part-time at a local after-school program twice a week.

It was Mrs. Baude who had put her in touch with a contact in Chesterfield, Virginia, which ultimately led to Story securing the part-time position. She offered tutoring services, and although the position wasn't for college credit, Story was fully invested in her work with the youth. Her relationship with her mother and Mrs. Baude—fondly referred to as "her cheerleaders"—had continued to deepen, and she found herself confiding in them, especially regarding her professional aspirations.

When it came to romance, Story began college mentally committed to staying man-free for as long as possible. Sure, the initial excitement of frat boys had tempted her, but she was committed to solidifying her academic standing and avoiding getting caught up in another toxic relationship like the one with Rakim. Throughout her senior year of high school, she successfully dodged commitment to anyone who showed interest. She went on the occasional date, but nothing serious. Naively, Story assumed college would be just as easy.

She didn't make it past freshman welcome before meeting an upperclassman who made her weak with desire. Terrance Curry was a point guard and kinesiology major from Jacksonville, Florida. He was well known on campus and liked by all. The ladies seemed particularly fond of him, but Terrance swore he wasn't checking for any shorties but her. And while Story recognized the obvious similarities between Terrance and Rakim, she couldn't help but feel honored to have been chosen as Terrance's "main" lady.

It didn't take long for Story to notice questionable behavior. If it wasn't a girl leaving his room just as she was arriving, it was friends telling her about unsavory situations they witnessed. There were also multiple times when Story was subjected to evil stares from Terrance's likely love interests—while walking with him and even when alone on campus.

True to the vow she made to herself, she decided to do something. And quick. She no longer stood for having her time wasted—or wasting the time of others. In her philosophy class, Story was introduced to the Law of Attraction, and she began to embrace the idea that if she put out positivity, she'd attract the same. She knew with certainty that she was not willing to compromise her dignity for a man ever again.

She sought guidance from her cheerleaders and they all agreed: Terrance needed to be cut loose. Ironically, before Story had the chance to do just that, Terrance ghosted her. She took it as a sign. He was *officially* free to see and do whatever—and whoever—he wanted. Story felt no way about it.

She still thought about Justine often, hoping her friend was well. Once, during a moment of weakness when she was debating what to do about Terrance, she dialed nine of the ten digits of Justine's home number, but just as she was about to press the final number, she could hear Mrs. Chandler's voice in her head:

Allow Justine the space that she needs to focus on the things that are really important. Justine will call you if or when she's ready. Otherwise, how about you don't call again.

She hung up before completing the call.

Mrs. Chandler was right: Justine would reach out if she wanted to speak. The best thing Story could do was allow her the space to focus on her studies and her life. If it were meant to be, they would find each other again. She pulled out the postcard of Rodeo Drive and smiled, rereading Justine's promise of their joint trip warmed her even now. She could still see it happening even if she didn't know how or when.

As Story hummed the sister chant to herself—*Istersay istersay, hatstay ymay istersay*—she remembered: she had never been able to give Justine her new phone number. Still, somehow, deep in her heart, she just knew their story wasn't over yet.

16

GAME TIME

Story

"Again!" Story instructed. "This time, go full out—more emotion, make sure you're smiling. And keep those lines clean. Five, six, seven, and..."

Story had been repeating cheers with her mentee, Amanda, for the past two hours. The two were rehearsing performance pieces for Homecoming—by far one of the most important events of the football season. As a sophomore, Story, along with the other upperclassmen on the team, had been assigned a freshman mentee. They were charged with guiding the newbies through their first year on the cheer squad, making sure they were up to speed on routines, and teaching them how to carry themselves as college-level cheerleaders.

Story didn't mind helping Amanda. In fact, the pair had grown quite close over the season—so close that she had begun seeing Amanda as the extended family she never had. Mentoring was becoming a part of who Story was: she thrived when helping others, but she had her limits. Amanda couldn't seem to nail the routine. She did back handsprings when the routine called for a back tucks. Turned left when she should have gone right. *And don't get me started on that baby voice she's using to attack the crowd,* Story thought in frustration. She was teetering on the edge of exhaustion. Her voice was going hoarse, her feet hurt and her problem knee was beginning to pulsate—all telltale signs that her body was ready to power down. Still, one thing was certain: they would not be embarrassed on Homecoming day. With the old-head alumni returning to campus, there was no room for error.

"I'm sorry, Story—my mind is all over the place," Amanda shook her head in frustration. "But I *am* going to get it. Can we do it one more time?

"You've got this girl! I know you can do this," Story encouraged despite her own exhaustion. "Take a deep breath and let's take it from the top."

If it took all night for Amanda to get it, so be it. There was no way Story was willing to let Amanda get caught slipping.

Justine

Oh my gosh, how long have I been asleep? she wondered, waking with start. She looked around at her surroundings. After a few moments, it registered where she was: Gregory's red leather couch.

Glancing at her watch, Justine gasped—1:32 a.m.

The two had gone to his off-campus apartment to study for their criminology exam. The last thing she remembered was quizzing Gregory when he suggested they take a break for dinner. She must have dozed off when he went to order their food; apparently, she was more tired than she realized. *I can't believe I slept this long, here, of all places, after midnight!*

"Welcome back, bighead!" Gregory said, disrupting her thoughts as he entered the living room from the kitchen. "Girl, you must've been really tired, 'cause you were calling the cows for sure!" He erupted into easy laughter.

"Shut up!" Justine said, blushing. "I do *not* snore."

"Here's some water," he offered before plopping down on the loveseat next to her. "Your food's in the kitchen."

Justine accepted the water gratefully, sipping from the plastic cup as she scanned her phone. Five missed calls. *All* from Daniel. She quickly dialed him, turning her back to her classmate for a bit of privacy. Not seeming to take the hint, Gregory leaned back, resting his arm on the back of the couch and propping his feet on the lacquer coffee table.

"Hey, baby, I... No, I'm fine... I'm sorry, I fell... Yeah, he's here... It's nothing, we were studying, babe... Ok, you're tripping... Alright, fine. *Fine...* I'll see you soon."

"What's good with ol' boy? Gregory asked, sensing her irritation.

"Nothing," Justine said shortly, doing her best to avoid the conversation before it got started.

"Everything good?" he asked. Justine couldn't discern Gregory's sincerity: his voice sounded concerned, but she could've sworn he was suppressing a smirk. Erring on the safe side, she replied, "Yeah, I better get going. It's super late—Daniel's on his way to pick me up." She handed him a now-empty cup.

"You sure? It's pretty late. You're welcome to stay here," he offered. He wiped his hand across his forehead, glancing around the room. Justine watched him, noting that he no longer seemed uninhibited. On the contrary, he seemed suddenly... shy or unsure. Whatever it was, it was a sharp turn from his usual boldness. Justine found herself intrigued by the sharp curvature of his profile, wondering if...

No! She thought to herself. *We are not going here.*

But she continued to study him as her desires and devotion warred. He furrowed his brow, then shook his head—answering a question only he could hear.

"Nahhh, it's fine. He's already on his way," she said with a smile, swatting her wayward thoughts. "I'm just going to head back to campus." Attempting to soften the rejection, she added, "Thanks for studying with me tonight though."

"You know I've always got you, girl," Gregory said, staring at her, reassuming his usual suaveness while reaching for her hand.

Heat rushed to her ears. Her stomach fluttered. In vain, she pretended to ignore the undertone in Gregory's gesture. Standing to her feet, the leather of the couch cushion *wooshed* as it rebounded back into position. Justine gently pulled her hand away and looked toward the door.

It's hot! I need some air, she thought—unsure whether the sudden hot flash was external or the chemistry she felt at Gregory's touch. His energy was electric. He was charismatic. Gentle. Attentive. And before this moment, the only person to have ever made Justine's temperature rise like this was Daniel. She squeezed her eyes shut at the thought.

"No, really, I'm cool. I'm going to head down to the lobby to wait for Daniel."

Things were getting more uncomfortable by the second. She definitely would need to put some space between her and Gregory—before she did something stupid.

"Ok, suit yourself. I'll catch you tomorrow." Gregory trailed her to the door and opened it. "Oh, and tell Daniel I said 'what's up.'"

Stunned by the comment, Justine turned to face him and found her forehead almost flush against Gregory's chest. Her breath caught in her throat. She dared not move. She was waiting for... for... *for what?* Gradually, she inched her eyes up to meet his, a head taller than her.

She wondered if her expression revealed how undone she became when close to him. As her eyes finally met Gregory's, she silently hoped he'd make a move. Sensing he was as conflicted as she was, Justine quickly looked away and stepped out of the apartment, hurriedly making her exit.

The trance was broken.

But just as the door closed behind her, Justine could've sworn she heard Gregory mutter, "You should be mine." As she waited for Daniel, the sound of the Brooklyn boy's voice, scent of his cologne and shape of his full lips—lips that had been *so* dangerously close to her own—stayed with her. It was as though he were standing right there, facing her. She could see his eyes asking the same question her body was: *What if—No!*

She commanded herself. *Ignore it; Gregory is JUST a friend. Nothing more.*

No sooner had she fought off the feelings than Daniel's sedan rounded the corner, and she hopped in. Just in time.

Story

    We did it!

Story pumped her fist in the air, a smile so wide she felt like her cheeks might crack. They had pulled it off! The football team won the Homecoming game in a total blowout: 21–0. The cheer team had done their thing too, especially after finding themselves in an impromptu cheer-off with the opposing squad. The alumni and fans loved every minute.

Denise had watched Story cheer for the first half of the game before heading back to North Carolina to work her night shift as a residential counselor at a shelter. Always about business, she didn't want to risk being late.

Perhaps best of all, Amanda had cheered her heart out—not a single ounce of nerves in sight. She nailed every routine flawlessly, and Story couldn't have been prouder. All that hard work paid off, as did her patience.

Running up to Amanda, sweaty and adrenaline-crazed, Story hoisted her into a bear hug and spun her around in a circle. "You did it, girl!"

"No, *we* did it!" Amanda replied as the two tumbled to the ground, laughing.

Story jumped to her feet before extending a hand to help Amanda up. She sobered when her mentee fixed her eyes on something in the distance.

"There goes that dirty old man again," she said, catching her breath.

"Who?" Story craned her neck for a better view.

Amanda nodded in the direction of an older gentleman in a heavy coat, wearing sunglasses and leaning on a cane. He wasn't looking directly at them, but seemed to be waiting for someone—or something.

"The one over there by the gate," she said, nodding her head in the man's direction. "He was mesmerized by you for practically the entire game."

"Hmmm…" Story finally saw him and felt an almost imperceptible pull toward the unidentified figure.

"You didn't see him?" Amanda glanced from the man back to Story. "He was sitting about three rows from the front, center field.

Every time I looked into the crowd, it was like his eyes were locked on you."

Story let her mentee's words sink in. She couldn't put her finger on it, but she didn't feel afraid. On the contrary, she felt drawn to him.

Hmmm, how crazy is that? she thought. *I don't know that man from a can of paint yet something about him feels almost comforting... like we're family.*

She willed the man to look at her. *If I can just see his eyes, I'll know for sure...* Story's thoughts compelled her in his direction, but as though sensing discovery, the mystery man turned and briskly walked away.

Story gasped. *Dad?*

"Huh?" Apparently her thoughts weren't silent.

Story snapped out of it and laughed, shaking off the thought. *I'm tripping.* She faced Amanda.

"Girl, I'm sure a LOT of people were looking at us today," she played it off. Trying to shake the weight of her unsated curiosity, she added with her characteristic flourish, "I mean, how could they not?"

Amanda played right along, "TRUE!"

The two laughed naturally, as Story returned to the spirit of celebration.

"Anyway, we should celebrate. Today was epic! Are you going to the party tonight at the Civic Center?"

"I might," Amanda replied with a side glance. "But first, I'm supposed to meet up with this dude I met last week. We'll see how *that* goes—and *if* I make it to the party." She winked.

"Ohhh, do tell," Story cooed, linking arms with Amanda and pulling her toward the stadium's exit.

"Well, it's kind of early to tell much. I met him on campus in front of the Student Union. He's an upperclassman. Super cute..." she squinted her round eyes thoughtfully. "But there's just something about him I haven't quite figured out yet."

"Well so far, he sounds like a catch," Story affirmed. "What's his name?"

"Terrance," Amanda announced, smiling wide.

Story stopped dead in her tracks. *You have got to be kidding me.*

"What? What's wrong? You look like you've seen a ghost." The lithe beauty tugged her arm to keep her moving.

"I feel like I might see one. Soon," Story muttered, shaking her head. "Just... promise me one thing: you'll be careful, ok?"

"Of course," Amanda vowed with a mischievous grin. "Aren't I always?"

Justine

"How long are you going to hold this over my head, Daniel?" Justine lamented, exhausted from the conversation. "I keep telling you, I fell asleep. *Nothing* happened. Gregory is *just* my friend. We have a few classes together and he's been a huge support in getting me through. That's it, that's all."

"Tuh! I'm sure he has been a support." Daniel retorted. "There is no way, you don't see what's going on here, Jus."

"What are you talking about? He's my friend."

"And if given the chance, he'll be adding 'with benefits' to that title," Daniel rebutted.

"I can't believe you would even say something like that to me. I think it's been made more than clear at this point that *you're* my man. It's not even like that with Gregory. Even if you don't trust him, you should trust me!"

Justine was growing more irked with each passing moment, and it wasn't because she felt Daniel was doubting her allegiance. She felt like a fraud—as much as she denied there being anything between her and Gregory, she knew he'd jump at the chance of something more. And Justine couldn't say that she was completely opposed to his advances. It felt good to feel wanted. Not to mention, the man was easy on the eyes. And while Daniel had her heart, they had been together for so long, the spark had turned into a steady simmer. Things were just too predictable.

Daniel pulled the car over to the shoulder of the road and put it in park. Turning to Justine he said "Look Jus, I'm not trying to be the jealous boyfriend. It's just that you mean so much to me. And I know how men think. Gregory has it out for you; I KNOW that. I'm not giving up on us or letting you go without a fight, so he's gonna have to step off!"

"What's that supposed to mean?" Justine asked. She hadn't seen this side of him before.

"I'm not comfortable with you two hanging outside of class anymore. I'm not stupid, I know you have to do what you have to do for your classes. But I ask that you respect me and quit all the extracurricular time with this guy."

Resigning herself to the fact she *was* getting awfully close to playing with fire, she nodded her head. "You have my word. I'll limit my time with Gregory."

Daniel stared at her. She could see everything in his eyes: love, fear, uncertainty, doubt. Justine knew the stakes were high; he was laying it all on the line with his request. Aiming to reassure him, she leaned in and echoed their sacred mantra.

"Trust me?" she asked.

"Always," he replied. A mixture of relief and melting apprehension in his voice. "Thanks babe. I love you."

"I love you too, Daniel," she spilled, her heart quickening as she leaned in for a hug. He had no idea how close she had just come to slipping up and saying Gregory's name.

17

PLAYING WITH FIRE

Justine

Wind whipped against her flushed face as several strands of hair escaped the bun at the nape of her neck. Clutching an overstuffed backpack even tighter, she pumped her legs as fast as she could without breaking into a full-on run. Refusing to look back, she could only hope she had managed to put some distance between them.

Justine's mind flashed back to the night she had almost ruined everything.

Ok, suit yourself, Gregory had said as Justine was leaving his place.

He had no idea how close she had come to doing just that. That night, she wanted to explore Gregory more than she let on. *Good thing you came to your senses,* she commended herself as she extended her stride. The burn that ripped through her calves threatened to induce a cramp; she kept pushing anyway.

Then she heard his voice again, closer this time.

"Justine, wait up!" Gregory called, slightly winded.

Knowing she couldn't outrun him without looking ridiculous, she came to an abrupt halt. Slowly turning on her heels, she found herself face-to-face with him.

"Oh, hey *friend*. I didn't even see you. Where are you coming from?" she lied, fumbling over her words as she shifted uncomfortably, scratching the back of one ankle with the toe of the shoe on the opposite foot. She tried to sound casual, even when she almost lost her balance.

Gregory stood staring at her quizzically, not bothering to break the extended pause.

"Yeah, ok," he said finally. "I thought you saw me when I waved outside the cafeteria. You were definitely looking in my direction, but then you just kept walking." He shook his head. "Anyway, how've you been? We haven't hung out in a minute."

"Oh," Justine chuckled nervously. "I'm good. Just been really busy trying to stay on top of my studies. As a matter of fact, I've gotta run, but it was good seeing you."

She turned to leave.

"Dang girl, wait!" he said, grabbing her arm. "How you gonna leave without giving me a hug?"

Reluctantly, Justine faced him again, this time stepping forward and offering a one-armed pat on the back. But as she moved in, Gregory pulled her into a full embrace—and before she could react, he planted a kiss on her lips.

Completely caught off guard, Justine knew she should've pulled away. *This is bad*, her mind screamed. But it was too late—her body was already engaged: head tilted, heels lifted, arms draped longingly around his neck. She felt her pulse quicken. The warmth of Gregory's lips heated her core. Her thoughts dissolved into the moment until reality snatched her.

Justine's eyes flew open. She pulled away, wiping her mouth with the back of her hand.

"I'm...I'm so sorry," Gregory stammered. "I've just missed being around you... I didn't mean to do that."

Justine just stared, speechless, head shaking slowly as she backed away. She was still processing what had just transpired when her senses returned. Her breathing stabilized and the warning alarms in her brain slowly quieted. She inconspicuously scanned the courtyard while adjusting the straps of her bag with shaky hands.

That's when she saw him.

Daniel.

His eyes locked with hers for a brief, crushing moment before he turned and walked away.

Justine saw in his eyes the immense pain. His fears were realized. *She* had done that. The ache was loud enough to wipe the fresh impression of Gregory's kiss from her mouth and mind. Her heart felt as though it were squeezed. Panic threatened to break the tears dammed just behind her eyelids. Shame crept up her spine and paralyzed her. She felt like she was sinking in quicksand. The frog in her throat refused to allow her to even call Daniel's name.

She had messed up. And she knew it.

Stupid, stupid, stupid! You're about to lose the purest love you've ever felt—for what? she berated herself as she rushed after Daniel, leaving Gregory standing alone in the middle of the courtyard.

Story

Story and a few of her cheer squad friends—Amanda, Torrey and Serita—were gathered in the dormitory basement, which doubled as a makeshift hair salon on Friday nights. They were getting ready for the next day's game. Music blared from Story's CD player while the girls sang, danced and added finishing touches to each 'do.

Torrey proudly pulled a bottle of Alizé from her backpack, having successfully smuggled it past the resident assistant. The group erupted in cheers, as Torrey poured cup after cup with little restraint. Not much of a drinker, Story nursed the same plastic cup and swayed to the beat, hips rocking in rhythm with the music.

"Story, let me finish your curls and wrap your hair, girl," Amanda called out.

"Ok, cool." Story flopped down into a folding chair. She glanced at the wall clock calculating how much time she had. She planned to head to her room soon—she didn't want to be too tired or hungover for tomorrow's game.

As Amanda worked, Story turned to Serita and started chatting about their top picks from the college's baseball team. All of a sudden, a familiar, unwelcome scent wafted up from behind her. Her scalp began to sting. The smell grew stronger.

Then it hit her—her hair was burning!

"Ahh!" Story yelped, whipping around just in time to catch Amanda fumbling to block her view of the curling iron. A thick tuft of hair was still attached to it.

"What the hell, Amanda?! Did you just burn off my hair?" Story's heart pounded as her hand flew to her scalp.

"Girl, relax. It wasn't even that much," Amanda replied tipsily, trying to steady herself against the chair. She had always been a lightweight.

When Story reached back, she didn't feel hair in one spot— nothing but peach fuzz remained. Heat rose to her head as her eyes locked on a drunken Amanda, coolly sipping from her cup as though nothing had gone wrong.

Without a second thought, she lunged for her. Torrey and Serita scrambled to hold her back, barely saving Amanda's neck from Story's grasp.

Amanda rolled her eyes and sucked her teeth. "Whatever. You're tripping. You act like you're not familiar with burning people."

"*What?*" Story blinked. "*You* burn *my* hair clean off, and now you're trying to flip this on me? What are you even talking about?" Her fists clenched. "You know what? You need to go before I mess you up!"

Amanda let out a nervous laugh, trying to mask her panic. She swayed unsteadily, her large eyes wild with alcohol and anger. "Oh, *now* you're all big and bad? Were you big and bad when you were passing around the clap?"

Silence fell over the room.

Amanda squared her stance as she glared at Story.

Story held her stare. Torrey and Serita fought their drunken haze, ready to restrain whoever took the first swing.

"Say what?" Her voice dropped an octave. "You heard that nonsense from Terrance, didn't you?"

Torrey looked between them, brows knitted. "Wait, what's going on?"

Amanda slurred, "I'll tell you what's going on. I have gonorrhea!"

"Ew!" Serita muttered under her breath. "I meeean... that sucks. I'm sorry, girl." She smacked the side of her own head in an attempt to sober up before subtly scooting her chair closer to the door and away from Amanda.

"Shut up Serita! The only person I've been with recently is Terrance. I confronted him and he told me all about how our little hoe friend, *Story*, was the last person he had been with, so he clearly got it from her." Amanda looked around, appearing to feel vindicated, before facing Story directly. "You didn't even tell me you knew Terrance! You two-faced *slore*! Now we *both* know what it's like to get burned."

"Wait, wait, wait," Story raised her hands to her temples. "You have the clap?"

"I already said that, dummy!"

"And you think *I* somehow gave it to you even though I haven't so much as laid eyes on Terrance since freshman year?"

Catching Amanda's attitude, she reminded herself to take deep breaths. "Terrance told you we had sex? That *I* gave *him* an STD? Are you crazy?"

Story squared her shoulders. "First of all, I've *never* slept with Terrance. Everybody knows he's the campus pass-around. I talked to him for all of a few weeks, tops. He ghosted me. Which was perfect for me because I was planning on dumping his sorry butt anyway."

Tears spilled down Amanda's face. Torrey rushed to her side, hugging her as she cried.

"I never told you about it because it wasn't that serious. You and Terrance are both grown. But you? You could've come to me woman to woman at any point. Instead, you burn my damn hair off?! This is crazy!"

Amanda opened her mouth soundlessly, face wet with tears, sweat and snot. Story looked at her—*she's a wreck!* She spoke deliberately holding her hands up as her mentee ventured to approach her.

"I'm so pissed right now..." she pointed toward the door avoiding Amanda's glassy gaze. "You need to go before I hurt you."

"Come on," Torrey whispered, guiding Amanda toward the door. "We should go."

Once they were gone, Serita held up the bottle of Alizé and tilted it toward Story. "Can you believe that crap?" she burped as she refilled Story's still half-full cup.

✣ 18 ✣

CONNECTED TO MY SOUL

Story

Several months passed, and Story knew she was growing when she found it in herself to forgive Amanda. After spending days replaying the incident, she felt sorry for her. Amanda was young, impressionable and emotionally caught up; Story knew about that all too well. She was clearly overwhelmed, and they had all probably drunk more than they should have that night. In hindsight, as her mentor, Story wondered if she could have done a better job of warning her about guys like Terrance.

As she pulled her hair into a high pony, allowing the loose curls to cascade to her shoulders, she slicked her baby hair back with Pro Styl gel. The showdown replayed in her mind. She was still pissed about the patch of hair missing from the back of her head, but she managed to reframe the incident. It helped that Story's hair was so full no one could even tell anything happened. Plus, her hair was growing—thick as ever—and so was her character.

Perspective had granted her grace for Amanda's momentary lapse in judgment, and grace for herself, too. The irony wasn't missed on how grace had been exactly what was missing in her fallout with

Justine. She definitely didn't want to make the same mistake with another good friend.

The two made amends after Amanda called to apologize.

She shared how she had been so sprung over Terrance that logic had taken a back seat. She knew deep down Story would never set her up and asked if the two could get past it. Story listened graciously, and agreed to put the whole situation behind them. She even accompanied Amanda to the campus health clinic for follow-up testing to confirm she had been fully treated for the infection.

Someday, Story hoped, they would be able to laugh at the absurdity of it all. And from the looks of it, they were well on their way. She smiled to herself remembering an encounter with Amanda in the cafeteria earlier that afternoon.

Are we still on for cheer practice tonight? her mentee had inquired.

You know it, and don't be late or you owe me five laps. With that, the pair were back to their pre-hairmageddon banter.

Justine

Misery was Justine's only company these days. The guilt of kissing Gregory tripled the moment she saw the hurt in Daniel's eyes. In the days that followed, she spiraled into a ball of self-pity.

Had she become the very part of her father she had spent years detesting—a self-centered lover of... many? *What would Mom think of me?* Justine felt swallowed by shame. She hadn't slept straight through the night since that day. She tossed and turned for hours, falling into a strained slumber, only to awake with the sun's rising disoriented and at a loss for what to do next. She had always prided herself on being responsible. She could count on one hand the number of times she acted recklessly. And short of the pregnancy scare, this was high on the list.

"Hello?" Justine said as the repeated ringing of the phone was replaced by silent airwaves. "It's me... Daniel, are you there?

The silence continued. Tears rolled wearily down her face.

"What do you need, Justine?" Daniel spoke her name for the first time in days.

Not knowing which direction to go, Justine apologized profusely. "I'm sorry... I'm so sooo sorry...You've got to know I didn't mean to—"

"Didn't mean to what?" Daniel erupted. "Let your tongue accidently land in his mouth? That's no accident Jus!"

It was Justine's turn to be silent.

"I *really* thought we had something special. Now, every time I think of your face, I see it glued to his." He sounded defeated. "Damn, yo! I told you what he was about!"

Justine heard the tick of her alarm clock as she let Daniel get it all out.

"I can't do this!"

"No! Don't say that," she whimpered, unable to keep quiet any longer. "We belong—"

"Look! I need to clear my head, ok? I need space." She heard an ache in his voice as he added, "You owe me that."

She agreed. She owed him so much more than that.

"Ok," her voice caught. "But Daniel..."

Daniel blew out a breath, "What?"

"I need you to know... I love you."

"Yeah ok..."

Then he was gone.

Justine cried as the familiar jingle resonated in her ear. *Beep, beep, beep... if you would like to make a call, please*—knowing what came next, she placed the phone back into its cradle where it belonged.

Story

Spring break of junior year, Story and her friends headed to Miami. As the sun streamed through the hotel window, she thought back to her teenage years when she and Justine would make plans to go to Miami once they got to college. The memory crashed into her like a wave, drenching her with sudden remorse. Florida had been such a dream for the two city girls back then.

All it took was one immature outburst, and the one friendship that had always been so rare, so inexplicably deep, was gone. Her connection with Justine had been authentic and easy, like they had known each other in another lifetime. Story hadn't experienced a friendship like theirs before or since.

From the moment the group arrived, an uneasiness trailed her like a single cloud blotting the sun from an otherwise perfect sky. Maybe it was the city. Maybe it was the unspoken apology. Maybe it was the memory of a friendship that made the current company feel like mere acquaintances. Whatever it was, even the blur of Spring Break chaos and inebriated antics couldn't eclipse it.

"Story, raise your glass," her friend, Megan instructed.

"I don't have one," Story whined.

"Someone get Story a cup," Megan yelled obnoxiously. "Come on girl, this trip is our chance to go wild. Snap out of it."

She nodded, determined to enjoy the much-needed vacation. Forcing a smile, she grabbed her cup and cheersed with the pack. But soon, she retreated to her room using the need to unpack as an excuse.

After unpacking, she pulled on her Kente-print bikini top and cut off shorts. But as she glanced out at the crowded beach below, hearing the tipsy shrieks of her friends, her mind drifted again—

I miss you girl. How are you?

Justine

Spring break of junior year found Justine home with her family. She was still on the outs with Daniel and saw no reason to stay in New York for the cheesy tourist adventures they had planned.

The second she stepped through the entryway of the family's high-rise condo, she knew something was off. The silence felt... wrong. Heavy.

"Mom? Dad?" she called out, making her way from room to room.

"We're in here," her father called back in a loud whisper. The usual pomp and circumstance her mother insisted on each time Justine returned from university was missing. No receiving line at the front door. No fragrant aroma of her favorite dish cooling on the stove.

What is going on? As much as Justine always fussed with her mother for being so over the top, she could have used an impromptu pep rally this go-round.

She traced her father's voice to the family room.

When she entered, Justine found her parents curled up on the loveseat. Action News murmured softly in the background. Barbie lay sleeping, her head resting comfortably in John's lap. She wore white silk pajamas, a matching floor-length robe and a royal purple scarf tied carefully around her head.

She looked angelic—beautiful even—as she breathed softly. Ragged little breaths fitfully punctuated what would have otherwise been a peaceful sleep. Justine couldn't remember the last time that she had seen her mother in a head scarf outside of her bedroom, let alone pajamas in the middle of the day.

And something else was different. Her mother seemed…frail.

"Hi Daddy," Justine began softly. "Is Mom not feeling well?"

"Let's wait until she wakes from her nap," her father said, lightly rubbing Barbie's back. "Then we can all talk about it together."

Justine's panic spiked. Her parents were clearly keeping something from her.

"What is it? What's going on?" she asked, her voice louder than intended.

Stepping closer to the couch, her concern deepened. Her mother's frame looked startlingly fragile. Barbie had always been petite, but she maintained a healthy weight for most of her adult life. Now her collar bones jutted out sharply and her eye sockets appeared hollow, shadowed by fatigue.

Justine stared, unable to tear her eyes away. *Someone needs to tell me what's going on. Right now,* she thought.

Before she could voice her thoughts, Barbie's eyes fluttered open.

"Oh, hey baby," she said, her voice tissue thin as she struggled to sit upright. John quickly helped her shift into a sitting position, tucking a few pillows behind her back.

"When did you get in?" Barbie asked, mustering a smile. "Are you hungry? John, grab the takeout menu," she added, trying to lighten the mood.

Justine stepped forward and wrapped her arms gently around her mother's delicate frame.

She ignored the questions. "Mom, what's going on?" she asked quietly. "You don't look like yourself. Do you have the flu or something?"

Barbie patted the cushion beside her and gave John a knowing glance. "Come sit down, honey."

"I don't want to sit down. Someone *please* just tell me what's going on!" Justine was shaking with anxiety.

"Sit. Down," John commanded firmly.

Justine sat. Reluctantly. Positioned precariously on the edge of the sofa, she awaited an answer.

"Well first, I want to start by saying I'm going to be just fine," Barbie glanced at John for reinforcement. "We all are," she continued. "A few months ago, I went to see Dr. Frazier for my annual well woman exam. During the appointment she did a routine breast exam and found a small, almond-sized knot on my right breast. She sent me for lab work, a mammogram and a 3-D ultrasound, which led to a biopsy. A few days later, I got the results," Barbie paused, shrugging weakly.

"Cancer?" Justine breathed, barely audible.

Her mother nodded. "I went back for more follow-up exams and testing. Ultimately, the results confirmed that I have stage II breast cancer, but thankfully, Dr. Frazier was on top of things. She immediately got me in to see the best oncologist in the state, Dr. Mufasa Agnew. We all agreed that I should have a single mastectomy, which is essentially where they remove the breast on the affected side. I had surgery last month and everything went well, but Dr. Agnew recommended I follow up with both chemotherapy and radiation to increase my chances of all of the cancerous cells being destroyed."

She took a breath as though merely recounting her journey was exhausting.

Justine gazed at the shape that was her mother, now blurred by the tears that had yet to fall.

Barbie held her daughter's hand. "I'm five sessions in with chemo and as you can see, it's made me a bit tired. But I'm fine. Once I finish my cycles of chemo, I'll have two weeks of radiation, then we will begin prepping for my reconstructive surgeries. I don't want you—or your father—to worry about me. I'm going to fight this. And I'm going to beat it."

John gazed lovingly at his wife—his admiration apparent. Justine could see that he saw something admirable in her mother, perhaps for the first time: strength, resilience.

His eyes never left hers as he spoke, "She's right, Little Lady. Your mother has been so unbelievably strong through all of this. She hasn't complained one bit and has strictly followed the doctors' orders. She's actually making it quite difficult for me to be her knight in shining armor if you ask me," he added. Barbie beamed at him. Even in her current state, the effect his words had on her was visible.

"Mommy, why didn't you tell me?" Justine's voice cracked.

"Honey, you have school. *That's* your priority now," Barbie patted Justine's cheeks, blotting a tear with her fingertips. "I couldn't live with myself if anything got in the way of that. Plus, I'm going to be just fine," Barbie reiterated. "Your father has been taking good care of me. I have my good days and bad. But I'm making it."

Justine took a shaky breath, sending a genuine smile her father's way. "So what's next?"

"Well at this point, I'm just focused on making it through my cycles of chemotherapy and radiation, then they'll do testing to be absolutely certain the cancer is gone and determine if I should also do hormonal therapy."

"What can I do to help?"

"Pray my strength and just support me as best you can," Barbie replied firmly.

"Consider it done," Justine leaned closer to kiss her mother's forehead. "I'm going to go make you some soup. I'll bet you haven't eaten anything today, have you?"

Barbie sheepishly shook her head *no*. "One of the side effects of chemo is constant nausea and loss of appetite. Food is the last thing on my mind most days. But you're right, I should try to put something on my stomach."

Justine barely made it out of the room before her shoulders began to shake. She hadn't wanted her mother to see her crying, but she was scared—more scared than she had ever been.

As she tried her best to gain control of her emotions, her hands poured the canned vegetable soup into the saucepan and turned on the burner. Her mind wandered. Barbie had always been the strength of the family. She had never seen her mother sick with anything more than a common cold. *How could this happen to her of all people? She eats a healthy diet, exercises regularly and always keeps herself up.* No one that Justine knew of in her mother's family had ever had cancer—though she did recall her grandmother having to have a hysterectomy for some reason.

Her mother had had to endure so much throughout her life already; Justine couldn't fathom why God was punishing her like this. Hadn't she already gone through her share of trials?

She continued her mental diatribe until the smell of burning soup hit her nostrils.

Carefully ladling off the top layer, she placed the soup in a bowl with a side of saltine crackers. Looking at the tray she did a mental check: Water. Spoon. Napkin. Food. As she lifted the tray, she focused all her energy into holding on and not spilling. Tears, water or soup. Before re-entering the family room, she paused to regain her composure.

You've got this Justine. You're a Chandler. You were built for the fight. Don't show weakness. Mom needs you to be strong, so snap out of it! Fix this! Taking a deep breath, she appeared with what she hoped was a neutral facial expression.

With shaky hands, she set the tray on the table and returned to the seat across from her parents. John picked up the soup and began to spoon feed Barbie.

Justine sat staring, trying to process it all.

What if she doesn't beat this? she thought to herself. *No, no, no, don't think like that,* she quickly suppressed any further negative thoughts. Doing so rapidly drained what little she had left of her energy.

"This is a lot," she blurted rather abruptly. "I'm going to go lay down for a bit." Before the waterworks could begin, Justine rushed off to her room.

As she lay in bed staring at the ceiling, she racked her brain about what she could do to further help her mother. She rolled to her side and stared at the Care Bear clock: 10:18 p.m. A smile found her face as she glanced around. Her mother had kept her bedroom just as it had been when Justine left three years ago. Pink fluffy duvet. Stuffed animals lining her shelf like hypervigilant soldiers. Vanity overflowing with the CDs from her youth. Where had the time gone?

Everything was the same, but everything was different. Justine tossed and turned, as innumerable outcomes flooded her mind. On one hand, her father was finally making himself available to support her mother through her treatments. But Justine felt the overwhelming desire to do her part as well.

Just then, Story came to mind. More than anything, she wished she could talk to the one person who knew her better than anyone. They would brainstorm on how to make everything better. Even just hearing her voice would have helped. But Justine still had no idea how to reach her. Then something strange happened: no sooner had she thought of her old friend than a plan came to mind—Justine would withdraw from school for the rest of the semester. She would learn as much as she could about breast cancer. And she would help nurse her mother back to good health. This time, when someone she loved needed her, she would show up. No matter how hard it was.

Story

Jolted awake, Story looked around, disoriented. The hair on her arms stood at full attention. She had an eerie feeling that something was wrong. Following the glow of the clock on her nightstand, she squinted—10:18 p.m.

Where had the evening gone?

She had laid down at eight for a quick power nap before hitting the town, and now over two hours had passed.

She reached for the hotel cordless and phoned home.

"Hello," Denise answered on the first ring, attempting to clear the sleep from her voice.

"Hey Ma, how's it going?"

"Story? Hey honey," she heard her mother fumble to maintain her grip on the receiver. "Everything alright?"

Story smiled as she envisioned her mother. Even when fighting sleep, she stayed ready to jump into mama bear mode at the drop of a dime. "Yeah... I just wanted to hear your voice and tell you I love you."

"How sweet, I love you too baby. Now go have fun —it's Spring Break, remember?"

"I hear you, Ma." With a heavy sigh, Story hung up and sank back onto her side. It looked like the club was a wash for the night, but she wasn't the least bit disappointed. She didn't feel much like partying with these unshakeable, unsettled feelings.

Story looked around the hotel room. Her luggage lay where she had left it. Her makeup remained on the vanity. The only light in the room came from the television—as it softly aired a rerun of *Full House* in the background. Still, something felt... off.

She couldn't quite put her finger on it, but an unease hummed somewhere inside of her. Staring up at the ceiling, she tried to name the sensation that pulled at the edges of her thoughts like a shadow just out of reach.

❀ 19 ❀

TAILSPIN

Story

 My dad left when I was two years old. One day he went to work and never came home. I was so young, I don't even remember him very much. My mom only has one picture of him because she was so angry when he left that she destroyed the rest. Somehow that wallet-sized picture must have slipped out of sight during one of her destructive rampages. When I was younger, I'd sit and stare at his picture for hours. I'd dissect what features we shared and try to guide him back to us just by staring into his eyes. Then, I'd imagine he was somewhere looking at my picture and devising a plan to come back.

Story paused to take a deep breath. She didn't expect the essay her after school student had written to hit so close to home. The eighth grade class had been tasked with writing a story about their own greatest loss; Natalia asked Story to review it. She didn't know what to expect when she agreed to support her, but she hadn't expected this. Story swallowed emotions evoked from their shared history—both fathers having left before either daughter could make any lasting memories. She too had daydreamed about her father often over the years, imagining him thinking about her, planning his return. As the years passed, however, and with all the moving around, Story had grown less and less hopeful that he'd ever find her.

My sisters remember our Daddy before things got bad. They used to tell me stories about how fun he was: how he'd take us to the park and play with us all the time. But they also told me stories I wish I could forget. Mommy and Daddy argued a lot, mostly about Daddy's drinking. I guess one day he just got tired of fighting and he needed a break. I spent a long time waiting for him to return. And when that didn't happen, I spent even more time being angry at him. These days, I just feel indifferent about it all.

Story understood that emotional rollercoaster all too well. Unfortunately, she didn't have any siblings to recount old memories. Justine had been the closest thing to a sibling she ever knew, and not a day went by that Story didn't regret how she had ruined that relationship. Whenever she asked her mother about her father, Denise always assured Story that her father *did* love her despite his absence. She never gave any more details, only offering that "circumstances" made it physically impossible for him to be there. For the life of her, Story could never understand what that meant—what circumstance could possibly keep a parent from their child? Still, she clung to the few stories her mother was willing to share.

Once such a tale included how Story's father had taken one look at her when she was born and beamed with pride—he even helped name her. He promised they would never want for anything, and in terms of money, he had fulfilled that promise. But while Story never came up short when it came to tangible needs, she still yearned for one thing: an emotional connection with him. She longed to *know* him, not just know *about* him.

Even at twenty years old, she longed for his affection, often wondering what life would have been like if he stayed. *I wonder if he ever wonders the same?* Her father had already missed so many of her firsts, and acknowledging that sometimes made her angry. The idea that he had a daughter out in the world and made no effort to connect with her seemed unfathomable: an offense she vowed to never commit with any children of her own. Weary from warring with what she couldn't control, Story made a promise to no longer be defined by the actions of her parents—or anyone else for that matter.

Her mind flashed back to sophomore year and the old man who

had been watching her from a distance. He felt strangely familiar, and, for a few days, she wondered if he might be her father. A week later she mentioned it to her mother, letting Denise know that she was finally ready to meet him. Story even offered to use her part-time income to hire a private investigator. But as soon as she began mapping out her plan, her mother shut it down. Hard. Feeling discouraged by her mother's refusal, Story decided she wasn't willing to upset the only parent she had left. Maybe one day, when the time was right, she'd find her father. On her own.

Story closed her eyes and rolled her neck. Left to right, right to left. The essay had deposited a palpable tension in her body. Flexing her fingers, she noticed moistened prints left on the paper.

Maybe I should take a break, she considered briefly. *Nah, I need to finish this.* Story took a deep breath, doing her best to flush the heart-achiness her student's account had awakened, and committed to finishing Natalia's essay. Tonight.

Justine

It had been just over a month since Justine made the decision to put university on hold. Initially, she made the choice quickly and definitively, but as the days passed and she ruminated on the logistics of her decision, she began to waiver. The stream of thoughts flooding her mind were endless.

What about school? This will set me back for graduation. What about Daniel? We aren't in the best space for long distance. What if we grow further apart? But whenever she saw her mother laying on the couch—frail, unkept, far from her prime—she knew this decision was more than worth it, even though both of her parents were completely against the idea. John tried to assure her that he had everything under control. Even so, he couldn't be available around the clock for Barbie—he had a business to run, prior commitments to uphold. And Justine saw no need to hire help when she was more than willing to step in herself. Once she made up her mind, she couldn't be swayed.

She took charge of getting her mother to and from chemotherapy appointments, cleaning up when Barbie got sick, and being a steady support for both of her parents. Thankfully their full-time chef and housekeeper were still managing the other household duties. But at night, while laying in her bed, when there were no duties to hide behind, the tide of feelings she successfully held at bay washed ashore. Her pillow caught her tears. Her hand held muffled wails. The moonlight kept her company. Her limbs trembled from fear-induced tension. When her nightly mourning ritual was complete, she'd fall into an exhausted sleep before waking the next morning, prepared for another round in the fight for her mother's life.

Justine had done a lot of research on breast cancer and discovered several holistic approaches, which they had since incorporated into Barbie's treatment plan. So far, treatment seemed to be progressing as expected.

As an added bonus, Justine noticed a shift in her parents' relationship. Her father really stepped up to be the husband her mother needed. He was gentle and protective with Barbie. Most importantly, she ceased to see any suspicious behavior that would suggest he was still stepping out on his marriage. Gone were the days of last minute red eyes to *God knows where*. No more inexplicable phone calls that needed to be taken in another room. John drastically reduced his travel engagements. He became more transparent about the daily operations of his company. And on more than one occasion, she had walked in on her parents snuggled up on the couch, simply holding one another as they slept.

Once, when Barbie was feeling an unusual burst of energy, the three of them went out for dinner. Throughout the evening, Justine basked in quiet excitement as she watched her parents giggling and exchanging flirty glances across the table. It had been a long time since the marriage she had always imagined her parents having matched the one they had in real life. It was a refreshing surprise.

And while it was unfortunate that Barbie's illness was the bridge to bring their family together, Justine was willing to accept whatever she could get. She couldn't be sure how long the family's honeymoon would last, but she chose to relish the good times and put aside the bad.

. . .

Story

She couldn't name it. After reading Natalia's essay, Story was a ball of unexplained emotions. In the month since returning to college from spring break in Miami, something felt off. Feelings she had long since buried arose to the surface. The bandage so firmly placed over the wound of her father's absence had been ripped away; left in its place were emptiness, sadness and resentment. She needed a reset—and decided she was long overdue for a visit home.

Being less than three hours away, she purchased a Greyhound ticket and was now en route to spend the weekend with her mom—her safe space. She believed that time with Denise would be just what she needed to get grounded. As the bus rolled along the short route to Raleigh, Story allowed the gentle hum of the engine and cool touch of the window pane against her temple to soothe the angst in her head. With the passing of each highway marker, she grew more excited at the thought of returning to what she knew.

When Story disembarked at the depot, her mother was already there. Running into her arms, she showered her cheeks with kisses. The floral scent of Denise's eau de toilette soothed Story—reminding her that she was right where she needed to be.

"Well, hello to you too," Denise said, enjoying her daughter's enthusiastic embrace.

"Mom, you have no idea how happy I am to see you," she whispered in her mother's ear. "This is just what I needed."

"How about you catch me up on what you've been getting into up at that fancy college?"

"Sure...let's grab a bite," Story chimed. "Lunch is on me."

"Ok, big spender. I could get used to this," Denise joked as the two walked hand in hand toward the car.

I could too, Story thought to herself.

Justine

Philly reminded Justine that she was there without the two people who had once been her biggest allies—Story and Daniel. She missed so many things about both of them. One look from Story could pause her racing thoughts. The firm press of Daniel's hand into hers assured her that she could take on anything.

But that life, those moments, were long gone. If someone had told her a few years ago that she wouldn't be able to turn to either of them for support now, she would've called them a liar. Justine felt herself spiraling. Her relationship with Daniel remained uncertain; she had no way of reaching Story to even try to repair their friendship; and her mother was battling a life-threatening illness.

She couldn't imagine, or handle, things getting any worse.

Story

During lunch, Story filled her mother in on college life, her trip to Miami and Natalia's essay. Denise listened without interrupting.

"That's a lot to unpack," she said once her daughter finally finished. "First of all, I want you to know that I'm so proud of you. I love watching the woman you're growing into. How you handled the situation with Amanda showed a lot of grace. I don't even know if I could've handled it better," she paused pensively. "Never let anyone dim your light, Story. Keep doing what's right, even when others don't."

"Thanks, Ma. I needed to hear that."

"You know I'm always Team Story, baby, and I'm not just saying what you want to hear—I'm telling you what I know."

The two sat eating in silence for a moment, as Story let her mother's affirmations fortify the parts of her that were weakened from worry.

"You mentioned that Miami would've been more fun if Justine had been there. I don't hear you speak about her much anymore. Do you two keep in touch?"

"Not since we moved. Why do you ask?"

"No reason. I just know how close you two were and wondered whatever came of that..." Denise's voice trailed off to a distant place.

She considered telling her mother about Mrs. Chandler's response to her after everything went down, but decided against it. Maybe there was some truth in what Mrs. Chandler had said: *Real friends don't hurt one another.* Story had replayed that phone call in her mind a thousand times, especially whenever she wanted desperately to make things right with Justine. Just as her thoughts began to drift, her mother spoke.

"I know reading that essay probably brought up a lot of questions for you. We've never really had an in-depth talk about your father..."

"We've never really had much of any kind of talk about my father, Mom..." Story ventured, careful not to ruin this rare moment.

"Believe me, I wish there was more I could share, baby—I really do. The best I can tell you is that your father and I met, and quickly fell in love. Things were complicated between us, and honestly, we should've never been together. But when I got pregnant with you, I knew that God was blessing me with the most beautiful gift." There was an uncharacteristic softness in her mother's voice when she said "love" and "gift."

"I've never regretted having you—not for one second. If anything, you saved me from continuing down a path I never should've started. Your father has his reasons for keeping his distance, and maybe one day, he'll find it within himself to be a part of your life." Denise reached for Story's hand. "But that's not something I can control as much as I wish I could. I'm sorry I can't give you more than that."

Story accepted what her mother had just shared. It was more than she had ever said about her father, and, this time, there was no irritation in her voice. While she still didn't understand why his identity had to remain a mystery, she felt a strange comfort in knowing she had been conceived in love and deemed a "gift" by her mother.

They spent hours chatting and catching up.

When Story finally retired to her room, she lay in bed thinking about Justine. What she needed now, more than anything, was a true friend. Deciding it was worth a shot, Story reached for the cordless phone and dialed Justine's home number.

After two rings, a voice answered.

"Hello?"

It took Story a moment to recognize Mrs. Chandler on the other end. She sounded either groggy or deeply unwell—she couldn't decipher which it was.

This doesn't sound good, she thought, now worried.

"Hellooo?" Mrs. Chandler repeated—more articulate with her second attempt.

Story couldn't bring her thoughts to the surface. Instead, she quickly hung up the phone.

❧ 20 ❧

REVIVAL

Justine

By November, Barbie had completed chemotherapy and begun radiation. Chemo had taken a brutal toll on her, but true to their word, both John and Justine stood by her side every step of the way. Justine had never been prouder of her mother. She had watched Barbie endure overwhelming fatigue, relentless nausea, frequent vomiting and even hair loss. Yet not once did her mother waver in her belief that they were all going to be just fine. And sure enough, they pulled through.

Together.

As radiation treatments continued, Barbie slowly began regaining her strength. Her hair started to grow back in soft, fussy ringlets, which she wore like a badge of honor—except on days when she chose to don one of the fancy wigs John had bought her.

Things were finally falling into place, Justine thought as she drove her mother home from a treatment session. She missed a semester and a half of school, but that was the least of her concerns. She was already in discussions with the dean of her department about re-enrolling.

"Want to go out for lunch, Mom?"

Barbie feigned a yawn and shook her head. "I think I've had

enough adventure for one day. I'd better get back to the house. Your father will be home soon."

Justine studied her mother for a moment, checking for signs of lucidity. "Dad doesn't return until tomorrow, Mom. His trip to South Africa was scheduled for a full week," she offered gently.

"Oh, is that right? Well, I'd best get home and rest up for his return," Barbie said with a coy smile.

"Oook," Justine responded, eyeing her mother.

Something was up.

Barbie had been through a lot, but she was typically sharp as a whip—she knew everyone's schedules like the back of her hand. Justine doubted she had genuinely forgotten her husband's itinerary. If she knew her mother like she thought she did, Barbie had something up her sleeve.

Still, she decided to let it go, certain it would eventually make sense. After everything Barbie had endured in recent months, she had earned the right to be a little off—or even secretive.

Story

Grabbing her cheer bag and preparing to leave the gymnasium after practice, Story waved to her teammates and headed toward the exit. It had been a great cheer practice, and she was more than pleased to see that her first semester as co-captain of the team was going so smoothly.

"Story, wait up," her fellow co-captain yelled out.

She turned and smiled as he jogged toward her. "What's up, Karl! How's it going?"

"Chillin'," he said, easily matching her stride. "So how you feelin' about the season?"

"It's going pretty well. The newbies are picking up on the routine's relatively quickly, and the old heads seem to be taking their mentoring roles seriously. Oh! And that cheer you taught today?! The bomb! I can't wait to see the crowd's reaction on Saturday."

Story's eyes settled on Karl's—a chameleonic hazel that, depending on the way the light landed in them, showcased flecks of gold, green or even blue. It was the first time she had noticed them.

Karl smiled, oblivious to Story's new discovery. "Yeah, I put that one together over the summer. Glad you like it," he said, stroking his goatee.

Reaching her Volkswagen Beetle, she attempted to wrap up the conversation. "I think we have a really good season ahead of us this year. I'm looking forward to it."

She unlocked the door.

"Wait!"

Story paused and looked back at him.

"Um." He scratched his head nervously. "If I were to ask you to hang out sometime outside of practice... what would you think?"

Story tilted her head. "Karl Fox, are you asking me on a date?" she teased.

The co-captain licked his lips and grinned, "I mean, it wouldn't be such a bad idea. You're single, I'm single. You're cute, I'm not too bad. We're co-captains—so aren't we kind of, technically, meant to be together?" he joked. "What do you think? Wanna grab dinner and catch a movie sometime?"

Story considered it. She had never thought of Karl in a romantic way before, but he *was* a cutie. Years of cheer stunts and lifts had built him solid. He was tall. He could dress. He was a biochemical engineering major—so clearly smart. He was kind, grounded and had always been respectful, which wasn't always the case in a female-led sport. Story had even overheard him mention his strong Christian upbringing a few times.

In so many ways, Karl was the opposite of the guys Story usually fell for: bad boys. But so far, her usual type hadn't proven to be a match. *What the heck, I don't have anything to lose,* she thought. *It isn't like there's a line of guys beating down my door.*

"I'd love to."

"Really?" His face lit up. "I mean, cool, cool. How about Friday at 8?"

"It's a date," she said, excited to see where this new adventure would take her.

· · ·

Justine

Justine and her mother had been home for no more than an hour when the doorbell rang.

"Justine honey, I'm going to go grab a shower," Barbie said hastily, hoisting herself off the couch. "Can you get the door?"

"Ummm, sure." Justine walked to the foyer, wondering why her mother was acting so strangely today. Peeking through the peephole, she nearly fainted—it was Daniel.

There he stood, holding a bouquet of white roses; she continued staring. He rang the bell again.

"Justine, *open* the door," Barbie whispered, peeking around the corner.

She caught her mother's eye just before Barbie's smirking face disappeared again.

Taking a few deep breaths to steady her heart, she opened the door, trying her best to appear calm.

"Oh hey, Daniel. I didn't know you were in town."

"Justine!" His eyes drank her in. Breaking his own reverie, he smiled sheepishly. "I mean... hey Jus, how've you been?"

"I'm alright," Justine said, smoothing her shirt and drying sweaty palms. "What brings you to Philly? Aren't you in the middle of the semester?"

"It was time."

"Time for what?"

"Can I come in?"

"Oh... yeah... sure."

As Justine guided Daniel toward the family room, she saw the hem of her mother's silk robe swish around the corner leading to the bedrooms. She smiled nervously, as she perched on the edge of the sectional.

"Have a seat." She pointed to the adjacent armchair.

The two sat in silence for what felt like an eternity: both captive to their own thoughts.

"These are for you," Daniel said, finally handing her the flowers.

"Thank you," she said softly. "They're beautiful."

"Justine, I..."

"Ohhh, Daniel! I had no idea you were coming," Barbie exclaimed, flamboyantly waltzing into the family room wearing a new maxi dress and asymmetrical shoulder length wig. "What brings you to town?"

Daniel looked at Barbie, clearly confused. "Well Mrs. Chandler, when I spoke to you on the phone—"

"Nonsense, it doesn't matter." Looking out of the window Barbie chattered on, "It's such a beautiful day, you two should go and get some fresh air. I'm going to rest for a bit and perhaps read my novel. You lovebirds have a good time now," she said while nudging Daniel and Justine toward the door. "Oh! And I'll put these in water," Barbie added, snatching the roses from Justine's extended hand.

There was no time to protest. Based on the top-grade performance her mother had just given, today seemed to be "a good day," which put Justine at ease with leaving her alone for a while.

The two walked down the hallway and rode the elevator in silence, Justine's fingers aching to reach out and touch Daniel. She felt as though her insides would turn to Jell-O as the scent of his aftershave wafted past her. *Gosh! I've missed him!* she thought. Daniel took an almost imperceivable step toward her, threatening to break down the wall that had been between them for the past few months. They stared at each other, their eyes communicating their unspoken feelings.

"Your mom looks like she's feeling well today," Daniel offered.

"Seems so," Justine smiled. "I suspect your visit had something to do with that."

Daniel just smiled.

As the couple exited, Mr. Arney waved a greeting.

"Want to go to Griffin Park?" Justine proposed.

"Sure."

As they continued walking, Daniel finally spoke.

"I came to town this weekend because I've missed you, Jus." He glanced at her, his tone sincere. "Don't get me wrong—I was pissed when I saw you in Gregory's arms, but I've had more than enough time to think. And honestly, I don't want to dwell on that anymore. What we have is stronger than anything else. You're the person I want to spend the rest of my life with, and I want you back."

Daniel's voice was steady now. "We can make this work. Even if you never come back to NYU; I'll wait for you. I can't let you go that easily. I have every intention of marrying you one day."

Justine sat on the park bench, stunned. He had just said everything she longed to hear for months.

"Daniel," she finally began, her voice thick with emotion, "I need to tell you again—I'm sorry. I'm so, so sorry."

She took a breath, gathering her thoughts. "I don't know why I didn't shut Gregory down long before that day. As much as I kept denying it to myself, I think deep down, I liked the attention. The challenge of it. But it was never about him. Not really." Her voice cracked slightly. "I never meant to hurt you. That's the last thing I'd ever want to do. And I am willing to fight for what we have—especially if you're still in this with me."

Daniel pulled Justine into his arms and held her tightly against his chest. He pressed a kiss to her forehead.

For a long moment, neither of them spoke. They just sat there, wrapped in the warmth of recommitting, allowing the quiet to hold them. It was as if, in that brief stillness, the chaos of the past few months had finally dissipated.

Story

Peeking out of her dorm window to see if Karl had arrived, Story flitted about the room adding last minute touches to her look. Almost on cue, her room phone rang.

"Hello?" she answered.

"Hi Story, it's Beatrice—you've got a guest waiting in the lobby."

"Thanks, Bea. I'll be right down."

She did one last spin in the mirror and smiled at her reflection. She had chosen a white tube top layered under a colorful button-down shirt and a fitted denim mini. A 24-karat gold link necklace with a cross charm gleamed at her collarbone, paired with chunky gold hoops and crisp white low-top sneakers. With a satisfied nod, Story patted her freshly-done hair and headed out the door.

Despite her usual confidence, she felt a flutter of nerves. She couldn't quite pinpoint why—maybe it was because she had never dated anyone like Karl before. Still, she reminded herself, *there's a first time for everything*. She was determined to see the night through. As soon as she stepped into the lobby, she saw him: a smile broad enough to turn the heads of several girls in the lounge. Low top caesar. Eyes deepened with specks of green, further complimenting his graphic tee. Well-defined shoulders. Karl was undoubtedly eye candy and Story's excitement surged at the thought of being on his arm.

His face lit up even more when he saw her. Words escaped him as he handed Story a bouquet of wildflowers and opened his arms for an embrace. She obliged.

"Dang, Story," he said, grinning. "You look *good*!"

She laughed and gave a quick twirl. "Thanks. Just something I threw on. I hope it works for wherever we're headed."

He doesn't need to know I've been obsessing over the perfect outfit since the day he asked me out, she thought, relieved he wasn't a mindreader.

"You look perfect," he said, meaning it. "Since it just came out, I thought we'd catch *Enemy of the State* at the theater in Colonial Heights. After that, maybe dinner at that new seafood restaurant, unless there is somewhere else you want to go."

"Nope, that sounds good to me."

Story grabbed Karl's hand, more than willing to follow his lead and impressed by the intentionality he put into the date. She examined his profile out of her peripheral vision. *This one just might be a keeper*, she mused.

⚜

When Story returned to her dorm later that evening, she was on cloud nine —Karl had been the perfect date. He opened every door, made sure she walked on the inside of the street, ordered for her at the restaurant, and— what really stood out—asked if he could kiss her at the end of the night. He was a true gentleman, unlike most of the guys she had dated before. He seemed tuned in to her energy, picking up on subtle cues and respecting Story's limits. When she mentioned, at the last minute, that she was suddenly craving soul food instead, he just smiled, made a u-turn and took her to a soul food spot he claimed had the best mac and cheese in the city.

No questions, no attitude—just a quiet, agreeable confidence. He was just smooth like that. Easygoing, attentive, and sincere. They had talked about everything and nothing, and he kept her laughing all night with his dry humor and quick wit. For the first time in a long time, Story felt treasured. She didn't have to decode mixed signals or pretend to be unfazed. It was just good, straightforward, grounded energy. She was still giddy with how much fun she had.

By the time she climbed into bed, one thought settled firmly in her mind: she wasn't letting this one get away. As far as she was concerned, she and Karl were in it for the long haul.

❧ 21 ❧

FINISH STRONG

Story

Senior year started with a bang. It was August 1999, and Story was still cheering for the university, working part-time at the after-school program and jumping headfirst into her final year of student teaching.

She had been placed in a third-grade classroom with a seasoned teacher at the local elementary school. Once a week, Story was responsible for leading the class the entire day. On other teaching days, she shadowed the head teacher and offered support wherever needed. It was exhausting but fulfilling work, and she was rising to the challenge.

Her students really took a liking to her theatrical means of storytelling. They snickered and squealed with glee as Story recounted what Snow White was left to endure after biting the apple. She welcomed such opportunities to share life lessons with the children: *treat others as you would like to be treated. All actions inevitably have a reaction. Mistakes are proof that you're trying.* She enjoyed following the evolution of insight that began forming in their developing minds. As the children grew, so did Story.

Through it all, Karl remained her biggest supporter and exactly what she needed to ground herself throughout the school year. When Story struggled to balance her commitments, he gave her the needed nudge. When she grew frustrated out of sheer exhaustion, he knew exactly what to say to bring a smile back to her face. He never ceased to be a consistent pillar of strength and joy in her life. And Story found herself mirroring his acts of kindness by being the best version of herself. Even when it was hard.

Things between them were moving quickly, but in a way that felt natural. As she worked toward graduating with honors, Karl was always in her corner—encouraging her, holding her accountable and reminding her of her *why*.

Although it was only two weeks into the fall semester, Story had already begun thinking about her next steps. She could stay in Virginia, which had come to feel like home over the past four years, or return to North Carolina to be closer to her mother. Then there was California—where Karl was headed, and where he was gently encouraging her to follow.

Each option carried its own weight, benefits and costs. And while she had yet to make a decision, she was wholeheartedly committed to taking the necessary time to make the choice that best aligned with the woman she was becoming—and the future she truly wanted.

Justine

Justine returned to NYU in the spring of 1999. Her mother was officially in remission after having completed all required treatments. With a clean bill of health, Barbie resumed her former social commitments, and John resumed his full-time schedule at Dream Makers Grow, Inc. With her parents settling back into their routines, Justine saw no reason to delay hers any longer.

Daniel came from New York to help Justine pack and return to campus. They drove back together and quickly got into the swing of their previous rhythm. While he was preparing for medical school, Justine was also fulfilling her academic career plan.

Due to her foresight and remaining in touch with her academic advisors throughout her leave of absence, they managed to map out a path for her to graduate by the fall of 2000. It would require maxing out her course load each semester and enrolling in summer classes.

After which, she planned to intern at a firm before starting law school. With Daniel graduating two semesters earlier, Justine took comfort knowing they were still on the path they had mapped out for themselves. Both individually, and together.

Still, as excited as Justine was to be back on track, she couldn't help but think about Story. It had been four years since they last spoke, and she still hadn't made any connections as strong as the friendship they once shared. Now that things were coming together academically, she resolved that it was high time she found her friend. It was important to her that they finish building the lives that they once dreamt of—together. There was just one major hiccup: she had no idea *how* to find her. Barbie suggested searching the white pages given Story's unique name, but she had yet to find anyone by that name in Pennsylvania or New York.

Feeling she had no other choice, Justine asked her father. His network was vast, and she felt confident his investigative contacts could reach further than she could. He promised to look into it and get back to her. The child within that had once been so deeply shattered by her father, and hero, now felt renewed hope. He had shown up for her mother in an unprecedented way, and now that the pieces of her life seemed to be coming back together again, she trusted him to show up for her also.

Story

Something wasn't right! Story was a ball of nerves as she drove as quickly as her Beetle would allow without risking a ticket. She hadn't spoken to Amanda in five days, though they usually talked every day. Seeing as it was finals week, Story initially brushed off the uneasy feeling that kept nagging at her. But a few minutes ago, she called Amanda, and someone picked up the phone—but didn't speak.

Story repeatedly called out until she heard what sounded like someone dropping the phone, emitting a weak moan. She strained to hear, craning her neck and pressing the receiver to her shoulder. Holding her breath, she waited. Her efforts met with continued silence. Amanda lived with a roommate off-campus, but it wasn't more than a five-minute drive from the university. *I can make it in three,* Story reasoned as she grabbed her purse and keys.

As she pulled into the parking lot of Colonial Manor Apartments, the hairs on her arms stood up. Her nerves brought prickly sweat to her temples and armpits. She was... scared. But sensing she didn't have the luxury of time, she quickly put the car in park and rushed to Amanda's front door.

Story banged, hoping she was overreacting, half-expecting the feisty persona to swing open the door, hands on hips, at any second.

"Amanda, open up!" She paused, hand suspended midair as she awaited any sounds of life behind the heavy wooden door. "Are you in there?" she yelled, resuming her pounding. *Boom, boom, boom!*

"I don't think they're home," said the neighbor, Ms. O'Hare, leaning out of her window with a cigarette dangling from her lip. "Kenya moved out last week after those two got into an argument about cleaning up. I haven't seen 'Manda since yesterday when she came home from class. She seemed pretty upset. But I don't get in folks' business none, so I ain't say nothin' to her 'bout it."

Story was in awe, listening as Amanda's notoriously nosy neighbor recounted everyone's whereabouts. She and Amanda had often joked about how Ms. O'Hare sat in her living room window like a self-appointed neighborhood watch. It was a shame that the one time Story actually needed her to spill the beans, Ms. O'Hare didn't seem to know where Amanda was.

"Thank you, ma'am," she said, turning to walk toward her car.

"Don't call me ma'am!" the eagle-eyed, nicotine-laced voice called out. "I'm not *that* old!"

Story paused, her hand on the car handle. Something told her to try one more time. She made her way to the rear of the apartment, where she knew Amanda's bedroom was. Peering through a slit in the blinds, she could just make out a bed and dresser. There on the other side of the bed, she saw her—Amanda was lying on the floor. Face down.

Squinting for a better view, Story noticed the faintest rise and fall of her slender back. She knocked frantically on the window.

"Amanda! Amanda, get up!"

After several failed attempts to wake her, Story knew her mentee was in trouble. Without wasting another second, she rushed to the front of the apartment and told Ms. O'Hare to call the police.

Justine

Daniel walked across the stage to receive his degree. He was officially on his way to NYU's Grossman School of Medicine. It had taken a ton of hard work and grit, but he stayed focused and remained on course. Justine could not have been prouder. She turned to his parents, Dawn and Nelson, and shared a warm embrace. He was officially the first college graduate in his family, and the moment was as much an accomplishment for his parents as it was for him. They spent years drilling the importance of a proper education. Having been teen parents themselves, they never wanted their son to experience the struggles they had.

Mr. and Mrs. McClendon had both taken on second jobs to help put Daniel through undergrad. Their contributions, along with Daniel's scholarship, had significantly reduced the amount he needed to take out in student loans. Mrs. McClendon wiped away a tear, grateful for the fruits of their labor; her tenacity reminded Justine a lot of her own mother, who was also the glue that held the family together. Both women possessed a kind of fortitude she aspired to.

After the ceremony, Daniel shook hands with a few of his classmates before setting out to find his family. Justine waved frantically to get his attention, unable to contain her excitement. When he got close enough, she ran into his arms. Daniel picked her up and spun her around, balancing his degree in the other hand. Setting her back down, he abruptly turned to his parents, presented a determined smile and dropped to one knee.

"What are you doing?" Justine gasped, covering her mouth.

"Trust me?"

"Always," she responded as she always did to this question—without hesitation.

"Justine Elizabeth Chandler, I have loved you from the moment I laid eyes on you sophomore year of high school. From the first *hello*, I knew I wanted you to be a permanent fixture in my life—and you have been that and more."

Justine stood. Speechless. She could hear her heart beating in her ears.

"We've had our share of challenges, but we've come out on top each time," Daniel continued. "I love seeing your smiling face: I go to bed with thoughts of you and I wake up eager to see you again. When we're together, nothing else matters. You make me a better person."

Where is this going? she wondered, glancing nervously at the gradually growing crowd. She held her breath and willed herself not to bolt from the stadium. She loved Daniel, but there was still so much she needed to accomplish before walking down the aisle.

"I want to be by your side for the rest of our lives. The last time we got back together, I told you I was going to marry you one day. Today, I give you this promise ring as proof that my plan hasn't changed. Jus, will you wear this ring?"

The bubble of anxiety burst as she exclaimed, "YES," feeling both excited and relieved. The promise of marriage was the perfect next step, almost as perfect as the solitaire diamond Daniel slipped on her finger. Beaming with pride, Justine relished in this symbol of intention—she was more than willing to commit to marrying Daniel. Someday.

Story

"Story Johnniece Brooks." Her cheerleaders went wild—Denise, Mrs. Baude and Amanda screamed at the top of their lungs as Story's name was called to receive her degree.

She did a quick happy dance before walking through the procession to shake hands. When Story returned to her seat, she slapped fives with her peers. She couldn't believe the day was finally here. She had fought her way through, dealt with more than she imagined possible and managed to graduate summa cum laude—an honor both she and Karl boasted.

Her mother, Denise, had taken off the entire weekend to celebrate this moment. Story knew her mother had worked hard to ensure she made something of herself, and seeing her walk across that stage made every sacrifice well worth it.

Mrs. Baude had become more than a mentor—she was a friend. Even after Story's relocation to North Carolina, she remained a person with whom she could share her deepest thoughts. Mrs. Baude had driven from Philly to Virginia earlier that morning just to celebrate this moment. Story felt deeply blessed to be surrounded by her greatest supporters.

Catching the attention of Denise and Mrs. Baude, she grinned and mouthed, *We did it!*

Yes we did! Denise mouthed back.

Mrs. Baude blew Story a kiss and winked. Their exuberance was powerful enough to span the length of the stadium.

Continuing down the row, Story gave Amanda a thumbs up. Their relationship had grown exponentially since their initial mentorship pairing. After Amanda's failed suicide attempt several months prior, Story's vigilance had saved her friend's life. She had gotten her to the hospital just in time for them to pump her stomach before any permanent damage could be done.

Reflecting on the incident, Story shuddered to think of how Amanda had fallen into such a dark place, and felt happy she was there when it mattered most. Even in this moment of celebration, she recalled a conversation during Amanda's recovery:

What were you thinking?

...That's the problem. I don't think I was thinking... Not clearly at least, Amanda admitted. *My roommate left. I couldn't cover rent. Then as if that weren't enough, Terrance told me he needed a change... whatever that means.*

Story listened as her friend unearthed the shadows that had almost pulled her under.

I couldn't keep up with all of that and my studies. It felt like it would be easier on everyone if I just went to sleep... forever.

An air of hopelessness hung around the woman she now regarded as a little sister. As soon as Story touched Amanda's hand, the dam broke. Story hugged her for what seemed like hours, letting her cry it all out—even shedding tears of her own. She had learned a valuable lesson from her last argument with Justine: judgment and chastisement were not what was needed. Love and grace were. And that is exactly what she gave.

In hindsight, Story was grateful to have found Amanda, and even more grateful to be celebrating this moment and milestone with her. After months of therapy, her mentee was finally in a space where she seemed to truly cherish life.

The only thing that could've made this day better was her and Justine walking across the stage hand-in-hand. She hoped that wherever Justine was, she was feeling the same sense of euphoria. As the group left the graduation stadium, Story was so caught up in conversation, she bumped into a man who had his back to her. The warm woody scent of his cologne filled her nostrils as a sense of familiarity warmed her. As her eyes traced the man's pointed loafers up to his zoot suit and tan fedora, he slowly turned around to face her. Story looked into the darkly-tinted lenses of the older gentleman with a goatee, full sideburns and gray afro. He smiled.

"My apologies," he stated in a voice that defied his larger-than-life stature. "I didn't see you coming."

"Oh no, it's my fault," Story quickly added, feeling her face flush for a reason she couldn't understand. "I wasn't paying attention. You have a good day Sir."

She walked away—already returning to thoughts of Justine, not noticing the man's mouth left agape with unspoken words. She rejoined her loved ones, but her mind was in another time and space.

This should be us, she whispered into the wind.

PART III: A LIFETIME

❧ 22 ❧

ANTICIPATION

Story

October 15, 2000

Dear Diary,

I'm going to meet my father today. I can't believe it! I have envisioned this day for too many years to count. I can't remember a time when I haven't wondered who my father is—even considered hiring a private investigator to find him. But without Mom's support, and with so little information to share with an investigator, I just gave up. I pretended not to care, and just shifted my focus to other things. But to keep it real, I cared far more than I admitted.

Ma has never offered so much as a name. Trust me, I've tried to get her to come up off it. Then, out of the blue, yesterday, she came to my crib and announced that we're going on a road trip to meet my father. Even as I write this, I'm still in shock. But I was way too ecstatic to ask questions. All I could do was hug her. I hope she can feel how grateful I am. There's something weird though because even in that moment, I felt a bit of hesitation from her. But honestly, yo, I can't even care. This is my chance! She's probably just nervous after keeping me from my dad for so long, but I'm not even tripping on that right now. It's a miracle that she's finally relenting, and I'm not about to screw this up by asking too many questions.

I barely slept last night. And when I did, I dreamt about him. Twice! Both times were so vivid, I had to write them down.

In the first dream, my father stood with open arms and a giant smile. I noticed I had his smile. We sat in a local diner for hours, catching each other up on the past twenty-three years. He said he was so proud of me. I couldn't help but admire the light that seemed to shine from him. His energy was so magnetic. So endearing. So... perfect.

In the second dream, I was chasing my father. Just as I reached out to grab him, he shook his head, as if to say he didn't want to be touched—then he disintegrated into thin air. I woke up in a cold sweat. After hours of tossing and turning, I finally drifted into a fitful sleep.

I woke again around 6:45 a.m. and jumped out of bed, unable to sleep any longer. Despite everything, I did my morning meditations and felt like my spirit was renewed. I've been practicing manifestation for a while now, and I'm hopeful things will turn out more like the first dream. Well, I better finish getting ready before Mom gets here. I can't wait to write again later.

Peace,
Story

Other than knowing they would be heading on a road trip, Story had no clue what the day would hold. Denise mentioned they would be meeting her father in Pennsylvania, but Story wasn't sure if he lived there or if it was simply a meeting point. Imagining her father living in Pennsylvania all this time and her never being allowed to meet him was unfathomable.

The drive from Raleigh to Pennsylvania would take roughly six and a half hours, traffic permitting. Story hadn't been back since she left at sixteen, but that didn't matter—she would've driven cross-country for this. If not for the significance of this trip, she might have even stopped by her old high-rise in hopes of seeing Justine, assuming the Chandlers still lived in Prospect Gardens. Still, she couldn't risk throwing off the trip by adding detours. If all went well, there would be plenty of opportunities to return—and maybe even visit Justine in Philly. By then, she might finally be able to tell her dearest friend in the world what her own biological father was like.

Denise told Story to dress comfortably for the drive and to bring a business casual outfit to change into. When she asked about these unusual instructions, her mother simply said, "You'll want to be comfortable for the drive but presentable when you meet him." That was that. Story still didn't know his name, where in Pennsylvania they were meeting, or when.

Wanting to look effortlessly put-together, Story chose a pair of soft fleece-lined leggings and an oversized tee for the ride. She packed a black pencil skirt, an off-the-shoulder sweater and her new black and gold stilettos to change into. Her accessories were simple but stylish: a nameplate necklace, diamond-studded earrings and the Fossil watch Karl had gifted her for her birthday.

Denise gave her a once-over and nodded. "He used to love the color black," she murmured, more to herself than to Story.

Story clung to that detail: if he liked black, she would wear black.

❧

They were well into their journey when Story remembered.

"Karl!" she gasped. Everything happened so fast she had forgotten to tell her boyfriend. *I'll fill him in later,* she thought.

She and Karl had been an item since junior year of undergrad. In three years, it didn't take long for her to learn how easygoing, compassionate and attentive he was. No other romantic relationship had made her this happy. Her only frustration was the distance—Karl moved back to California after graduation, while she returned to North Carolina. Long-distance was wearing on her, especially since she couldn't afford frequent flights to Cali. She missed the spontaneity of their in-person dates, but still believed their relationship was worth the effort. Giving up on the healthiest love she had ever known for a reason as temporary as physical distance wasn't so easily justifiable.

She decided to call Karl once they were settled—after she met her father. He was protective, but she was sure she could easily get back in his good graces with some sweet talk—and perhaps a touch of phone sex. The angel on her shoulder told her to clue him in, but Story wanted this moment to be hers and hers alone.

By 8 a.m., they were northbound on I-95 in Denise's Toyota Camry. Denise drove while Story daydreamed in the passenger seat.

Hi, I'm Story Brooks, she imagined herself saying. *No—that's silly. He'll know my name... right?* Well, just in case—*Hi Dad, I'm Story...*

"What time are we meeting him, Ma?"

Exhausted by Story's persistent questions, Denise sucked her teeth and rolled her eyes. "We're actually going to get a hotel for the evening. It will be too late to see them when we arrive."

Story felt her heart sink. *Them?* Someone else was going to be there. So much for it being *her* moment.

"Who else is going to be there?" Story asked, trying to sound casual.

"Why are you asking so many questions?" Denise snapped. "You'll see when you see."

Sheesh, what's up with her? Story rolled her eyes and looked out the window. Her mother's zesty replies were becoming annoying. Her question was more than valid. Still, she knew the conversation was over. She'd just have to wait to find out.

Justine

Justine stood frozen in her New York City apartment, listening silently as her mother spoke on the other end of the line. She could hear the words, but her brain had ceased to comprehend them.

"Justine... what is it?" Daniel asked gently from the sofa. He watched with growing concern as the color drained from his girl-friend's face. He had come to pick her up for their weekly date night, but right as they were heading out the door, the landline rang. They paused, waiting for the voicemail to pick up.

"Justine, it's your mom. Call me as soon as you get this message. This can't wait… just call me, please?" Barbie's voice trembled with a faint sniffle.

Justine answered the phone just as her mother was about to hang up. "Hey Mom, what's going on?" Daniel waited anxiously, trying to make sense of the one-sided conversation. Justine finally put the call on speaker and began pacing the room.

"Mom, Daniel's here with me. Can you repeat what you just said?" she asked, staring out the window.

"Hi Mrs. Chandler," Daniel called out.

"Oh, hi Daniel. I'm sorry to interrupt, but this couldn't wait. My husband is missing."

Daniel gasped just as Justine broke into barely audible sobs.

Barbie continued through tears. "He's been at an empowerment retreat in Raleigh for the past five days. He was due home tomorrow. But Judy, his assistant, called me this morning. She said no one's been able to reach him since yesterday evening. It's not like him not to check in. Judy usually reviews his return flights with him, so when she couldn't reach him, she waited a few hours, then contacted the retreat organizers. They got back to her last night, but no one could say when they last saw him. Everyone assumed he left early for Philly."

"Mom, have you called the police?" Justine interjected.

"I did. I called the Wake County Police Department this morning after I spoke with Judy, but since no one could confirm when he was last seen, they said that he needed to be gone for a full 24 hours from the time that he was deemed missing before they could file a formal report. I just don't know what I'd do if something happened to John." Barbie broke down into loud, inconsolable sobs.

"We're on our way," Daniel said, looking at Justine for confirmation.

❧ 23 ❧

GOODBYE, HELLO

Justine

Life, as Justine remembered it, had always played out like a soap opera—a mirage of the American dream. Everyone thought she was so poised and put together. If only they knew what really went down in that penthouse. Of course, there were good times, but there were also bad. Lies. Betrayals. A life built around grandiose façades. Justine learned just as much from her parents about what *not* to do as she did about what *to* do. The reality was, until Barbie got sick, Justine simply saw her family as great actors. But when they had to pull together to save their matriarch, everything changed—seemingly for the better.

People often praised Justine as the model of perfection. And aside from the pregnancy scare and that one kiss with Gregory, she had lived up to her golden child persona. She maintained honor student status throughout her academic career. Even though she finished college just under a year behind schedule, it was worth it—helping to nurse her mother back to health during her battle with breast cancer was priceless.

After that, Justine made it into law school and finished her first year at the top of her class. But today—today was the test of all tests.

She had no idea how she'd make it through the day that was ahead of her.

Just a week and a half ago, Justine's father, the world-renowned activist and motivational speaker, John E. Chandler III—better known as "The Dream Maker"—passed away from a sudden brain aneurysm. The crazy thing was, no one even knew he passed for two full days: he was found unresponsive in his hotel room while attending a retreat near Raleigh, North Carolina. Housekeeping found him.

Justine and Daniel had driven down to Philly from New York within hours of learning he was missing. They were both at her parents' house when the Wake County Police called to inform her mother of his death—they made it just in time. As Barbie listened intently to the officer on the other end of the line, Justine watched her mother's body go stark still. Her eyes rolled back, and she collapsed. Had they arrived even minutes later, her mother would've crumpled to the floor, alone and unsupported.

Story

On the morning of Story's reunion with her father, she woke bright and early. Her outfit had already been ironed, her makeup lightly applied, and her hair unwrapped. She was waiting on the sofa when her mother finally emerged from the bedroom in a hotel robe. Story stared in disbelief, silently awaiting further explanation—she dared not say anything that might upset her mother and risk the reunion being called off.

"Good morning," Denise grumbled, avoiding eye contact. "I need coffee," she muttered, heading for the kitchenette.

Story watched, baffled, as her mother prepared the coffee machine. It took everything for her to bite her tongue.

She mentally barraged her mother with questions: *Can you hurry up?! Why aren't you dressed? What the heck are you waiting on?* But she remained silent, shifting her body to look out of the window. Her attention was drawn to a woman on the street below pushing a toddler in a stroller. The child happily kicked his feet, completely oblivious to Story's precipice.

After a few sips, Denise mumbled to herself, "I can't do this."

"Can't do what?" Story snapped around, shaken by her mother's words.

With a heavy sigh, Denise looked at her. "I can't just throw you to the wolves. Before you meet your father, there are some things you need to know."

Her mother plopped onto the sofa with a heavy thud and grabbed Story's hands. Slowly raising her eyes to meet her daughter's, she mustered a smile—a small peace offering. A plump tear slipped down Denise's face, landing on her robe where it sat, undisturbed. Story scooted closer, her hands firmly clasped in her mother's.

"What is it Mommy?" Story spoke softly.

"Your dad..." Denise sniffled and inhaled deeply, "...I never should have kept this from you..."

"Ma, what is it?" Story's patience gave way to fear.

"John Chandler *is...was* your father."

The words sat there, like an invisible wall suddenly revealed. Impossibly steep and thick.

"Wait what!" releasing her mother's hands, she jumped to her feet. She looked down on her mother who remained seated on the couch. She needed this to make sense. And quick.

The silence became unbearable. "What do you mean Mr. Chandler is my dad? And did you say *was*? You're talking crazy... What *are* you actually talking about? There's no way..."

Pacing the living room, Story fought to make sense of it all.

Denise sat with her head hung, her own hands now grasping one another in support.

"SAY SOMETHING!" Story demanded as she stood in front of her mother.

Slowly raising her head, Denise reached for the tissue box on the coffee table. Taking a deep breath, she tried again. "I never wanted you to find out like this. John *is* your father. I've always known and so has he..."

"So *I* was the only one..."

Denise held up her hand to stop Story from going on another tangent.

"Let me finish," Denise said firmly.

Story slowly sat on the armrest of the chaise across from her mother, folding her arms across her chest.

"Was I wrong for getting involved with John? Yes," Denise admitted as the tears tumbled down her face. "Did I ever mean for things to go as far as they did? No! I didn't know he was married when I met him. I should have ended things once I learned the truth."

Story could no longer look at her mother; she was too disgusted.

"But Story, you have to know—you were made out of love," Denise proffered. "I spent *years* trying to right my wrongs as best I could. I made sure you had a relationship with your father. We moved here just to make that happen."

She stared at her mother, wanting to ask for more and yet, capsized by all that had already been given.

"I don't know what else to say," she barely whispered.

Over the next two hours, Story learned the details surrounding her conception. *For twenty-three years, my life has been a lie*, she thought, processing this revelation. Even if someone had offered her a million dollars, she would've never guessed things would end like this: *John Chandler is my father*. She had lived, quite literally, under his nose for more than half her life without the faintest idea.

To say Story was angry was an understatement. Disappointed. Ashamed. Mistrustful—those were just the beginning. She knew she'd never see her mother the same way again. Sleeping with a married man was bad enough—but getting pregnant? Story tried her best to process it all. Then she did the math: *I'm only five months older than Justine, which meant both mom and Mrs. Chandler were pregnant at the same time*. She shook her head in disbelief. This all felt like a sick joke.

As if things couldn't get worse, Story was being denied the chance to meet Mr. Chandler as her father. Denise shared the news of his death, overcome with guilt, confessing she brought Story to Philly for one final goodbye. Until today, she hadn't been able to bring herself to speak a word of this to Story. She even admitted that the original plan had been to bring her to the funeral and tell her the truth at the last moment—before Story had time to react or ask questions.

Story replayed her mother's confession. *This morning, something changed. Seeing you sit on that couch so full of hope, snapped me out of it. I owed you the truth, especially before we went to the service.*

This can't be happening to me. The sense of betrayal threatened to overtake her. The two of them had talked and cried for hours. At one point, Denise suggested they just head back to Raleigh instead of opening the wound any further. But Story refused. She needed to see him. And right now, she needed a moment alone to just sit with her thoughts—without her mother's voice in her ear. So when Denise went into the bathroom to get ready, Story quietly slipped out the front door. She'd find her own way to her father's service.

She didn't know what she expected to gain from looking at him in a 7-foot-long, 2 ½-foot-wide box—but she had waited twenty-three years to lay eyes on the man she was entitled to call *hers* and *Daddy*. Come hell or high water, she was going to see her father—and say all of the things she had never been afforded the chance to. Until now.

Justine

Dad was always the life of the party. Anyone who knew him never forgot him. He had a way with words...

Justine recited her father's eulogy from memory. Her therapist suggested she speak from the heart, but there was no way she could leave such an important moment to chance. Since her father's passing, Justine had stepped into the role of being the rock of her family. She busied herself with organizing the funeral arrangements, picking out her father's favorite suit and tie, consoling her mother, finalizing details with the caterer for the repast and numerous other "to-do's" on what seemed like a never ending list. No stone was left unturned.

From how "together" she presented herself, no one would ever know she was breaking down internally. Except Daniel. *I'm here for you no matter what, Jus. I know this is hard, but I've got you. Always.* His promise held her together when she felt the threat of falling apart.

Her therapist said she should allow herself to feel and stay in the moment. *But who had time for that?* Justine felt her focus would be better spent ensuring her father went out in style. And she gladly embraced the distraction.

She brushed off the imaginary lint on her cream A-line dress and bent down to put on her matching Manolo Blahnik cream patent leather pumps. Justine topped off her look with a string of fresh-water pearls around her neck and pearl stud earrings. Glancing in the mirror, she gave herself a nod of approval, took a deep breath to steady her nerves, squared her shoulders and walked out of her bedroom in search of her mother.

"Mommy, are you ready?" Justine asked impassively, walking into the kitchen.

Barbie continued staring into space as though she hadn't heard her.

"Mom?" The look in her mother's eyes cracked something.

Unable to keep her composure any longer, she tipped her head forward until her brow rested on her mother's shoulder. For the first time since skinning her knee in second grade, Justine allowed her mother to see her tears freely flow. She was spent. Fresh out of any means of holding it together. Tired of seeming *ok*. Barbie started at her touch before jumping into action. Enveloping Justine into her arms, she smoothed her daughter's hair as she whispered, "It's all going to be alright, baby. Let it out."

With this new pain, Justine had no qualms about showing someone, other than Daniel, that she wasn't made of Teflon. She wept until there was nothing left.

Then Barbie delicately pushed Justine's shoulders until she was standing upright. Smoothing over the collar of Justine's dress, she nodded her head encouragingly.

"We are going to get through this... *together*. *Again*. Let's go."

❦

The white Lincoln Town Car was waiting in front of the building as instructed when Justine and Barbie exited the elevator. Arney regarded the two compassionately, "My deepest condolences, Mrs. and Miss Chandler."

"Thank you, Mr. Arney," the Chandler women replied, feeling more appreciative than their voices could convey.

Both ladies slid into the butter soft leather seats, bracing themselves for the thirty minute ride to Guiding Light Funeral Home—a ride that felt at once too long and too short. After the driver closed their door and set travel time expectations, both women sank into the silence. Barbie stared off into space. Justine busied herself trying to recall the driver's name. Even the tires were silent, navigating bumps with a reverent soundlessness.

After a while, Barbie released a loud sigh as a tear trailed down each of her foundation-laced cheeks.

"It's going to be ok, Mommy," Justine consoled, gripping her mother's hand in solidarity.

"Tuh," Barbie scoffed. "I don't know if I should be laughing or crying these days."

"What do you mean by that?"

"I can't believe he's gone," Barbie began. "But I also feel... *free*."

Justine's brow furrowed.

"There are some things about your father that you didn't know. You were too young for me to share such things," Barbie continued. "And plus, even as a young girl, you were an anxious child. I think you got that from your Grandma Carol."

"Mommy, what are you talking about?"

"John... your dad lived a very public life—"

"I know," Justine interrupted.

"Girl, you don't know the half of it!" Barbie shot back, uncharacteristically brusque. "Your father lived a very public life in more ways than one. I don't know who we are going to see today at this funeral. I'm just hoping we can all carry ourselves as ladies."

"Mom, you're scaring me... what are you saying?"

Barbie sat reflecting before speaking again, "Have you ever heard that song about a rolling stone?" She cast a sidelong glance at her daughter.

"Yeah..." Justine's eyes bulged then darted around the backseat of the town car as if seeking the quickest exit. *Does she know about the women?* Justine's worst fear was becoming her reality. "And?" she hesitantly said, still unsure of where the conversation was headed.

"Well, I couldn't have written it better myself. Justine, I don't know who is going to be at this funeral today because there is no telling who was the latest and greatest in John's fold of... of... concubines," Barbie said, as though the word burned her tongue.

"Mom!"

Barbie shrugged without any visible emotion, "It's true. Your father had his fair share of ill-timed 'dalliances' shall we say. At any rate, we are almost there. We will talk more later."

Justine was speechless. She had spent so long trying to shield her mother from this secret when all along, she knew. *Does she know I knew too?* Justine gazed out of the window, wishing there were another half hour so she could empty her eyes of fear—fear her mother could read her mind.

What was she supposed to do with her mother's revelation? Everyone was counting on her to get up there and sing her father's praises. She tried to calm the shaking in her leg. Then switched to rubbing away the goosebumps that appeared on her bare arms, undoing all efforts to appear unruffled. Nevertheless, the internal warfare Justine was feeling threatened to bubble over any second.

Suddenly feeling the need to escape the suffocating air in the town car, she began square breathing.

Inhale 2, 3, 4. Hold 2, 3, 4. Exhale 2, 3, 4. Rest 2, 3, 4. And repeat. Gradually, Justine's pulse returned to normal as she mentally regrouped and prepared to exit the limo. But with her mother's forewarning, she figured she had better keep that square breathing technique on tap.

24
REUNITED

Story

The service was nearly standing room only with increasingly more people waiting their turn to enter the sanctuary. Fortunately, Story found a seat near the back, arriving just as the viewing was underway. The podium, more than half a football field away, was lit in a rainbow of colors, brought to life by the sun's reflection through the stained glass windows.

Not wanting to cause a disturbance, she waited on her pew until her row was called. From Story's vantage point, she could make out the white casket with gold trim at the front of the church and the very top of Mr. Chandler's short black afro. In the sea of people making their final procession to view the body, Story didn't recognize many faces. She assumed Justine and her mother were at the front, but had yet to spot them. Even if she had, she had no idea what she might do or say.

She wondered if Justine already knew that they were sisters; and if so, how long had she known? The cocktail of emotions pulsing through her body muddied her ability to separate her assumptions from reality. When her row was called to join the viewing line, she stood abruptly, legs shaky, mind determined.

Just then, her mother appeared from the crowd and stood beside her. Story didn't know where Denise had come from or how she knew to find her, only that her tension melted at knowing she wouldn't have to go through this moment alone. Though they were both at a loss for words, she felt supported and protected by Denise's presence.

Her eyes caught a glimpse of Denise wringing her hands, betraying the truth behind her best attempt to appear composed. Story understood. The circumstances of this reunion were admittedly less than ideal. Still she had waited her entire life for this moment. And as fate would have it, she'd never have the chance again—this was her one chance to meet her father and she had every intention of speaking her peace.

As Story moved toward the moment, she became aware her mother was not following her.

"Mommy, please come," she pleaded. As disappointed as she was in her mother, she needed her now. Her mother owed her this. At the very least.

Denise returned Story's gaze with eyes that replayed history. It was at this moment, the young woman realized she wasn't the only one hurting. Wrong as it may be, Denise had also suffered a loss. Her mother needed a shoulder to lean on just as much as she did.

The ladies made their way to the front of the church waiting their turns to say their final goodbyes. Denise walked up to the coffin first and stared down at John. She closed her eyes, said a silent prayer and discretely gave his hand a squeeze. Not ready to truly face her current reality, she refused to look in the direction of John's wife and other daughter on the front pew.

Instead, she stepped to the side with her back to the crowd and allowed Story to step forward, feeling the need to stand guard—she wouldn't allow more than an arm's length between herself and her daughter. When Story saw that it was her turn, she nervously fiddled with non-existent dust on her sweater before walking slowly to the coffin.

There he was: the man she had only ever known as "Mr. Chandler," nestled in the satin, pillowy encasement of the white box. Story took in his features. She never noticed it before: they had the same almond-shaped eyes, pointed nose and full lips. Closing her eyes, she envisioned him from memory. She inhaled softly as she recalled they had the same slanted smile, just like in her dream. It was a smile that winked. The irony made her swallow. Hard. Story continued to scan his body laying so impossibly lifeless in the coffin. Her eyes rested on his hands. They both had short, stubby nail beds.

How did I miss all this?

Whoever chose Mr. Chandler's outfit for his homegoing service selected a perfectly-tailored tan suit with a crisp white shirt that opened at the collar to expose a paisley printed ascot with a neutral color palette. Even against his ashen pallor, Mr. Chandler lay there like the distinguished gentleman she had always known. Story continued scanning his body until her eyes snagged on his designer chocolate, Italian leather loafers. Instantly, she was back at Homecoming night of her sophomore year in high school.

The memory came closer than yesterday: the mystery man boarding the elevator after having been caught in a *very* affectionate kiss with her mother. The memories of a flowing trench coat and brown leather shoes sweeping into the elevator filled her mind. Story had been so caught up in her own saga with Rakim, she hadn't been focused on putting the pieces together. Those shoes were custom and high quality, fashionable, just as she had always prided herself in being. Her mind hadn't been playing tricks on her: Mr. Chandler *had* been at their apartment that night! Story breathed deeply as memories of the moment filled in the missing pieces to her life's puzzle.

If there was one thing that Mr. Chandler taught her, it was to seize the moment. She had come a long way to meet her father and say the unspoken things. She could feel her father's presence in that very moment nudging her to do just that. While Story reached for words that suddenly became elusive, she remembered the years spent unknowingly in his presence. Her lived years provided the perfect draft of all she needed to express. Story steadied herself to speak from the heart. Closing her eyes, she connected with his energy and allowed herself her first, and final, conversation with the man that she now knew was her father:

Hi Mr. Chandler?... I guess I should call you Dad. Wow, I can't believe this. Never in a million years would I have thought we'd reunite like this. I've dreamt about you my entire life. Always wondering what it would be like to have a father. I've longed to know if I looked like you. I've longed to hear someone say, 'You act just like your father.' It's crazy because when I was a kid, I'd hear my friends call their fathers 'Daddy.' It felt like nails on a chalkboard. I'd never want them to be denied such a luxury, but I just wondered what it'd be like to relate. And it hurt that I couldn't.

I've always wanted to have a constant fixture and a protector in my dad. I envisioned you as my very own savior carrying me on your shoulders in the good and bad times. I've longed for someone to teach me life lessons from a man's perspective. Someone to share my love of sports. Someone to tell me corny jokes and laugh well before I had a chance to grasp the punchline. Can you imagine what that must have been like? Have you ever experienced a thirst that couldn't be quenched? A sense of longing that was never fulfilled? Well, I'll be the first to tell you, I wouldn't wish that fate on my worst enemy.

If I'm being honest, growing up, I always imagined you as my dad because you were the closest thing that I ever had to one. You were the epitome of how I thought my father would be. Yeah, you had your shortcomings, but I saw past that to your heart. At your core, I pray that you loved and accepted me as your daughter, just like you did Justine. Who could have known that the man I pictured and the man that stood before me were one and the same?

I could stand here and fixate on why you never told me your true identity, but that is all water under the bridge now, huh? So, I choose to spend my final moments in your physical presence focused on the positive. As much as I always felt I was lacking when it came to having a father, I do want to thank you for sharing so many special moments with me. I had no idea how much I'd need them. But through the years, I've found myself recalling many of the lessons you taught me and Justine.

One of the things you taught me was to trust my gut. I choose to trust that if you and my mother didn't tell me about my true identity after all those years, it had to be for good reason. And I can forgive you for that because I know with all my heart that even in your silence, you must have been protecting me: shielding me from years of confusion, shame and second-hand guilt. No child should ever have to experience the repercussions of their parents' wrongdoing. So, thank you for protecting me in your own way.

I don't know whether I should be happy, sad, mad or all the above. But I think I'll choose to be happy. Life is too short to not savor the moments that made me who I am. In this moment, I vow to you to cherish the memories we were able to make, short lived as they may have been. Again... thank you... Dad. I hope I've made you proud. Story slowly opened her eyes, and turned to go back to her seat.

It was only then that she locked eyes with Justine: her sister.

Justine

Justine couldn't believe what she was seeing. She had spent years dreaming of the day she'd see Story again, but never in a million years would she have guessed today would be that day. As she gazed into her best friend's eyes, she heard their childhood chant as clear as day, *"Istersay, istersay, hatstay ymay istersay!"* The memory ejected Justine from her seat and into Story's arms. The saddest day of her life might just become the best: they were finally being reunited!

Justine grasped Story's hand, turning triumphantly to face the congregation as though announcing the special moment they had just shared. Daniel gave the two a knowing nod topped with a smile.

Barbie sat next to Daniel, her face the epitome of dismay. Justine's own smile darkened as clouds of memory wafted across her mind: her mother's words before the funeral service stole the shine. *"There are some things about your father that you didn't know. You were too young for me to share such things."*

Glancing from her mother back to her best friend, Justine let her hand fall from her bestie's grasp. *What did Mom mean by that?* The look on her mother's face said one of those secrets had to do with Story. In her heart she knew now was far from the moment to investigate.

"Talk after service?" Story proposed, her eyes glued on Mrs. Chandler.

"Yes...let's," Justine replied absentmindedly, her thoughts continuing to dissect why her mother looked so incredibly dispirited by Story's presence.

To the outsider, John's service and burial were uneventful. Justine stood by her mother, relieved to have made it through her speech, but at a loss for what came next.

She had never known life without her father—a layered, imperfect man with whom Justine hadn't always seen eye to eye. Beneath his veneer, though, there was a catch: she had still been, and always would be, his daughter, a title and truth Justine wore as a badge of honor. She could never deny the power of his presence throughout her life.

How was she going to carry on without him? She couldn't help but smile to herself at the thought that her father would likely know exactly what to do after suffering such a great loss. *We Chandlers never fold: we pick ourselves up and keep fighting for a brighter day.* She could hear him as clearly as if he were standing next to her.

Justine shifted her attention to her mother. As Barbie watched him being lowered into his final resting place, tears silently crept down her face like secrets spilling over. She knew her mother was going to miss John Chandler; after all, they had spent the majority of their lives as a unit. At some point, she'd have to release the gut-wrenching pain she must have felt as a result of everything she held on to. For now, though, she maintained her image as the pillar of strength all the onlookers had known her to be. She dabbed at her tears and met Justine's eyes with a grief-laden smile. They both knew there was a lot of mess to tidy up in their talk later.

Just as Barbie and Justine turned to leave the burial grounds with Daniel in tow, they came face to face with Denise and Story. Justine stood in silence awaiting a cue from her mother that she was fine. When Barbie nudged her head in the direction of Story indicating that Justine should leave her to talk to Denise alone, she took the hint. While Story, Justine and Daniel stood off at a distance catching up, Barbie decided it was high time to settle the inner tension that was now filling the cemetery.

"I can't believe you're actually here," Justine said. "Thank you so much for coming."

Story just smiled, unsure of what Justine did or didn't know about their father, the phone conversation years ago... all of it. She opted not to bring it up. Not now, at least.

"I've missed you so much throughout the years. But I had no idea how to find you—"

"And believe me, she tried," Daniel interjected.

"This is all so... surreal..." Story began, letting her voice trail off.

Justine nodded. "I wish it were under better circumstances, but I'm so happy to see you."

"Maybe we could exchange numbers? There's so much for us to catch up on," Story said tentatively, searching Justine's eyes for even the slightest hint that she also knew the truth.

❦

"Hello there," Barbie started. Denise ignored the coldness in the woman's tone; she knew neither of them would ever be "ready" for this moment.

"Hi. I'm ..." Denise shook her head, averting her eyes before finally meeting Barbie's gaze again. "I'm so sorry for your loss."

"Likewise," Barbie mumbled.

Denise was surprised. And a little relieved. Glancing around the cemetery, she caught Story's raised eyebrow and knew she had to finish what she had started.

Barbie shifted her body so as to inconspicuously block Justine and Story from hearing any more of their conversation. Lowering her voice, she spoke plainly, "Look, let's not beat around the bush here: there are some things that finally need to come to light. I think it's best we meet at another time to discuss it all."

Denise was relieved that Barbie seemed to be taking the lead.

"Will you two be in town for very long?"

"We were going to stay one more night and then hit the road, but I agree: I can't keep living this lie. Our girls deserve more," she paused. "And John would have ultimately wanted this, too," she finished.

Barbie looked away, as though swallowing a retort. "Fine. Shall we get together and talk before you go? Or should we meet up one day in the near future?" Denise sensed Barbie was hoping for the latter.

"Let's get it over with before Story and I leave town."

They agreed to meet the following day at Salvatore's, hoping that meeting in a neutral setting would help keep things in check. With plans finalized, Denise motioned to Story that it was time for their departure. Story gave Daniel and Justine one more hug, promising to call when she could. As she walked to their car, Story grabbed her mother's hand and whispered "Why do I get the sense that Justine has no idea?"

Denise hesitated before responding, "Your father used to always joke that he'd mastered taking people's secrets to the grave. I imagine that included his own, baby." Her words hung like an unclassified omen as the two women prepared to face tomorrow, and whatever truths it would bring.

25

AFTERSHOCK

Justine

Justine rubbed her arms to ward off a chill. The sky was a curtain of iridescent gray, occasionally ripped open by streaks of lightning.

Seeing Story yesterday had been great, but now the clouds were rolling in. Emotionally. Yesterday, after the funeral, Justine and Barbie had sat in the living room sharing fond memories of John.

"Remember that time we went to Disney World?" Justine smiled.

"You cried and cried when Mickey didn't return your wave at the parade," Barbie chuckled softly. "Later that day, your father cornered Mickey by the teacups and paid him twenty dollars to come speak with you."

"No way! Dad bribed Mickey?! I thought Mickey had come to find me on his own!"

"Your Daddy wouldn't have his princess being upset."

The two had laughed at the memory before settling into a pregnant silence.

"Today on the way to the funeral, I mentioned, I wasn't certain who would be at the service. That wasn't entirely true... I had a feeling about a specific person who might show."

Justine nodded, her body rigid with anticipation.

"Years ago, I learned about your father's affairs... including one with Denise." Barbie paused, her voice catching. "I never told you. I told no one."

"Story's mom?!" Justine choked.

Her mother nodded and continued. "I confronted him, but I always got the sense your father knew I'd stick by his side no matter what." She wrung her hands, clearly uncomfortable by the admission.

"Wait... that can't be true—"

Justine's mind raced, remembering Story's admission during their big blow-up. *Story wasn't lying... she was telling the truth.* She hated to admit it now.

"Today at the church, I saw Story standing next to the casket—"

"Yeah..." Her stomach lurched with anxiety.

"The moment I saw her, all of my suspicions about their relationship were reconfirmed." An aging, yet still-elegant, hand flew to her mouth, trying to catch the tears. "They share an undeniable resemblance."

Justine tried to make sense of what her mother was telling her. "Are you saying that Daddy was Story's—"

"—father," Barbie had finished the sentence for her. The words took up the space her father had left.

Justine said nothing then—and still could not—so she continued staring as the lightning split the sky, yet again.

But her mind kept reminiscing on the previous day's conversation. Barbie went on sharing how the finality of it all had nearly decimated her during the service. She couldn't understand how Denise could flaunt the piercing fact of John's infidelity—and her daughter's paternity—in her face at a time like this.

Justine remembered how her mother had briskly wiped her face after the admission, as though the tears were the culprits themselves. "The deed is done. The dust has settled," she sighed, composing herself. "This won't be the first time I have had to clean up John's mess."

The initial denial of her mother's admission flew in the face of Justine's secret knowledge of her father's indiscretions. But when Barbie recounted everything she knew about Story's mother's and her father's relationship, there was no more room for denial. Barbie's comments echoed: *Your father had his fair share of ill-timed dalliances...* Then there was the way she had looked at Story and Justine during the service—a look of sheer disgust. That was when alarm bells had begun to go off.

I wonder if Story knows about all of this?

Returning to the present, Justine turned from the window, offering her mother a weak smile as Barbie entered the room. "Hey Mom, you ready?" She walked over and gave Barbie's shoulder a light rub.

Barbie flinched, not only from her daughter's touch, but also the clap of thunder followed by a streak of light.

Justine watched as her mother continued staring off. As much as they both sought peace from the many years of family secrets, misdeeds and heartache, Justine was also well aware that they could no longer feign ignorance, as blissful as the pretense had seemed.

Fresh disappointment bubbled. *Damn, Dad! It's just like you to uproot our lives and leave us*, she vented mentally.

"Look..." Barbie spoke in a soothing tone as though reading her mind, "I know this is a lot, but we *will* get through this. Let's get going. From the looks of the weather, I don't want to risk being late." Although her tone was assured, Justine knew her mother was having her own internal struggle.

"Let's do this."

She took Barbie's hand in her own, absentmindedly stroking the back with her thumb as they exited the apartment. She needed to set her sights on the meeting ahead and protecting her mother, come what may.

Story

Fighting the urge to roll her eyes, Story placed a sturdy hand on her mother's knee to steady its shaking.

"Mom, you're doing it again," she said gently.

Denise glanced at Story and crossed her ankles. "Sorry dear," she said with a hollow laugh. "I guess my nerves are getting the best of me."

They arrived at Salvatore's a bit early in order to secure a table and eliminate the element of surprise when Barbie and Justine arrived. They had been sitting at the table in complete silence for at least ten minutes—taking turns anxiously glancing toward the door in anticipation of the inevitable. At exactly noon, Barbie and Justine walked through the entrance. They appeared to float, as though above the matter of business today.

Justine

"Barbie! Amore mio," the owner affectionately addressed her mother as he walked toward her with open arms.

"Come stai, caro Sal?" Barbie effortlessly replied. Making a sweeping gesture with her hand, she directed his attention to the table. "Sal, this is my daughter and our... um..."

"Friends," Justine completed her mother's sentence.

Barbie nodded graciously. "We'll have the usual," she added politely. With raised eyebrows, Sal gave a slight nod and went to get drinks.

Story greeted Justine with a bear hug. Arms pinned to her sides, Justine gave her an awkward smile and shake of her head. She always did have an animated nature.

I've got to stay focused: I came here for clarity and I don't plan on leaving until I have it.

"What did they say?" Story whispered in her ear.

"Bar-bie, my love"... "How are you Sal, dearest," Justine whispered back in a mock Italian accent.

With curt smiles, Barbie and Denise exchanged pleasantries as Barbie took her seat.

The moments following their initial greeting felt agonizingly long as each woman glanced around the table, uncertain where to begin. Barbie glanced towards the kitchen in search of food and drink to cut the tension. Denise, sitting rod straight, fussed with her blouse. Justine mindlessly picked at her fingernails, searching for "just the right words." Story glanced at the mothers waiting expectantly for either to break the ice.

"I have four glasses of red wine, compliments of the house," the waiter announced as he approached the table.

"How kind," Barbie said, welcoming the interruption. "Please be sure to thank Sal for me."

More silence followed as each woman took sips of wine to calm spent nerves. Justine was the first to speak.

"Ok... I know my mother agreed to this meeting today so we could talk. She told me everything last night, but I still have questions." She turned to face Story's mother.

Denise gave Justine her full attention, "I figured you'd both have questions. And I'm here to—"

Disinterested in Denise's perspective and eager to release her pent up feelings before she lost her nerve, Justine cut her off. "Denise, I can't wrap my mind around what you could possibly have to say for yourself. You *knew* my father was a married man. Seduced him. Got pregnant to ensure you sealed the deal. Then spent years *flaunting* what you'd done under my mother's nose." Justine counted each transgression on her fingers.

"Now Justine—" Barbie interjected.

"No, let me finish, Mom," she cut in without ever taking her eyes off of Denise. After all the secrets that had been concealed and revealed, no one was about to silence her now. NO. ONE.

Story

Caught off guard by Justine's tone, Story snapped her head back, looking from her mother to Justine—uncertain of who needed saving the most. This felt so unlike the gentle spirit she had known most of her youth, and so unlike the warmth she had felt from Justine less than 24 hours ago.

"If there was a photo next to the word *homewrecker* in the dictionary, it would undoubtedly be yours." The words flew like daggers at Denise.

"Justine!" Barbie clutched her chest. "We didn't come here to behave like this."

So it's HER who's gonna need saving, I see. Story pushed her chair back, but her mother caught her eye and shook her head. *Stand down*, the motion said.

With great restraint, she fought to calm her nerves as she sat back. Cautiously. As she calmed and surveyed the moment she noticed something: the look in Justine's eyes wasn't venomous—just hurt.

Give her grace, Story reminded herself. *Just listen.*

"And Story, how long have you known about this? Did you only befriend me so you could secure your spot in *our* family?"

Story shook her head in disbelief. She felt the first sting of tears. "There's no way you actually believe that—"

Justine continued her tirade. It was clear she was desperate to make sense of her thoughts through a hailstorm of emotions. "Unbeknownst to me, my mother has had to carry this burden for my entire life. I'll bet you both would have loved to see her crumble under pressure. But clearly you didn't do enough research on *my* family because we *always* bounce back."

Story felt for Justine—for her anger, for her hurt, for her confusion, for her desire to protect "her" family. She understood the feelings. There was a pause, as though she were expecting something. *But what?* Story couldn't quite tell. But she was determined not to fight with the friend—and sister—she had just newly found.

"So, what are we doing here? Did you two want to apologize? Or were you hoping for some sort of hush money to prevent you from further tarnishing my father's legacy?"

Once out of words, the storm that had knotted Justine's brows and commanded her tongue seemed to pass. No one had expected her to go so hard—least of all, Story and her mother. But aside from the matter at hand, she was proud to see her sister had finally found her voice.

Denise

"Now wait a minute..." Feeling her mother's hand gently tug her arm, Story swallowed her words.

Say something, Mom, Story's eyes pleaded with her mother.

Denise didn't like the tone this meeting had taken any more than her daughter. She was saddened to see the girls upset and divided, each fighting to protect the image of their own mother. But knowing she had a huge part to play in this mess, she set about the business of fixing it. As much as she could.

Denise took a deep breath and exhaled. "I get it," she began calmly. "This is a lousy situation, and it looks really bad. Justine, I understand why you're angry, hurt and an array of other emotions—all valid."

She dug in her purse for a tissue to blot the fresh tears. Story squeezed her mother's knee in encouragement, and when she looked in her daughter's eyes, she could see the judgment was melting away.

"Alright, ladies. We have Salvatore's family style meal for you today," the waiter announced. A procession of waiters followed and laid the medley of foods on the table as the lead waiter introduced each item: "grilled chicken caprese salad...sicilian meatball soup... lasagna... pasta carbonara... and breadsticks."

"Thank you," they each chimed, appreciative for the interference.

"My pleasure, can I get you anything else?" the middle-aged Italian man continued, oblivious to the mood of the table.

"No, you've been wonderful," Barbie said with a forced smile.

Turning to the table, she encouraged, almost as a peace offering, "Dig in ladies."

The minutes ticked by as platters were passed and selections made. Eventually, they returned their attention to a somber, but patient, Denise who was clearly more invested in clearing the air than indulging in the aromatic dishes placed before them.

"I'm so sorry to have ever been the cause of your pain, Justine. Barbie, that extends to you as well. I never meant to fall in love or get so recklessly wrapped up..." Her voice trailed off. She suddenly felt torn about continuing, unsure if her apology was enough to heal the hurt she helped create. "Are you willing to hear my side of the story?"

Denise looked from Justine to Story, allowing her gaze to linger a moment longer when she reached Barbie. "Perhaps, we'll all have a better understanding of how we got here."

"We're here, and this clearly isn't going away," Barbie said, her voice quivering. "I'm listening."

With a nod of her head, Denise continued. "I met John in March of

1976. We were both volunteers at the *Stand Up, Stand Out* rally in Hartford, Connecticut. I was a junior in college; he was knee deep in his career. I actually couldn't stand him after our first meeting: the entire rally, he came off loud and arrogant, demanding all the attention." She chuckled.

"That's my John," Barbie said absentmindedly, forgetting for a moment the present company.

Denise felt a hint of kinship. They both knew him in their own way. "I wanted to focus on the rally while he seemed focused on working the room. But by the end of the day though, he somehow managed to win me over, and even asked me out for drinks. I agreed to meet him at a local bar under the guise of debriefing from the rally, but when we got there, all that pretense and showiness just..." she fluttered her fingers, before finishing in barely a whisper, "...fell away.

"We spent hours drinking, laughing, talking about everything under the sun. And with a little liquid courage, we both ended up getting a little handsy, but nothing more than kissing happened that night. Not once did he mention having a wife. I even asked him if he was seeing anyone. And I can still hear his reply: 'No one to be concerned about,' he had said."

Justine gasped at her father's audacity. Barbie's forehead crinkled. But neither refuted Denise's claims.

They all waited for her to continue.

"Maybe in hindsight, I should have dug deeper as to what he meant, but in the moment I assumed he meant that he was casually dating, as was I."

Barbie began blinking rapidly to ward off tears. Denise reached out a hand to console her. Surprisingly, she accepted.

"I remember that," Barbie said. "We were separated. It was maybe a year into our marriage and I'd already grown sick of John's wandering eyes. I knew he was a cheater ever since our dating years, but I never expected him to bring that behavior into our marriage. I was shattered when he did.

"The first time he stepped out on me, I caught him with my best friend. He hadn't even tried to be 'careful'... he took the heifer to *my* favorite restaurant of all places." Barbie looked away as she recalled the memory.

"Silly me, I ditched her and *kept* him. He *promised* me that he loved me and only me. And like a fool, I believed him.

"But there was always that nagging feeling that I wasn't enough for him. There were plenty of times I wasn't sure if we should even stay together. I told him, on more than one occasion, that I needed a break."

"Mommy, you never told me that," Justine said in disbelief.

"You weren't even a thought at that point. And that's certainly not something that would have naturally come up in conversation with my child. Plus, you *adored* your father; I never wanted to take that from you."

Justine nodded her understanding.

"When he left for that rally, I decided to get as far away from him as possible. I just wanted time to think without any reminders of him crowding my mind. I had a little spending money, so I purchased a ticket and took the greyhound back home to Birmingham." Barbie met Story's mother's eyes again. This time they were full of compassion.

"I had no idea," Denise said, pained. "I'm so sorry."

Story offered Barbie an empathetic smile. The tension eased around the table as the ice began to melt between them.

Taking a deep breath, Denise continued, "After the rally, I never really expected to see John again. That night at the bar, we'd connected in a way I'd never felt before, but we didn't exchange numbers. And when I returned from a bathroom run, he'd already snuck out of the bar. I spent days wondering if the encounter was merely a figment of my imagination... Eventually, I chalked it up to us just being two passersby in the night.

"I did think about him from time to time, but I never thought I'd see him again. Then one day about three months later, he showed up. I was walking across my college campus when it felt like the crowd parted and there he was. It took a minute for my brain to catch up and register that he was really there. But my body..." Denise shrugged, almost apologetically. "I ran straight into his arms before he had a chance to disappear. He told me he was in town meeting with some elected officials. After asking around, he figured out where I went to college and came to find me."

"Well wasn't he a modern day Sherlock Holmes?" Barbie smirked.

Justine and Story stifled laughter.

"John knew all of the right things to say. He told me I was beautiful. That God had shown him from the moment we met that we were meant to be together. How unworthy he was of my time. How he hoped I would give him a chance to prove otherwise. There were also gifts. An African violet since I'd told him when we first met how I always thought flowers were a waste of time. They never last. My favorite chocolates. A journal and pen set because he knew I loved to write. I was so impressed that he'd remembered my interests from that one night at the bar, he just charmed the socks off of me... Tuh! And apparently my pants... *and* my panties."

"Mom!" Story yelped, fighting off an ill-placed chuckle.

"Gross," Justine said while crossing her arms, although the sight of Story's efforts to remain serious did soften the blow.

Barbie's eyebrow raised again, now joined by the slightest tilt of her head. She took a sip of wine, but remained quiet.

"Sorry," Denise caught herself. "By the time I found out that I was pregnant with you, Story, I was three months along... and your father was long gone. Thankfully this time, we exchanged numbers, although I hadn't called him—and if it weren't for you, I wouldn't have."

"Why not?" Story asked.

"A long-distance relationship never seemed realistic to me. And besides, shortly after our extremely brief affair, I met someone new." Denise shrugged. "Initially, I was on the fence about keeping you or giving you up for adoption."

At this admission, each woman's heart quivered.

"Ouch," Story said.

"It wasn't because I didn't want you. It was just my family was furious with me for having gotten knocked up without a husband. So I did what I had to do: I called him. But the way he spoke to me that day..." Denise cringed. "He blamed me for our 'situation.' Said he wasn't ready to be a father and told me to do whatever I wanted."

Barbie flinched hearing her late husband's response. It was her turn to give comfort. She reached out and squeezed the arm of the woman who had been her enemy only minutes before. It was the slightest of gestures, but in that moment it let Denise know she no longer saw her as just "the other woman."

"I was furious! I called him everything but a child of God and told him to lose my number!"

"So he never knew that you kept Story?" Justine asked.

Shaking her head, Denise said, "A few days later, he called back and apologized. He promised to be there for me and our baby. I can admit it now... I was young...*and* naive. I wanted so desperately to believe him... so I did."

Justine passed Story's mother her cloth napkin, her heart softening at the torment she had also endured.

"I gave birth to you on April 23, 1977. You came into the world screaming and looked directly at John. When you two locked eyes, there was no denying it: he was your father. You looked just like him and it was like you organically knew you were his. He insisted on naming you himself. *Story* because he knew of my passion for writing and dreams of Hollywood and *Johnniece* because you were his first born. Clearly, making you a Junior was out of the question with you being a girl."

"Wow," was all Story could muster.

"John cradled you in his arms and whispered in your ear. You never took your eyes off of him for one second. The connection was undeniable. He held you and promised you the world. For years, I held on to that promise."

Story smiled at the thought, as her mother held her gaze. Her truth had finally given her daughter the reassurance she needed—and rightly deserved—all these years: *My daddy loved me*.

Barbie

Picking up where Denise left off, Barbie mused, "John managed to get back in my good graces after showing up in my parent's living room a week or so after I left. I've always suspected my parents—namely my mother—played a big part in that."

Looking at Justine, Barbie confessed, "Your Grandma Carol had very compelling ways. Within a few days of his arrival, we were headed back to Philly. We were eight months or so into rekindling our relationship when I found out that I was pregnant."

Justine perked up at the mention of her beginnings.

"John never gave me further reason to believe he was anything less than faithful until well after you were born…" Barbie looked up at the ceiling, gathering her energy, "but from the sound of things, he just got better at hiding it… I can't believe I let him back into my heart."

"There was no way for you to have known, Mom," Justine offered, trying desperately to relieve her mother of any further sadness.

"I had you on September 8, 1977," Barbie continued as though she hadn't heard a word. "John was the proudest father. All the nurses in the labor ward gushed over what a 'great man' I had. He doted over you day and night for our entire hospital stay. He even sent the staff a fruit basket when we were discharged. Maybe a month after you were born, I received a call."

Story shot her mother a look.

"It wasn't me," Denise said out loud.

"No, it wasn't," Barbie admitted. "It was someone named *Genevieve.*"

"Genevieve?!" Justine yelped as though even the utterance of the name stung.

"Who the heck is that?!" Story piped up, her voice overlapping.

Denise fanned while sharing a knowing glance with Barbie. She could feel what John's wife was thinking: *This man was a real piece of work!*

"Here I was still on a high after having had my first baby, and Genevieve was sharing with me how she was pregnant with John's baby boy."

"What?!" Justine slammed her hand on the table.

"Oh baby, calm down." Barbie continued. "I was shattered! When I confronted John, he adamantly denied it. I wanted so badly to believe him, but given his track record, I needed peace of mind. John agreed to a paternity test once the baby was born—"

"Well if he hadn't at least slept with Genevieve he wouldn't have reason for a paternity test," Story blurted, stating the obvious. Denise shot her daughter a look.

"Exactly. But at the time that was enough. I had nowhere to go if I left him again. I wasn't working. I had a new baby. My family had already shown that they were on his side. Seeking the help of a friend meant divulging what was going on within our home, which was out of the question. I had no choice but to take it. I kept my mouth shut, developed tougher skin and I convinced myself to believe my husband —or at least pretend to."

"I'm so sorry, Mommy."

"You've done nothing to apologize for, honey. It was your father's doing." Barbie raised her glass, signaling to the waiter that they were ready for another round. Then she looked to Denise as though to tag her in.

"Through your early years, John would come and go as he pleased. He blamed his career for why we couldn't be together all of the time. I've viewed marriage as a broken institution since the moment my parents split as a girl. It never even occurred to me to pressure him to marry me. I just accepted whatever scraps he was willing to share."

Story shook her head defiantly.

"Your father always took care of you financially, just as he promised. When he could, he surprised us with sporadic visits. You knew him as your father until you were about three years old."

Turning to Barbie with a question in her eyes, Denise pressed on. "Then one day, everything but the funds dried up. He stopped calling. He stopped visiting. It was as though he disappeared into thin air."

"When Justine was almost three, I found out about Story, though I never knew either of you by name," Barbie rushed to explain. "I found a Toys R' Us and Woolworths receipt based out of stores in Connecticut. There were hundreds of dollars worth of children's toys and clothes listed in plain sight. John hadn't returned from his trip with anything for Justine. It took me weeks, but I pressed John until he finally came clean. That was when he told me all about you and the baby."

"You knew *all* of this time?" Justine queried.

Barbie nodded, at a loss for anything she could say to take away the hurt in her daughter's eyes.

"After allowing myself to grieve the loss of the picture-perfect life I thought we had finally settled into, I decided to stay. John told me we were separated when Denise got pregnant and the timeline added up, so yet again I chose to believe my husband."

Turning to Story, Barbie spoke, "I know I may not always seem like it, but I do have a heart. I couldn't bring myself to allow John to turn his back on you. I accepted him continuing to support you financially. I even wrote and mailed the checks from time to time. But I couldn't stomach him gallivanting off to Connecticut to play house with you and your mother. I made him promise me and—yes, I threatened his career and our relationship—that if he turned on me it was over."

"But he didn't stop," Justine said—part question, part statement.

"John reached out again when Story was about eight," Denise answered. "In all of those years, I purposely kept the same phone number, so he would always have a way to reach his daughter."

Barbie noticed Story's eyes beginning to tear up, and felt an ache in her chest. Her mother had tried her best to make it easy for John to stay in touch, but he had dropped the ball. She knew that they, the mothers, had carried the weight of his choices and sacrificed more than either daughter could imagine.

"Before I could even ask where he'd been, he persuaded me to meet for lunch to 'talk about things.'"

Barbie laughed to herself, "His infamous *talks*" she added wryly. Denise shook her head. She watched as a shared sadness, agreement or humiliation played across Denise's face. She didn't know her well, but it was very evident that she was rattled.

"I asked my mother to keep Story and met him at a local pub. That's when he dropped the bomb: he was married, and had been for nearly ten years. I was sick to my stomach. It was like we were in some alternate universe. I refused to believe this was the life meant for me... and my daughter.

"I decided then and there that I would protect you from ever feeling that kind of pain, baby." Denise directed her statement to her daughter. Barbie admired all the ways she had tried to protect Story.

Turning to address the group, she continued, "He apologized profusely and explained that things had been rocky for years in his marriage. He told me that he'd recently officially separated, and convinced me that we were what was missing from his life. John was either a master of persuasion or I was the biggest simpleton known to humankind because I fell for it. Yet again. When he asked me to move to Philly so he could be in his daughter's life, I agreed.

"I told him we wouldn't make the move until Story finished the school year; I wanted her to continue to have as much familiarity and stability as possible."

"That was why we moved so much?"

"That was why we moved to Philly—I wanted more than anything for you to have your father in your life. Somehow, I convinced myself that I was making the ultimate sacrifice for my child. By the time we moved to Philly and he set us up at Prospect Gardens, I really thought it was finally time for us to have our happily ever after. That dream shattered the moment I learned we were living in the same building as his ready-made family."

Barbie sniffed, not sure if she was more annoyed by the casual reference to her family or hearing another one of John's lies.

As if sensing her upset, Denise addressed her directly. "He was nowhere near separated from you, Barbie. But what was I to do? I didn't want to leave with my tail tucked between my legs. So, I chose to make the best of things and redesign a life for us here in Philly."

Barbie understood. Since her youth, she had witnessed firsthand how it was often left up to the women in her life to *fix it* when their men went astray.

"I'll never forget the first time I saw you and Story in the elevator. There was something so familiar when I looked into Story's eyes, and her smile was captivating." A fondness sweetened the bitter feelings as she recollected the moment. "I remember complimenting you on your hair beads."

"I remember that," Story replied. "You said my hair was, and I quote, 'absolutely darling' and said your daughter would probably love to have those kinds of beads."

Barbie smiled warmly, for perhaps the first time that afternoon. "It was a brief interaction, but..."

"Impactful," Story completed, as though reading her mind. "Your compliment was the reason I asked my mom to put beads in my hair on the first day of fourth grade. I remember thinking you were a really nice lady and hoping your daughter would be just as nice. I also remember hoping that if she liked my hair too, maybe it would make the other kids at school like me. It was the first spark of hope that I had that living in Philly, far away from everyone I knew, wasn't going to suck," Story said with a tired laugh.

"You sat next to me on the first day of fourth grade and I thought you were the coolest kid I'd ever met." Justine reminisced." I had no idea at that time that you were my..."

"Sister..." they both said, letting the word dangle.

The two held each other's gaze, a mixture of awe and excitement. Suddenly none of the *how*s and *why*s that brought them to the moment mattered.

Justine offered a warm smile. "I'm so sorry for the things I said earlier. I spoke out of line and I hope you both won't hold it against me. It's been a really rough couple of weeks. First Dad died, now this."

With that, Justine finally allowed herself to come undone. Barbie gently rubbed her daughter's back as tears cascaded from her own eyes. When she glanced up, she saw something she had never noticed before in Story's eyes: love. She could tell it hurt Story to see Justine hurting. And she realized it wasn't the first time she had seen that look in the girl's eyes.

"Is it fair to say that we have had enough tears for one day?" Barbie offered, dabbing her eye delicately. "Maybe we can spend the rest of our lunch getting to know the *real* us."

Hopping at an opportunity to lighten the mood, Story jokingly added, "Ok cool, so we can eat now?"

The entire table erupted into laughter as they tidied tears and began shaking off the gravity of all that had been shared. Each woman had survived John's choices in her own way. And while each of them was still managing to gather the scattered pieces of herself, somehow, together, they were beginning to find that some of those missing parts resided in each other.

❧ 26 ❧

THE MOTHERS

Denise

Denise expected the road ahead to be tough. After a day of grief and reckoning, she was mentally and physically drained. Still, she was committed. She was finally willing to give Story the answers and clarity she had denied her for so long. Whatever questions her daughter might ask, she was prepared to answer. But she needed someone beside her. Just in case she faltered.

When Story disappeared from the hotel room before the funeral service, Denise completely unraveled. She thought she had lost the one person she spent most of her life trying to protect. With no idea where or how to find her, she called Story's childhood mentor, Mrs. Baude. After all the birthday cards, graduations and long-distance phone calls —even after the move from Philly—a genuine friendship had formed. In time, the relationship deepened, and she proudly came to think of Mrs. Baude as family.

Years ago, in one of her more fragile moments, she had confided the truth about Story's father. To her surprise, Mrs. Baude never judged her. Instead, she offered quiet support and encouraged her to share more with Story when she felt ready.

When she explained her crisis the day prior over the phone, her confidante listened in her characteristic gentle way. After thinking for a moment, she suggested checking the funeral parlor. As soon as Denise heard the words, heat rushed to her face; how had she not thought of the most obvious place to find her daughter?

Following this day's events, Denise was spent and wracked with guilt. Projecting her own overwhelm, she feared she wouldn't be able to get through to Story. When she requested Mrs. Baude's presence for any fallout from the lunch meeting with the Chandlers, they agreed to meet at the hotel. Riding the wave of courage, Denise steadied herself for whatever was to come from any potentially life-altering confessions. She hoped Mrs. Baude's support would help guide their family forward after such upheaval.

Surprisingly, Story had handled the lunch well. Denise suspected that had something to do with her finally having the sister she always dreamed of. Still, she knew the emotional floor could give out at any moment—and welcomed Mrs. Baude as a cushion to catch her daughter's fall.

Story was overjoyed to see her mentor and friend standing at the door when she answered the knock. The day had been a whirlwind, and it helped to have a familiar face there as she tried to process her life's latest revelation. After a warm hug, the three women settled into the hotel room's sitting area.

"I'm so glad you could make it, Sasha," Denise said, rising to embrace her. "I really appreciate you coming."

"You two are my family. There's no way I'd ignore a call for backup," she replied with a smile.

Once everyone was seated, Denise began. "Story, I asked Sasha— Mrs. Baude—to support us through this. As you know, she has a background in counseling, and I thought she'd be the perfect person to help walk us through any remaining questions."

"I appreciate that, Ma," Story replied. "I do have more questions— ones I didn't want to ask in front of Mrs. Chandler or Justine. Maybe we should start from the beginning. I feel like I've only scratched the surface of who you are and how we got here."

"I'm willing to answer anything you want to know."

"That sounds fair," Mrs. Baude agreed. "You've both come this far, let's push through so you both have the closure you need."

"Ok, so I'll start from the beginning, and fill in answers as I go. Does that work?"

Story nodded.

"Well, as you know, I was born in Connecticut—in a small town called Mystic. I was the second of three children, each of us about two years apart. We moved to Hartford shortly after your Uncle Leonard died in a boating accident when he was thirteen. I was fifteen at the time. Our parents were never the same after that. Even relocating couldn't mend what had fractured between them. They tried, but nothing quite soothes the heartache of losing a child."

"The loss of your brother had to have been a huge blow to all of you. Did you ever do family counseling?"

Denise shook her head, "No. We couldn't afford that. We just carried on the best we knew how."

"After two years in Hartford, my parents sat me and my sister, Coretta, down and told us they were divorcing. I was seventeen at that time. Coretta was nineteen, and already out of the house. Since I still had two years of high school left, I stayed with Mommy when Daddy moved out, so I could graduate with my class."

While she had told Story about her upbringing before, her daughter seemed to frame it with new eyes, more compassionate and understanding eyes.

I should have told her all of this sooner, Denise thought before continuing.

"At first, we pretended things were fine—but Mommy couldn't keep up the façade. The pain of losing Leonard and dissolution of her marriage made her unravel. She became critical, short-tempered and paranoid. Nothing I did ever seemed good enough. Living in that house became miserable."

"That sounds agonizing," Mrs. Baude empathized. "I can only imagine what your mother must have been going through. No parent can ever truly prepare for such a loss—and if she didn't know how to cope, she couldn't help you cope either."

Denise nodded. "I tried talking to Coretta, but she was wrapped up in her own life. I brought it up to Daddy once during a weekend visit, and he promised to talk to Mommy. That gave me some relief—I'd started feeling depressed, like I was suffocating. But their talk led to a huge blow-up, which only made me feel worse, like I had caused more harm. I withdrew. I felt safest when I shut my heart off to anything that could hurt it.

"College changed my life. Slowly, I chipped away at the years of feeling neglected, misunderstood and invisible. I made friends and joined a group called United Connection—UCONN for short. It was a play on the university's name, but our mission extended beyond the campus, into the wider Hartford community. For the first time, I felt like I had purpose. My spirit was revived. I was in a good place when the *Stand Up, Stand Out* rally came around.

"Granted, my relationships with Mommy and Coretta were still rocky. Coretta had taken Mommy's side after the divorce. *Stop being a brat. You're overreacting again,* she'd say whenever I told her anything about Mommy. And Daddy was battling his own demons, numbing his pain with a fifth of gin most days. To this day, the smell of hard liquor turns my stomach. It's like the scent of gin used to seep out of daddy's pores, but by that time I had learned to hold on to the things that made me happy and find comfort there.

"Like I said at lunch, your father wasn't my type when we first met —but he grew on me. He sold me the dream of a fairytale life, and I fell for it. I did love him, which is part of why it took me so long to tell you the truth. Even after our romantic relationship ended, I felt a need to protect him. I never wanted you to see him in a negative light. But the longer I waited, the more cracks showed in our foundation. I always thought I had time to make it right..."

Mrs. Baude leaned in, placing a hand on Denise's back as she gathered herself. The weight of holding these secrets had really taken its toll, and digging it all up now let her know that she couldn't proceed with business as usual after this.

"When your father passed, I knew time had run out. I couldn't let him be buried without you knowing who he really was. And it broke my heart that my fear had kept you apart."

Denise shook her head as tears trickled more freely now. For the first time, Story could see just how sad her mother had been all these years. She wasn't the only one feeling something was missing: her mother felt it too. Not only that, she blamed herself for it.

"Were you still with Dad when we moved to Philly?" Story asked, needing reassurance that her mother hadn't purposefully tried to disrupt his marriage to Mrs. Chandler.

Without hesitation, her mother replied, "No. I came to Philly for you. I thought being closer to John's home base would give you two a chance to build a relationship. I'd be lying if I said I didn't sometimes imagine us trying again, but when I got here and learned he was still married, that hope died. I shifted all my focus onto you. Honestly, him admitting he was married was probably the best thing he ever did for me—it set me free. I no longer felt the need to keep my life on pause waiting for a man that wasn't willing to give all of himself to what we had. For the first time in years, I acknowledged how worthy I was of the *right* type of love."

"What about that time after the homecoming dance, when I saw you two by the elevators?" Story asked.

Denise closed her eyes, recalling the moment she had long hoped Story hadn't witnessed. She knew she had made a mistake letting John into their home that day. He claimed he just wanted to drop off Story's monthly stipend, but when he kissed her before leaving, Denise had a momentary lapse—she kissed him back before thinking.

"I've regretted that moment ever since. I never should've let him get that close again. But I promise, it never went beyond that kiss. I'm ashamed it even went that far."

Story hesitated before asking, "The news said he died in a hotel in Raleigh. Did you see him while he was in town?"

Denise shook her head. "He reached out. Said he'd lost too many years and wanted to be your dad. I was hesitant. You were just stepping into adulthood, and I wasn't sure if it was the right time. But I agreed to meet. I knew it was finally time to tell you the truth. We never got the chance to meet because he... well... you know. It was all so sudden and heartbreaking."

Her voice trembled at the end.

Story sat, collecting her thoughts.

Mrs. Baude glanced between the two, breathing gently and deeply.

"That's everything. That's my truth—as imperfect as it may be," Denise finished. "I don't expect you to understand or approve of my actions; only know, I was doing the best I could and I hope you don't hate me for it."

"Story," Mrs. Baude said gently, "I know today has been intense. It's healthy to take time to process. What matters is that the heart of the conversation is out there. You may feel many emotions in the days and months ahead—and that's valid. Let yourself feel them all. Lean on your village: your mom, Karl, me. We all want what's best for you. Just know that this truth doesn't define you or your mother. Let it build you, not break you."

Story nodded quietly, and for the first time, Denise saw her daughter as a woman, not just *her child*. She was not only learning about her family history, but possibly deciding how to make her own way as a woman, a lover, a life partner and potential mother one day. There was so much to take in, she hoped it wasn't "too much."

"Thank you both for being here for me," Story began. "Mom, I'm not angry. I'm not even sure what I'm feeling right now—but it's not anger. I just need time to find my way to making meaning out of all of this."

She stood slowly with an inhale. Stretching to resolve any residual tightness, she exhaled—focused and controlled. The other two women followed suit before Story hugged each of them.

"It's like my entire life has new meaning. I'll never be the same. I guess that's both good and bad," she said thoughtfully. "Mom, I know today was tough on you too. I really appreciate everything you did to make this happen for me and to answer my questions. I needed this, but I'm beyond exhausted. I'm going to turn in." Then added with a smile, "You two young ladies don't stay up too late, ok?"

As she disappeared down the hall, Denise leaned toward Mrs. Baude and whispered, "Leave it to Story to still try and act like the mother at a time like this."

Barbie

Barbie couldn't believe she had spent so many years fighting to uphold the image of perfection. In the end, she learned a hard truth: the pursuit had cost her more than it gave. Justine was, undoubtedly, the best thing that had ever happened to her. And despite all his faults, she could honestly say John had been the second best. In the later years of their marriage, after her bout with breast cancer, they began counseling, and it did wonders to mend what had long been broken. Now that she had found peace with John's past, she was willing to do whatever it took to help Justine find her own.

"Honey, it's more important than ever that we keep our lines of communication open," Barbie said gently. "I've spoken with my therapist about all this, and she offered some helpful tips about how we could move forward. I want you to feel supported as we navigate this new normal. Just tell me how I can best do that."

"Why did you stay?" The words tumbled out. "Mom, you are hands down the strongest person I know. For years, I thought I was protecting you from the things I knew about Dad. I believed telling you what I saw as a child would break you. But you already knew—all this time—and still, you never wavered. Why? What made you stay?"

It didn't surprise Barbie that Justine had seen more than she would've hoped.

"You know how your father was, Jus—he was a charmer. He made me feel invincible when I was with him." Barbie smiled, pausing to fiddle with the leaves of a floral arrangement on the side table.

Her smile slowly faded as she continued, "But my ideas about marriage were set long before I ever met John. Your Me-Maw and Pa-Paw were married for over sixty years before he passed," Barbie said matter-of-factly. "And for as long as I can remember, Pa-Paw was a serial cheater. He didn't even try to hide it."

The grandfather clock began to chirp, alerting them of the hour. Momentarily distracted, Justine looked at the large clock—it had been a gift from her grandparents on her parents' first anniversary. Twenty plus years later, the clock had outlived the marriage.

Barbie, seemingly oblivious to the semblance of the moment and sound of the clock continued, "Growing up, it seemed normal—almost expected. I remember my mother and her friends sitting around, griping about their husbands' 'roaming ways.' *Men will be men. As long as he takes care of home first. Always remember, he chose you.* Those were the types of toxic affirmations they threw around like gospel."

Justine scrunched her face, shaking her head in shock at the past generations' mindset about respect and faithfulness in marriage.

"After hearing that over and over, it just felt like a good wife stuck by her man, no matter what. I believed I could hold your father's attention if I tried hard enough. I spent years—and thousands of dollars—on my appearance. I catered to his every whim, tried to be the supportive, doting wife. In the end, it still wasn't enough."

"Do I have a brother out there somewhere, too?"

"Who?" Barbie blinked, caught off guard.

"At lunch... you mentioned a woman named Genevieve being pregnant with a baby boy. What came of that? Did Dad take the paternity test?"

"Ah, yes. I'd nearly forgotten," Barbie said with a tired smile. "Yes, he did the test. And based on the results I saw, he was right—the baby wasn't his. It was a relief for both of us. But in my heart, I knew I didn't want another scare like that. That was before I knew about Story.

"Either way, I convinced your father to get a vasectomy. I knew it meant I'd never carry another child, but I was at peace with that."

Justine looked at her mother in surprise. She had no idea the depth of what her mother had sacrificed to keep their family together.

"Having you felt like more than enough." Barbie rushed to assure Justine. "And if stopping any more illegitimate children meant I'd have to let go of experiencing motherhood for a second time, I could live with that.

"It was years before I realized why he had agreed so quickly—he already knew he had two beautiful, healthy girls. Thankfully, I've never gotten notice of any other children." She crossed her index and middle fingers superstitiously.

"You never said how you found out that Story was Dad's child," Justine said. "When did you put it together?"

"After that initial encounter in the elevator, I couldn't shake her face from my mind. At first, I didn't know why she looked so familiar. But once you two became close, I had plenty of time to study her—her eyes, her smile, her mannerisms—they all screamed John.

"Is that when you confronted Dad?"

"Not quite. I was still putting it all together. *Should I confront him? Maybe corner Denise the next time we crossed paths? But, what could I even say without proof?* I felt like I needed solid evidence.

"One day, you casually mentioned that her family was originally from Connecticut. And it clicked. I remembered the old receipts from years before. I couldn't let it go after that."

"So what did you do?"

Barbie's eyes held a new sense of determination as she recalled the memory, "I never really wanted to know the name of your father's mistress and child. But from that moment, I became obsessed with learning the truth. I guess your father was tired of running from his past: it didn't take much for him to confirm who Denise and Story were. I was absolutely against them living in the same building as us."

"How old was I when you found out?"

Nibbling the tip of her finger as she did the mental calculations, Barbie guessed. "You must have been around nine going on ten by then. I was even more opposed to you two being friends, once I knew, but John made it clear he wouldn't turn his back on his daughter... his firstborn."

Barbie noticed her daughter wince at the mention of Story being John's first born. She had gotten used to being an only child, and had long since given up on asking for a sibling.

"You and Story were so close, there was no separating you two without it bringing on additional questions from you. So, I resigned myself to the fact that I'd lost the battle and ended up just like my mother. The rest is history," Barbie concluded, relieved that there was no more to tell. The first tendrils of peace crept into the pause as she watched her daughter fit these new pieces into the puzzle of her life.

"Are there any other questions I can answer for you?"

"I knew there was something special about our connection. Since fourth grade, when I first met her, I just felt this unexplainable connection. Who would have thought she was my blood sister," Justine mused, recounting the bond she had felt with Story—her sister—even when they were estranged. "Part of me is happy to have a sister, but another part of me feels guilty almost... I don't want to be happy at your expense." This was more intimate than she and Justine had ever been, especially in recent days. "I'm so angry at Dad!" she admitted.

"Baby, I appreciate your consideration, but I need you to live your happiest life. It has taken counseling, time and lots of tears to accept that your father's ways weren't about me," Barbie paused, unsure of how much she should share. "I'm still learning to accept that. But my prayer is for you to one day forgive your father for his imperfections, just as I am learning to do."

Barbie never admitted her flaws or allowed herself to be seen as anything other than perfectly put together, but she didn't want her daughter thinking that's what it meant to be a woman. She wanted her to know that true self love could only happen with complete vulnerability and honesty. She wanted her daughter to know now that a man's actions were never her fault or responsibility—good, bad or otherwise.

"Now before I forget, your father always planned to tell you everything himself. But we can never predict when our time is up. A month ago, our counselor suggested he make this video for you, just to practice getting all of his thoughts out. You know him—he was so proud of it, he made me promise to pass it on if for some reason he never got to speak the words himself." Barbie handed Justine a DVD and stood. "I'm going to go to bed, but you watch that whenever you're ready. And remember, I may have held in a lot before, but I'm here now. If you need me to fill in any blanks, after your father has spoken his peace, you know where to find me. I love you, honey."

"I love you too, Mommy," Justine replied, gazing at the disc with fresh tears brimming.

27

COMING CLEAN

Story

It had been a *long* day. Story paced the length of the hotel room, trying to let off steam before retiring for the evening. Still she was grateful for the sense of resolve that now washed over her.

At the end of their meeting, Barbie surprised Story when she grabbed her hands and looked her directly in the eye. Story had been taken aback by her transparency and humility:

I owe you an apology for how I've treated you throughout the years. There were times when I hated you so much, I wished you and your mother would disappear. I see now that my anger was misplaced. You were a child and I had no business treating you with such malice... that day on the phone when I spoke so harshly to you, I was only protecting Justine. She told me you two had a falling out and without even knowing the details, I saw red. When you called, I honestly thought God placed you in my lap to get rid of you once and for all. I was so wrong! And I'm ashamed of myself.

Speechless, Story blinked rapidly—anchoring herself amidst the tidal wave of Mrs. Chandler's words.

None of this is your fault. If anything, I now see what a blessing you are. I loved your father, And in many ways, your existence means his legacy now lives on two-fold.

Barbie had then reached into her purse and withdrew a bubble-wrapped envelope. Placing the envelope in Story's hand, she folded the young woman's fingers over the package.

Your father wanted you to have this. In his later years, he spoke openly to me about you. And I'd come to terms with it all. There is nothing like a health scare to adjust your perspective on what's truly important in life. Please take this and watch it when you are ready. I know it can't right all of his wrongs, but I hope it brings you some solace.

Tears sprinkled her shirt as Story soaked in every word Mrs. Chandler spoke. Justine and Denise stood at the distance allowing the two a moment of privacy. Until that moment, Story hadn't realized how much she needed to hear those words. She placed the envelope in her purse, wrapping both arms around Mrs. Chandler in a tight embrace. Barbie let her. They stood there uninterrupted, their tears falling without any care of make-up. Story didn't know what was in the envelope, but she felt strongly that it held the missing pieces she needed to heal what was hurt in her for so very long.

⚜

Story tossed and turned for what felt like forever before accepting that sleep wasn't in her immediate future. After speaking with her mother and Mrs. Baude, she had gone to bed while the two of them stayed up talking. She thought her brain had been ready to power down, but sleep evaded her like a criminal on the run. Finally, she gave in and sat up in bed. Looking to her left, she realized her mother had come to bed at some point in the night, which meant she must have drifted off, despite feeling as though she hadn't slept a wink. She never even heard her mother enter the room. Looking to her right, she noticed the time: 1:11 a.m.

Quietly getting out of bed, she grabbed the bubble-wrapped envelope and made her way to the living room. If she couldn't sleep, she figured she may as well find out what was inside the package. Carefully breaking the seal, Story flipped the envelope upside down and allowed its content to fall onto her lap. A faded photo rested atop a single DVD. The photo was of her and Justine right before their tenth grade homecoming dance. They stood proudly, their dates positioned a respectful distance away on either side. Sandwiched between the girls was their father. Story had never seen the processed photo, but seeing it now transported her to the moment—a moment she missed in all the excitement.

Her father's pride and love for *both* of his daughters couldn't have been clearer. The image impressed a feeling of fullness onto her heart. Perplexed as to what could be on the DVD, Story popped it into the hotel's entertainment system, and dropped onto the couch, one leg tucked beneath her. Once seated, she pressed play. Her father's image appeared on the screen—shirt unbuttoned at the collar, tie resting on the arm of the chair, manicured nails folded on the desk.

Story scanned his background. She could see an award of some sort just over his left shoulder. A framed photo of Justine and Barbie stood proudly on his desk. Based on the high-back black leather executive chair, he seemed to be in his home office. The camera shifted slightly bringing her dad into center-frame. *I wonder if Mrs. Chandler is on the other side of the camera,* Story allowed her mind to drift for a moment before focusing on the man before her.

As though John had anticipated Story needing a moment to take him in, he sat quietly before beginning to speak. Then as though on cue, he began:

Hey Little Lady, I hate that you're seeing this recording because if you're seeing this, it means I never got the chance to tell you your true identity myself. Her father's smile went from effervescent to crestfallen, at the realization of his own words.

I'm sure you know by now that I'm your father. As much as I've cherished that role, I was too much of a coward to openly admit it. It's important that I follow up by saying I'm sorry. I hope that one day you will find it in your heart to accept that.

Story uncrossed her leg and leaned slightly forward in the seat, now fully engaged in what her father was saying.

There is so much I need to say, but my fear is that none of it will truly justify my actions. For your entire life, I put far too many things before you and your wellbeing. I was selfish and I can acknowledge that now. I didn't do right by you or your mother.

You can say that again, Story thought.

I was living a single life as a married man and that was wrong. I dug myself into a hole that I eventually couldn't get out of. You deserved a father that was there for you. A father who told you they loved you. A father to make memories with.

Story nodded her head in complete agreement, forgetting for a moment that her father was on the big screen and not sitting with her.

I tried to be all of those things. John rubbed his face. His eyes drifted from the camera, as though it was hard for him to face himself. Taking a deep breath, he spoke again, *Because you never knew I was your father, it feels presumptuous to assume you could feel my efforts. There were so many times I wanted to wrap my arms around you and tell you how much I loved you.*

I wish you had, Story wiped her eyes, now raw from days of crying.

But my pride wouldn't allow me to drop the mask of all that I'd built in the public light. I loved you from the first time I saw you. That can never change. And even though I was on the outside looking in, I followed your progression through life.

Story wondered how.

When you and your mother left Philly, I would make a point of coming to Raleigh just to be close to you. I've driven by your home more times than I can count, never working up the nerve to ring the bell. I went to a few of your games to watch you cheer. The way you performed was magnetic! You've always been so driven, a quality much like your mother. Speaking of which, I hope your styling business is booming by now. John beamed. *You thrive most when engaging with others, kind of like me.*

I even attended your high school and college graduations. I would cheer so loud, I'd lose my voice. I would make a game of how elaborate I could make my disguise. You never once caught me. But at your college graduation, you bumped into me, and stared at me as though you couldn't place how you knew me. I guess it's true when they say the eyes are the windows to the soul because even when I tried to hide, you saw me.

It only took a moment for the memory to bubble up in Story's mind. *The old man!* Her eyes flashed with recognition. She took two shaky breaths.

It took me a long time to hold myself accountable for my actions. But I did try, Baby Girl. I only wish I'd had more time to prove it to you. I can't tell you which way your heart should sway. What I've done was pretty crappy. Please try not to hold any of this against your mother or Justine's mother. They were just casualties of the game I played. I take accountability for my actions with no excuses made. I hope you're able to forgive me. Look out for your sister. One thing I got right was ensuring you two had a relationship. She needs you and you need her. Remind her to give herself some slack and embrace life. We only get one. And never be afraid to shake up the world a little. He added with a mischievous grin.

Looking directly through the camera and into Story's heart, he concluded: *I guess there is nothing left to say but I love you, Little Lady. Take care and know that I'll forever watch over you.*

Justine

Justine had been fighting to rest her mind from the moment her head hit the pillow. But sleep seemed to be as much the enemy as her father. Sighing in frustration, she rolled over and glanced at her alarm clock: 1:11 a.m.

Since she couldn't sleep, she decided to try watching a little television. Propping herself up in bed, Justine cut on the television and watched as the screen came to life. After a few minutes of flipping through infomercials, she cut it back off and let out an uneasy sigh.

She was so angry with her father! He had made a mess out of all of their lives, and was nowhere near to clean it up. After all the years spent covering for him, she felt stuck, trapped even, as to how she should move forward. Keeping with Chandler traditions, she tried her best to allow him to keep his cape as the superhero they all knew and loved. But in the end, even Superman lived his life as a mere mortal. Justine was hurt to know her father had been living a double life completely outside her scope of comprehension. She, too, felt like a pawn in his game. The wounds were fresh. He had gone on, and left them all to pick up the pieces. Justine wasn't certain she could ever forgive his lies and deception. Life as she knew it would never be the same.

As thunder cracked outside, Justine reached for her cordless phone and she dialed Story's cell.

"Hello?" Story said, picking up on the first ring.

Justine laughed. "Somehow, I knew you'd be up," she said.

"Somehow I knew you'd be calling," Story countered.

The two fell into easy conversation for hours, picking right up where they left off. They talked about everything and nothing at all. There was comfort in the silent moments and laughter in between.

"Did you watch yours?" Story asked.

"What? The DVD?" Justine feigned ignorance.

"Nah, the feature film," Story joked. They both laughed. Justine knew her sister felt her tension; she couldn't bring herself to admit how angry she was and had no desire to hear more of her father's excuses.

"Yeah, Mr... I mean Dad really messed up, huh?" Story said. "I can't explain why, but I forgive him. At least he got it right when he brought us together."

Justine was quiet for a while. "I'm just not ready."

"I get it," Story offered. "I support your decision, and I'm here for you when you decide the time is right."

"Thanks for that, Story. You've always been my biggest cheerleader." She smiled.

"And always will be!"

Looking out her window, Justine realized the rain had stopped and the sun had risen. She pressed the cordless phone between her head and shoulder as she walked to the window. As she looked out, she gasped.

"Story, go look out of your window!" Justine said excitedly.

"What is it girl?" Story asked.

"Just go look! Hurry!"

She heard Story moving on the other line.

"Do you see it?" Justine asked.

"A double rainbow," they said in perfect harmony.

"Sis, I may be mad as hell at him, but I think Dad *is* watching over us."

"He is indeed, Sister. He is indeed."

EPILOGUE: A LIFETIME OF FOREVERS

Justine

It had been three years, but Justine finally felt ready. She gave her apartment a final once over before closing her suitcase. As best she could tell, she had everything she needed. The DVD on the dresser caught her eye. She was finally ready to check one final task off her to-do list. She walked over to the television/DVD combo that claimed a corner of her bedroom, turned it on, and placed the disc in the tray. Justine took a deep breath, her mother's words echoing in her mind: *"Watch that whenever you're ready."*

She needed closure in order to move forward with her next chapter. She needed to know what his intentions had been. After her world had been turned upside down, what justification would he offer? She needed to know that his heart was somehow in the right place. She needed to hear him say he loved her, even if it was for the last time. Taking another deep breath, her finger pressed play. Her heart rate quickened as her father popped into view.

He leaned into the frame, fingertips tented and lips pressed together, fighting an uncommon quiver of nerves. Justine scanned the familiar plaques, photos, pen well and stack of files in her father's home study.

Hey Little Lady. Where do I begin? I know this message is long overdue. Sadly, I also know if you're watching this video, I never worked up the courage to say these things. Your mother and I had every intention of telling you everything after I had the chance to tell Story—in person.

John paused for a breath. *I know what you're probably thinking... how did I find her?*

Justine pursed her lips, awaiting his response.

Truth is, I've always known where to find her. The day you asked me to help you track her down, I nearly told you everything. But my gut told me Story deserved to hear everything from me first. I'm sorry for not being honest with you. I wish things could have been different—that I had done them differently. I'll forever have to rest knowing I failed all of you, at least in this way.

Justine's chin dropped, meeting her chest in the descent. Her vision blurred with tears as her mind ran through the many times her father had failed her.

And I am so sorry. His apology landed, as though he could read her mind all these years later.

I'm sure your mother has told you by now that Story is my daughter and your sister. I've made a lot of decisions I wish I could take back, but Story was never God's mistake.

For the first time since the video began, Justine felt optimistic. *Story is far from a mistake. She's actually God's greatest gift to me.* She stacked her hands over her heart embracing the joy that surged through her body.

I can see now that the only mistake was not taking responsibility for my actions. A moment of weakness should have never turned into a lifetime of hiding. I need you to know I apologize with everything in me: for breaking my marital vows repeatedly... for hurting your mother... for letting you down... for being an example of everything a man SHOULD NOT do.

John leaned back as though reconciling his inability to be the role model to the very people who deserved it most. *I am so deeply sorry for how I handled the situation with the... with YOUR baby. It's taken me longer than most to recognize that I spent a huge chunk of my adult years being selfish and shooting for my next dream. But one thing I stand strong on is this: I love you and I love Story.*

I love you too Daddy, Justine whispered.

I may have not always shown it in the best way, but I hope you still felt it. Her father's smile filled the screen. *Remember how we used to race each other at the pool on hot summer days? Me teaching you to drive at Griffin Park? The day you graduated from NYU—sights set on joining the fight for equality and justice... just like your old man.*

John dabbed his eye with a handkerchief. *I'm not asking you to turn a blind eye from anything I've done, but I do hope you're able to remember it wasn't all bad. I do hope you hold the good right alongside the hurt.*

I know I don't have the right to ask anything of you, but if I may, I have one final request: I need you to take care of yourself and your mother. And look out for your sister. Remember to slow down enough to enjoy the fruits of your labor. You two need either other. Please don't hold anything that I've done over Ms. Brooks' or your mother's head. I accept full responsibility for the web I've woven. All they did was try to protect you girls in all my mess. Never forget, as flawed as I am, that I love you. Always have, always will. Never doubt that I'll always be with you, Princess.

Justine sobbed in a way she hadn't in years. She still had a ways to go, but she was finally on the path to reconciliation.

Story

True to her name, Story's life had played out like a book. Her mother may have not made it to Hollywood, but she had lived a beautiful tale. If ever there was a testimony of making lemons out of lemonade, she was living it. The past 26 years of her life had been a whirlwind of love, hate, turmoil and forgiveness. Still, she wouldn't change one minute of it.

Although her journey was far from over, Story had a lot to be thankful for. Number one on the list was reuniting with her sister and partner in crime. She also planned to continue growing her relationship with Karl, who had proven to truly be the love of her life and reliable backbone when she needed it most. She had finally convinced him to move to North Carolina—not an easy feat considering his West Coast roots. Nevertheless, they'd both agreed their love was worth it.

She had once again begun accepting styling clients on an as-needed basis. And though her client list was growing steadily, education remained her primary source of income and life calling. Her career as an elementary school teacher was on the right trajectory. She had her sights set on becoming a principal within the next five years. But perhaps the most pivotal development in Story's life was discovering who her father was. Though their time together had been short, she was able to reconcile that it had run its course. She and her mother had grown closer now that that secret no longer stood between them. All ill feelings toward Denise for any of the decisions she made while raising her had dissipated into compassion and understanding, and her mother remained her biggest supporter.

She checked her room making sure she had everything for a trip of a lifetime: she was preparing for her first flight with one of her favorite people. Story couldn't wait for her skin to be kissed by the sun, to feel its warmth and shop amongst her favorite celebs on Rodeo Drive. Things were looking up for sure.

Justine

From the outside looking in, Justine had lived the perfect life, but she knew better than anyone that that couldn't be further from the truth. It had taken years of prayer and perseverance for Justine to love herself completely. The growing pains and family trauma she had endured now held new meaning. She had put in the work and gotten to the bottom of her desires for perfectionism—in its place now were forgiveness and grace.

Of course, it had taken time and therapy, but Barbie's prayers were answered: Justine no longer held any animosity towards her late father for his actions or lack thereof. She accepted that she might never completely understand why her father had chosen to live a double life, but she had forgiven him nonetheless. For her, forgiveness was less about understanding, and more about acceptance of what was without always needing to "get it." It was a lesson that had helped her heal and grow as a partner in each of her relationships.

Reconnecting with Story was one of the biggest blessings in her life. Their bond felt unbreakable. In fact, the two were preparing to go on a trip to celebrate their many new beginnings. New jobs, new perspectives and most importantly—new titles: sister-friends.

Justine stood at the airline gate and spoke briskly into her phone. "Girl hurry up, we're going to miss this flight!"

"I'm coming," Story said in a winded tone, "I was up half the night catching up on that series, *Unbreakable*. Walter had me playing all types of detectives while trying to figure out where he was and who he was with when he left Camille. I messed around and overslept. I can't believe I didn't even get to finish the series after all that. *That's* a connection that needs to be broken." Her sister chuckled in her ear.

"Just hurry up! This trip is not about that silly show!" Justine gave her phone the side eye. "I don't know why you watch that mess anyway."

"Sometimes I need a little comedic relief, to watch someone else's life play out for a change. I'm so glad I don't live in that 'toxic relationship' space anymore. But you're right, this is the trip of our lifetime. It's not every day that I get to celebrate my sister-friend passing the bar! I can't wait to see what, or who, we can get into in L.A."

"Ew, you nasty," Justine said, scrunching her face. "*And* you're fronting —there is no way you would do anything to jeopardize what you and Karl have going on."

"I know, I know," Story said, rolling her eyes, "and you've only got eyes for your Dorky Daniel. Blah, blah blah. But a girl can dream, right?"

The women giggled into their respective phones the same way they did as girls. Story snuck up behind Justine and tapped her shoulder. They embraced, squealing.

"Eek! You made it, let's go!"

As they walked toward the ticket counter, she proudly faced Story, "I finally did it!"

Her sister already knew what she meant. "You watched dad's DVD! Woohoo," Story cheered, hands raised triumphantly in the air.

Justine shrunk into herself before remembering the lyrics of her new favorite song: *I'm a work in progress, I'm a seed grown into a flower...* Renewed in her a reminder to never camouflage the person she was growing into, she joined Story in a happy dance, ignoring the onlookers.

"I'm so proud of you! How do you feel?"

She pondered the question for a moment before responding, "I feel... free! Dad had his demons, but he can rest in peace knowing that we're going to be just fine. Justine hooked her arm around her sister's shoulder. Story's arm slid around her waist. They fit. Just like that.

"Istersay, istersay, hatstay ymay istersay!" they said together. The two recited the chant 'sister, sister, that's my sister,' from their childhood secret language. Walking in sync the Prospect Girls boarded their plane *to the stars*. Neither could quite pinpoint what they had done to deserve each other, but as they reflected on their lives, they knew one thing was certain: soul ties were not easily broken.

ACKNOWLEDGMENTS

Whew, we did it! My first novel is officially in the books (pun intended). I'm so grateful to my village for planting the seed in my mind to even carry out this venture. To my birth mom,

Kathryne Enoch, and bonus mom, Barbara Brown, thank you for playing such a key role in making me who I am today. Your guidance in this journey called life has been immeasurable.

Thank you to my husband, Thomas Bray, for—strangely—finding me interesting enough to encourage putting my random thoughts into a book. You don't always get this Philly girl humor, but you rock with it nonetheless. Your support means a lot. Roll Tide... Go State... something something boom boom. LOL.

Made in the image of God—thank you to my daughter, Gabriella. You are my mini. You are my reason. I have loved you from the moment you were a concept and will continue to love you well beyond my last breath. Your existence is like medicine to my soul. Thank you for being an all-around awesome being.

I need my soul sistas to step to the front of the congregation. Melody Poindexter, Marie Burns and Me'Chel Tyson, the creation of each of our bonds has been so organic and intentional. God out did himself when he gave me y'all. We are twenty plus years in and our connection never gets tired. Thank you for being my sounding boards, confidants, motivators and comedic relief through this project.

Thank you to my unofficial alpha readers: Thomas Bray, Maurice Brown, Mikia Clemmons and Melody Poindexter. Your feedback and encouragement during the writing process made this book so much more than I initially envisioned.

To my editor, Asha Tané, you were the piece that I didn't realize was missing. Wow, who could have known that a chance recommendation, could turn into such a magical experience. You challenged me to find my voice in this project. I have expressed more feelings while refining this book than I ever knew were in me. LOL. Your expertise and gentle guiding were major in getting me to the finish line. For this, I say thank you, thank you, thank you. I look forward to our next project.

Fariss Ryan, calling you a jack of all trades is no exaggeration. You took my vision and bought it to life. Thanks to you and Victoria Davies, my final product is so pretty!

Last but most certainly not least, I thank God. How does one put into words the level of gratitude held for the Most High? There is no me without you. Thank you for breathing life into my body. Thank you for thinking I was worth saving. Thank you for being my comforter, protector, provider—my all and all.

REVIEWS

Enjoy this book? You can make a big difference!

Reviews are the most powerful tool when it comes to getting attention for writing a book. Not only would I love to read your kind words, I'd really like to hear your honest feedback.

If you've enjoyed reading this book, please consider telling your friends about it or take five minutes to write a review on the book's Amazon page. I would be very grateful.

Thank you,

Colleen

ABOUT THE AUTHOR

Like her characters, Colleen Bray is multifaceted. Born and raised in the Philadelphia area, Colleen's journey has been filled with a multitude of twists and turns. She proudly served her country in the United States Army followed by years serving her community as a social worker and nurse. Currently based out of Maryland, Colleen spends her days as an Army wife, soccer mom, registered nurse and novelist. In her spare time, she enjoys pampering her fur baby, reading, community service, traveling and building memories with family.